PENGUIN BOOKS AND BLUE SALT

BARD OF BLOOD

Bilal Siddiqi is the author of three books, *Bard of Blood*, *The Kiss of Life*, co-authored with Emraan Hashmi, and *The Stardust Affair*. He wrote his debut novel, *Bard of Blood*, when he was only nineteen. It has now been adapted as an original series for Netflix, of which he is the creator; he has also worked on the screenplays. He is working on his fourth book and screenplays for a few feature films and series.

D1254154

S. HUSSAIN ZAIDI PRESENTS

BARD OF BLOOD

THE SECRET WAR IN BALOCHISTAN
IS ABOUT TO EXPLODE

BILAL
SIDDIQI

BLUE
SALT

PENGUIN BOOKS

An imprint of Penguin Random House

PENGUIN BOOKS

USA | Canada | UK | Ireland | Australia
New Zealand | India | South Africa | China

Penguin Books is part of the Penguin Random House group of companies
whose addresses can be found at global.penguinrandomhouse.com

Published by Penguin Random House India Pvt. Ltd
7th Floor, Infinity Tower C, DLF Cyber City,
Gurgaon 122 002, Haryana, India

Penguin
Random House
India

First published by Penguin Books India and Blue Salt 2015
Published in Penguin Books by Penguin Random House India and Blue Salt 2019

ISBN 9780143423966

Typeset in Sabon by Manipal Digital Systems, Manipal
Printed at Replika Press Pvt. Ltd, India

www.penguin.co.in

MIX
Paper from
responsible sources
FSC® C016779

For Parwaiz Gul
Nana Abba, you live on through your
beautiful wife and daughter.
If what they say is true, maybe some day you and I
will meet up there and discuss this book . . .

Contents

Acknowledgements

Bard of Blood is a work of fiction interspersed with facts, which draws from actual incidents and characters to give it a realistic backdrop. Creative liberties have been taken, and in no way does the book look to educate more than entertain. And in that endeavour I hope I have succeeded.

I have always been intrigued by the secret world of espionage and its role in the contemporary world. *Bard of Blood*, though entirely a work of fiction, is my way of thanking the silent forces at work for ensuring that our country remains safe. These are men and women who place our interests above theirs, so that we can have a good night's sleep.

This book wouldn't have been in your hands had it not been for S. Hussain Zaidi. My mentor, teacher, a father figure and truly one of India's best crime-writers, Hussain sir is a treasure trove of knowledge. He has guided me and entertained my questions at the unearthliest of hours. Hussain sir, Velly ma'am and their two children, Ammar and Zain, are my second family. Thank you for being there!

I am also indebted to the immensely knowledgeable Brijesh Singh, Inspector General of Maharashtra Police, who bailed me out of the helpless position a writer often finds himself in. Thank you, sir, for your invaluable inputs!

I would also like to thank Glenn Carle, who was a career field operations officer of the Central Intelligence Agency. He helped me get my basic facts about terrorism in place before I set out writing this book.

Thank you, Chiki Sarkar, for reposing your faith in this project. It is an honour to be published by Penguin Random House, and I thank the entire team who worked on the book for making this possible. Thank you, Rachita Raj, my editor, who has ensured that the book reads well. Thank you, Shruti Katoch, for working on the publicity. Thank you, Gavin Morris and Saurav Das, for a great cover design!

Thank you, Pallavi Pawar, my English teacher from school. She is my friend and confidante, and words cannot express my gratitude. Love you, Miss P!

Mamatha Shetty, one of my other school teachers, had always told me that I have what it takes to be a writer. I didn't quite believe it until now. Thank you, ma'am!

Vibha Singh ma'am, thank you for your helpful feedback on the story.

And then, of course, I would like to thank all my friends who didn't quite contribute to the book directly, but have placed their confidence in me and have been there through thick and thin—Nabeel, Veer, Abdul, Siddhesh, Maria, Sonia, Nikita, Ketaki and many others who know who they are! I'm grateful to have friends like you! I would also like to thank all my colleagues at Red Chillies Entertainment who have taught me a lot in the past year!

A special thank you to Shah Rukh sir. I remember handing him the first ever copy of this book that Penguin had sent me. And today, because of his support and guidance, it is a show on Netflix! He is and always will be someone I look up to.

Emraan Hashmi is someone I met because of Hussain sir when I had completed writing this book. He had launched this book for me way before there was a possibility of it being adapted for the screen. And now, he is playing the lead character. He nothing short of a brother to me and I will always love the Hashmi family for their warmth.

And finally, I would like to thank my family—my parents, Mansoor and Farhat, my sister, Zayna, and my Nani, Hamida, for simply being the best in the world! I love you all beyond measure.

I had told myself at the tender age of thirteen that I would write at least one book before I die. Well, seven years later, here we are. Now, on to the next one!

PART I

'Come What Come May'

Prologue

26 August 2014
Quetta, Balochistan

A fourteen-year-old boy, the youngest in the crowd, watched the four men rolling on the rocky ground. Their faces were caked with blood. Their bloodshot eyes were half open. A white discharge seeped from the corner of their mouths. The sun beat down hard upon them. The boy looked up at his father's animated face, quizzically.

'Watch on, son.'

The boy's gaze shifted back to the four semi-conscious men on the ground. The people in the crowd, all members of the Taliban, jostled with each other to get a better look at the wounded men. It had been almost two hours since they had been waiting at the venue—a large, barren ground, enclosed within high steel grilles and barbed wire. This killing field was perched atop a low hill. The men wore black kurtas and covered their faces in chequered scarves as protection from the gusts of dusty wind that blew about. As the clock ticked, they began to grow impatient and belted out uncouth

slogans. But none left, because they were about to witness
the beheading of four nationals of a country they had been
taught to loathe. And the moment they had been waiting for
had finally arrived.

Two white Toyota off-road vehicles made their way
through a metal gate and up the low hill. The crowd gasped
collectively in awe as a turbaned man stepped out of the rear
seat of one of the vehicles. He was tall, around six foot four,
and had a black eyepatch to go with his black salwar-kurta.
He was rather elderly, as the grey in his beard revealed.
The man glanced around at the soldiers waiting to catch
a glimpse of him and raised one hand to greet them. They
cheered raucously.

'Who is that, Abbu?' the young boy asked his father,
curiously.

'That, my son, is the Amir al-Mu'minin.'

The boy's gaze shifted back to the mysterious man.

'Amir al-Mu'minin?'

'The Commander of the Faithful, my son. When Allah
summoned our beloved Prophet Muhammad, peace be
upon him, to *jannat*, his spot was left vacant on earth. The
Almighty needed someone to lead the faithful Muslims on
this planet.'

A few questions popped up in the boy's head, as he
saw machetes being sharpened. The Amir was circling the
four Indian prisoners, staring at their twisted forms on the
ground.

'So, this is our new Prophet?' the boy asked innocently.

'There is only one Allah, and Muhammad is his Prophet.'
His father smiled. 'But Mohammed Omar is the new leader
of the Muslims, son. In the city of Kandahar, there was a
large mosque that held our Prophet's cloak in a series of
locked chests. The Prophet had said that anyone who could

retrieve the cloak would be his successor. Many tried and failed. Until a Pashtun, like you and me, came along.'

The boy gazed in admiration at the old man with the eyepatch. The blowing wind made the dust swirl up behind him, making him look heroic. The eyepatch added to the mystery that surrounded him. He had been wounded severely during the 1989 battle in Jalalabad, during the Afghan Civil War. He survived, but his left eye couldn't. A fragment of shrapnel had destroyed it completely. Since then he had worn an eyepatch. His eye bled sometimes, a sign that he was furious. And when *his* eye bled, people bled.

'Son, I have brought you here to show you our leader. All of us here are a part of his Taliban. We fight for his cause, because his cause is Allah's will. You should consider yourself lucky. Not everyone gets to see him because men from foreign lands, the kafirs, are waiting to kill him.'

'He is a good man if he is carrying out Allah's will,' the boy reasoned. 'Why would they want to kill him?'

The father was about to reply, when the Amir's voice boomed from a megaphone. He was pointing at the four prisoners that lay near his feet, trussed up like turkeys.

'Four Indians,' he bellowed into a microphone, to the people that had gathered to witness the execution. He had taken his place behind the four prisoners on the ground. His men stood respectfully behind him, each with a machete of his own.

'Hindustanis,' he continued, his voice climbing up in decibels. 'Friends of the Americans. Enemies of Our Cause. Above all, enemies of Islam!'

He looked down briefly at the captives, as the crowd cursed in unison.

'Yes, my soldiers. These four have been caught spying on us,' he continued. 'Indian agents. *Jasoos.* They don't seem to understand that meddling in our business and meddling with Allah's will isn't good for them. But they still do it. The Indians, the Americans, all of them. Above all, they fail to realize that interfering in my mission to create an Islamic caliphate is going to cost them, and everyone like them, their lives! Today, my loyal mujahideen, I will set an example!'

The crowd cheered raucously, as the Amir took a machete in his hand and held it high.

'My aim, as many of you know, is to get the haram Americans out of our beautiful land and direct the Talib insurgency against them and the Government of Afghanistan. After that, I will create a greater land . . . Pashtunistan!' His voice boomed through the speakers. 'But how can I possibly do this if people like these keep getting in my way?'

He waved his machete in the air.

'I had promised to destroy America. But I will also destroy its allies,' he sneered. The crowd cheered as if they were witnessing a well-fought cricket match.

'I want four volunteers,' he said as he held the machete out and walked towards the crowd that consisted mostly of the members of his army, ranging in age from fourteen to fifty. He scanned the crowd for worthy volunteers with his one good eye. It settled on a group of young boys, who, like everyone else, had their arms stretched out, hoping to be bestowed with the honour of executing the prisoners. He liked young boys.

'Raise your hand, son!'

The young boy raised his hand. The Amir stopped in front of him and motioned him to step out. The boy walked out, warily. His father's chest puffed with pride.

The boy and the other volunteers were handed a machete each. The men had their heads rested on a tree trunk.

'Enjoy the fear in their eyes.' He smiled as he goaded the young boys. They were just young teens, but the power of having someone's life at their mercy felt intoxicating. Cries of *Allah-o-Akbar* echoed through the mountains. The crowd had readied themselves to witness the act. They didn't notice a Mercedes pulling up right behind the parked SUVs.

A burly middle-aged man got out of the car and ran hurriedly towards the prisoners. The boys with the machetes had braced themselves, as instructed by their Amir. They raised their machetes and the four captives closed their eyes, ready to accept their fate.

'STOP!'

The Amir turned to look at the burly man who had just arrived running towards him. He motioned the boys to stop. They lowered their machetes.

The man stood on his toes and whispered into the tall Amir's ear. The Amir looked at him angrily and shook his head. 'No,' he said. 'I do not negotiate when it comes to such matters.'

The other man continued to reason. The Amir was visibly furious. The crowd looked on intently, watching their leader lose his cool.

'Let them live for now and then we get to kill more like them,' the other man said through gritted teeth, holding the Amir's arm. 'I have a plan, Amir. At least hear me out!'

The Amir contained his fury and paused to think. He stroked his wild grey beard and motioned the boys to drop their weapons and go back. They obeyed. The four agents opened their eyes, wondering if they were dead already. Strangely, they were not. They shot confused glances at each other. They saw the Amir walk up towards them and then turn to the crowd.

'My friend here insists that these kafirs should not be killed,' the Amir said. A collective gasp went through the crowd. And then he made a dismissive gesture. 'That is all I can tell you for now, my faithful soldiers. Please leave peacefully.'

The crowd murmured as they walked out. He then turned towards the four agents, and knelt next to them.

'I wanted to kill you,' he said, 'but this man and his people have other plans.' The Amir looked at the four bewildered faces with sadistic pleasure.

'I'm going to give your country a chance to let you live,' he continued. 'It is up to them to take this chance . . . which I know they won't. You come from a country of selfish people. And I will kill you soon enough . . . soon after you realize that dying for them isn't worth it.'

He was uncomfortably close to one of the men. The agent spat on him. The Amir, enraged, stood up and sent his boot into the agent's face, knocking off several of his teeth. The man buckled and fell to the floor, unconscious.

Before he could do anything more reckless, the other man held his arm firmly and led him towards his car.

Maulana Mohammed Omar's—Amir al-Mu'minin's—right eye began to bleed. And when his eye bled, the people bled.

1

28 August 2014
New Delhi

A silver Honda sedan drove into the garage of a rather ordinary-looking bungalow in Vasant Vihar. The driver, a tall bespectacled man with carefully combed thinning hair, parked the car and stepped out. Lieutenant General Sadiq Sheikh liked this part about his evenings the most: parking the car in the garage and relaxing until the drive back to the grind the next morning. He usually took the day off on Sundays, unless, of course, he was absolutely required to get down to the Wing, as his office was informally called. Not a rare occurrence for a man in his profession.

Sadiq was two years short of sixty, and felt it was time to hang up his boots in the coming year. He had served India for thirty-two years. Initially, he spent his time as a field agent for the Military Intelligence—MI—and then rose through the ranks to become the Lieutenant General. But soon enough, his guile and uncanny ability to strategize led to his induction into the Research and Analysis Wing—

RAW—overseeing covert operations in Pakistan. Sadiq's induction was definitely surprising. Not many Muslims had applied or gone through the rigorous preparations to be a part of RAW, solely because of their perception of a non-existent bias. But Sadiq stood as an example for those who felt this way. For a while, he was the link between RAW and the MI. And then he returned to head the MI, as the Director General from the office at Sena Bhavan. He had had a good run so far. A few downs, but more than a few ups. Sometimes, a victory in his profession was all about minimizing damage, and Sadiq had done a good job of that. The current RAW chief, Arun Joshi, had been rather vocal about how they would have a tough time looking for an appropriate replacement for the void that Sadiq was about to leave behind.

He slipped off his shoes, but kept his socks on. He pulled off his vest, ruffling his neatly combed, scanty hair, and threw it on the single bed as he entered his room. He dropped his car keys and wallet into a drawer, and unstrapped his watch and placed it inside, delicately. He then proceeded to the kitchen to make himself a strong cup of coffee. He slid his hand into his pocket and searched for his pack of Marlboro cigarettes. Smoking wasn't a habit he liked, but he firmly believed that of all the things he had survived in the world of intelligence work, smoking would be the last thing to kill him. He lit one and took a long drag, while the coffee was brewing. It was during moments like these when he wished he had a family. Someone to welcome him back after a taxing day at work. It had never troubled him in his youth, but now he thought of it almost every other day. He wasn't celibate, of course, but having a family would have put his loved ones directly in the line of fire. For a man like him, a family would be a weakness.

A weakness he couldn't hide. Though he didn't regret his decision, he often found himself wondering what it might have been to have a wife and, perhaps, even a son. The coffee was ready, and he poured it into his large ceramic mug. He picked it up in the same hand that squeezed his cigarette between his fingers, and walked into the living room.

A son. A face flashed in his mind that led him back to his MI days. *At least I have known what having a son would be like. And I screwed that up. I wish it hadn't ended the way it did.* He switched on his reading lamp and sat on the sofa beside it. The rest of the room was entirely dark. Sadiq sipped his coffee and then grabbed the television remote. He checked which films were airing. Unlike yesterday, when he had watched Marlon Brando's *Julius Caesar*, today had nothing interesting to offer. He enjoyed watching the news as much as some people enjoyed watching TV soaps. For him, the news was his other source of fiction on television. Only a few channels were credible, and Sadiq, in a bid to relax, often turned to the other ones to entertain himself. He liked the fact that he could segregate lies from the truth, propaganda from reality, all the while sipping his evening coffee after a long day of work. He kept his coffee aside and could almost feel himself drifting into a nap that he often took before dinner, when the phone rang.

He felt the phone vibrate against his left thigh and reached into his pocket. It was the cellphone the Wing had provided him. He put on his spectacles and squinted at the screen. There was no identifiable number on it. His secure phone seldom rang without reason, and though Sadiq wasn't quite in the mood to answer it, he did.

'*Salaam aleikum*, Sadiq Sahab,' a calm voice greeted him. Sadiq was unfamiliar with the voice on the other end.

'*Waleikum as-salaam*,' Sadiq replied with an equal measure of courtesy. 'Who's speaking?'

'That's not important, Sadiq Sahab,' the caller said. The voice had a slight metallic ring to it. A voice modulator, Sadiq realized.

'Well, if you've called me to exchange sweet nothings, now is not a good time.'

'I can assure you it is more than that,' the voice on the other end replied.

'What's stopping you?' Sadiq quipped.

'Remember Vikramjit Singh?'

Sadiq fell silent. It had been over seven years since the RAW agent Vikramjit Singh was killed in action in Quetta. Someone had sold the operation out.

'What about him?' Sadiq said softly.

'I'm going to read out an address to you,' the voice resumed. 'You meet me there, and you'll get answers to the questions that are bottled up inside you. You know me, but I'm afraid I can't let my real voice be heard over the phone.'

Sadiq scrambled hurriedly for a pen, and grabbed the first piece of paper he could find. He urged the man to go on. The man dictated the address clearly. A place in Dhaula Kuan. 'I want you here within half an hour.'

The line went dead.

Sadiq, suddenly feeling very alert, picked up his mug of coffee and began to walk towards his room. The coffee had gone cold, he gulped it down. This case was back to haunt him. One of the few mysteries that he hadn't been able to crack in his long and otherwise illustrious career. He tried to live with the fact that he might never get to the bottom of it, but it needled him every single day. As he poured the thick brown dregs at the bottom of the mug into the sink, he began to recap the information he had about that fateful day in the city of Quetta, in the Balochistan province of Pakistan.

Sadiq still remembered the time he had briefed Vikramjit personally, with the intention to embed him in Quetta and spy on the Shura's elements. Vikramjit had always been a bright agent. Even though his physique and strength may not have been the best in a crunch situation, despite being well built, he more than made up for it with his well-honed ability to think on his feet. He had always dropped hints about wanting to work there, and Sadiq was impressed with his enthusiasm. So when Sadiq did eventually offer him the assignment, Vikramjit agreed without batting an eyelid. But in 2005, the year when Balochistan was at the height of turmoil, Vikramjit was killed under mysterious circumstances. His death was one of the few cases that disturbed Sadiq the most. Closure evaded him. Along with Vikramjit, Sadiq had also lost the man he considered a son. The man he had put into Balochistan himself. The man who had never spoken to him since he was forced to bow out of the game.

Just recently, Sadiq's officers had intercepted a few messages that were directed to the Quetta Shura from a location in India. *There has to be a connect,* he thought, as he opened his drawer and picked up his car keys. He chose one of the few watches lying in his drawer and casually slipped it on. He forced his feet into his shoes and walked briskly out of his house. It was almost 9 p.m. Sadiq had half an hour to reach his destination. He cursed himself, realizing his car was now parked comfortably in the garage. He jerked the large door open and got behind the wheel. He reversed the Honda City out of the driveway and on to the road. He switched the air conditioner on. Sadiq checked the dashboard for his pistol. *Just in case,* he thought. He looked at the address on the bit of paper he held in his hand one last time and then put his foot on the gas. For a man advanced in years, Sadiq drove with the precision of a professional race-car driver. Within a half hour, Sadiq had pulled up in front of his destination.

He adjusted his spectacles and looked at the abandoned cottage. It was slightly smaller than the standard Delhi bungalow. He took his handgun out of the dashboard and concealed it under his shirt, in the small of his back. He parked his car and looked at his watch, fiddling with it as he walked up to the door. He was about to knock, when he realized the door was already ajar. He pushed it further open softly. A musty smell welcomed him. The corridor was dark, and Sadiq found his way into a small room that was dimly lit and smelled of cigarette smoke. He strained to see a figure sitting on a rocking chair, in the corner of the room. The man's silhouette was vaguely familiar.

The man got up and walked into the lit portion of the room, leaving his rocking chair swaying smoothly. He wore an oversized black coat, and was smoking a cigarette.

'Oh, I should've known it was you,' Sadiq said with a sense of dread. 'Tell me what you've got.'

The man's reciprocated smile did not reach his eyes. He took a step towards Sadiq.

'The insider,' he said, holding the cigarette, 'the man who sold the operation out in Balochistan in 2006 and has leaked many secrets ever since is still in the organization.'

Sadiq nodded. He was about to speak when the man interrupted him.

'But you knew that already, didn't you?'

'Do you know his identity?' Sadiq asked calmly.

The man took in a lungful of his cigarette and then dropped it, extinguishing it with his foot. He ignored Sadiq's question.

'I'll get to that. But as we speak, know that four of your agents in Quetta have been compromised.'

Sadiq stood silently as he tried to process this latest bit of information. The man walked up to him quickly and put his hand right behind Sadiq's back. He pulled the hidden gun out.

'Old bastard,' the man spat out.

And then it all fell in place. The missing piece of the Balochistan puzzle. The insider that they could never catch stood right before him. The reason Sadiq had to suspend his favourite agent. The man walked back to his initial position, pocketing Sadiq's gun.

'It was you,' Sadiq muttered softly. He shook his head and squinted down at his feet. When he looked up, the barrel of a silenced 0.22 Walther PPK was pointing at him. He smiled sourly. 'I should've known.'

'There you go, Sadiq Sheikh. What started in Balochistan had never really ended. It will end now. Right here in India,' the man smiled cruelly. 'Not with your death alone, though. You have failed, Sadiq.'

Sadiq nervously fiddled with his watch. The man continued, 'Soon, the people who consider you a hero will remember you as the man who met a sorry death, not the patriot who served his country well. And that thought should scare you. Balochistan has always been a grey area for you, Sadiq. You may have been able to delay the imminent attacks, but you could never have stopped them.'

Sadiq said through gritted teeth: 'You're killing me now because you're afraid. Afraid that I will get in the way again.'

'I like your sense of self-importance.' The man grinned, his gun steadily aimed at Sadiq's head. 'But the country will burn. And there's nothing you'll be able to do about it.'

'You underestimate the love for the country that people in our agency have,' Sadiq said. 'Not everyone is like you.

Believe it or not, some of us will go to any extent to prove our patriotism. Rest assured, there's no way you'll get out of this alive.'

The man laughed throatily.

'The same old Sadiq Sheikh. You let me do the worrying about that,' the man said in a patronizing tone. 'Any other famous last words?'

Sadiq stood silently, looking at the ground. And then, with a dry smile, looked the man in the eye and said clearly:

Of all the wonders that I yet have heard,
It seems to me most strange that men should fear;
Seeing that death, a necessary end,
Will come when it will come.

The man looked confused on hearing Sadiq reciting poetry. He addressed him with a wry smile: 'Always been one for theatrics, haven't we? I'm glad you're accepting your death with a smile.'

'Your death will come, too,' Sadiq said. 'Sooner than you expect. But not before you realize that you've failed again.'

He closed his eyes and prayed silently in his mind. And then there was a muffled gunshot. Lieutenant General Sadiq Sheikh had found closure . . . in death.

2

29 August 2014
Mumbai

A slight drizzle had sputtered to a stop as the final schedule of the day went under way. The weather was beginning to get pleasant after one of Mumbai's perpetual hot afternoons. It was the most enthusiastically awaited part of the day's play for the students of Francisco's College. For the teachers, not as much. Having earlier beaten the students at lesser games like carom, the teachers now had to face them at a more physically taxing sport at the large Azad Maidan opposite the college.

The students had the upper hand, obviously a no-brainer. Since the past few years, the students had been consistently outdoing their professors at the game of football. They were young, athletic and knew the game better than their older counterparts. The college organized a sports festival every year, and one of the events included the teachers and students playing against each other. The teachers, portly and unfit, played the game without nursing any serious hopes of winning. And so, just like every other year, they were accepting their defeat gracefully and with smiles all round. It was mutually decided that a forty-minute game would be played, since the teachers' midriffs wouldn't allow them to pretend to play more than that. The students laughed and agreed. It was the only time of the year they could humiliate their teachers without getting a dressing-down for it.

At half-time, the score was three goals to none. The teachers formed a huddle and spoke generally of a strategy that involved not conceding any further goals. Scoring a goal, they all agreed, was not even a remote possibility. One of them even suggested forfeiting the match and going back to the sidelines.

'Twenty minutes, and they've already scored three goals,' Mr Reddy, the maths professor, said. 'Another twenty minutes, and another three goals are a certainty. And that's if they're in the mood to be nice to us.'

The other teachers nodded in agreement.

'We've still got twenty minutes to win it,' said a distinct voice, softly.

The teachers broke out of their huddle to see the literature professor, half-smiling, behind them. He looked rather different today. His eyes beneath his perfectly arched eyebrows were black and cold, like two bullet-holes. He had his greying hair tied up in a short ponytail. He hadn't bothered shaving. He seldom did, unless it got out of hand and became itchy. He stood a little short of six feet, and wore a black form-fitting T-shirt and Adidas trackpants that complimented his well-toned physique. Both the lady teachers and girl students agreed, albeit secretly, that he was the best-looking professor in college. He was forty-one, single and stayed alone in a small flat in the suburbs of Mumbai. He never mingled much, save for the occasional greetings he returned to fellow professors and students. He was somewhat mysterious, in that sense. People just took him to be asocial. But they also agreed on another point. He was possibly the best Shakespeare teacher that had set foot in the institution. He was a changed man when he began to read out the Bard's verses and plays. His was probably the only class in the day when the students would give a teacher their undivided attention.

'So you finally decided to come out and play with us. To what do we the owe the pleasure?' Reddy asked him.

The Professor smiled. 'The fact that you get your asses kicked on a consistent basis, year after year. I'm here to change that.'

The students noticed the new player on the field and nudged each other. Was he really going to play football with the rest of the teachers? The students on the periphery of the field clapped wildly and began cheering this addition to the team. They had never, in the past six years, seen the Professor anywhere but the classroom. He used to be there on time, and would leave on time. But today, it seemed, was different.

'We still can't win,' Reddy said. 'Do the math.'

'What is past is prologue,' the Professor quoted Shakespeare with a smile. 'I'm replacing you on the field. Go do the math on the sidelines.'

Reddy walked away silently, wiping the sweat off his brow. The rest of the teachers seemed amused and even slightly surprised at the treatment meted out to the math professor.

'Now, we're going to play to win. If we lose the match, we can take solace in the fact that we tried,' the Professor said. 'So here's the plan.'

~

The physics professor, Mr Nimkar, and the literature professor stood opposite each other, waiting for the referee to blow the whistle to commence the second half. Nimkar, probably the fittest professor on the team, tapped the ball lightly to the Professor, who touched it and controlled it lightly under his foot. He looked up to see the openings in the field and motioned to Nimkar to position himself a few paces ahead. As soon as Nimkar did so, he tapped the ball back to him and ran in a blur, ahead of a clueless defender. Nimkar sent a clumsy pass down to the Professor, which he controlled with visible ease. He dodged another enthusiastic defender and, in a swift motion, closed in on the goalkeeper. With a neat touch, he finished the ball along the ground, into the back of the net. The students in the audience fell suddenly silent—it was probably the first time they had seen a professor score a goal as brilliant as that. And then, suddenly, they roared in delight.

The Professor just smiled to himself. *Two more to equalize, three more to win.* The teachers themselves looked shocked. The Professor raised a hand and motioned the crowd to calm down.

The ball was set rolling again, this time by the students. They passed it around, manoeuvring it nicely around the less-talented professors. Their ace striker, a young boy of twenty, was closing in on the goal and was just about to take a shot when he realized the ball wasn't with him any more. The literature professor had it at his feet and was shooting through the empty spaces on the field. One enthusiastic, muscular defender came running towards him and rammed into his shoulder. The Professor lost his footing for a second, but not the ball. Instead, it was the defender who lost his balance, after colliding into a shoulder made of what seemed like iron. The Professor saw the goal clearly this time. He dribbled the ball to attain a suitable angle. He made enough space and then, with calculated strength, hit the ball with the arch of his foot. The ball swerved inwards into the net. There was nothing the keeper could do about it! He kicked the grass in frustration and turned to retrieve the ball dejectedly.

The crowd erupted into a louder cheer this time. *Ten minutes. One to equalize. One to win.* Could the Professor actually pull it off? He was single-handedly taking on the college's best footballers. The odds were still stacked against his team, though. He strode over and muttered something into Nimkar's ear. Nimkar nodded and in turn went and whispered something into the Hindi professor Mr Shukla's ear. He nodded, but it didn't look like he understood fully.

The students broke out of their huddle and clapped and shouted words of encouragement to each other. They looked charged and ready to take on the Professor's team. They kicked off and passed the ball backwards to a defender. They were passing the ball around, trying to get time off their back. It was the safest way they could win, they reckoned. The Professor understood their ploy and began to judge their passing rhythm. He jogged slowly to where he knew the next pass would be and, just as soon as the student tapped it, he ran wildly towards the ball. He gained possession of it and had the ball in his command. He dribbled past the final defender faking a shot at the goal and stopped mockingly right in front of the goalkeeper. The goalkeeper ran towards him to grab the ball, just as he kicked it aside and dodged the goalie cleverly and, in a languorous sweep of his foot, landed the ball into the goal. The crowd went berserk! They couldn't believe their eyes. Not only was the literature professor beating the students, he was doing it in style. They had equalized!

Three minutes to go. One goal to win. The Professor loosened his ponytail and opened up his sweaty hair. He allowed himself a dimpled smile as he looked at the students yelling out his name. The students knew three minutes were not likely to be enough for the professors to win. But, given today, they had already suspended their belief so far. The opposition team came together in a huddle yet again. They discussed the situation heatedly, throwing in an abundance of cuss words for good measure. The other professors, however, were speechless. They didn't say a word to their colleague, and he didn't say a word to them either.

It was time, the referee said, to resume the match. The opposition started with the ball again. They decided to take a shot at the goal themselves. It was win or lose. They didn't want to settle for a draw at this point. Their two best strikers ran furiously, dodging a few professors along the way. Nimkar stuck his leg out and got the ball. He passed it to Shukla, who, by fluke, managed to hold possession of the ball now. There were just two minutes of play left. Shukla looked completely out of place with the ball at his feet, as he moved clumsily towards the goal. Suddenly, a defender came running into him from behind and knocked him off balance. The crowd laughed and then quickly tried to contain themselves.

The referee blew the whistle. It was a free kick. There was a deafening silence as the literature professor bent down to tie his laces. He placed himself behind the ball and set his eye on the spot where he intended to send the ball. He was pretty accurate at shooting . . . *even if it was a football this time.* He skipped lightly, readying himself to take the shot. The goal was at quite a distance, and there was no margin for error. He narrowed his eyes, cut out the environment from his system and, then, with a quick run-up, shot the ball as hard as he could. The ball ricocheted off the top of the goalpost and bounced into the goal. The crowd went silent for what seemed an eternity. And then they suddenly erupted into a wild and rapturous applause. The students, the teachers, everyone regarded the literature professor with new eyes. It was possibly the most dramatic football game they had ever witnessed!

The Professor walked back, unable to contain his smile. He took a towel and wiped the sweat off his ash-grey temples and the tip of his long nose. He picked up a bottle of water and emptied it over his head. His T-shirt was drenched with sweat. They had never seen the Professor like this before. He was usually dressed in a crisp white shirt and well-ironed trousers. But today, here he was, smiling like a young boy who had just managed to pull off the impossible.

The other teachers came up to him and began to pat him on the back and shake hands with him joyously. They still couldn't believe what had happened. It was a thoroughly enjoyable evening. The Professor smiled at them all and some even heard him laugh—a rarity. The losing team, meanwhile, faced the jeers of their classmates, which they were just not prepared for.

This is when they spotted the Principal of the college, a tall, elderly man with a slight stoop, scurrying towards them. 'Professor Anand,' he gasped, his mouth agape. 'There is a call for you. It's from the PM's office!'

The Professor turned and narrowed his eyes at the Principal. The other teachers shot each other confused looks.

The Principal continued, almost out of breath. 'Two men are here, at my office, waiting to take you back to Delhi.'

And then, suddenly, to all those within earshot, the football match they had just witnessed became the most believable part of the day. The confusion amongst the teachers turned to shock and bewilderment. Within minutes, a distorted version of the news spread through the campus like wildfire. Professor Kabir Anand had been summoned to Delhi by none other than the Prime Minister of India himself.

~

'Hello, Professor Anand,' a voice greeted Kabir curtly as he answered the phone in the Principal's office. 'I'm Arun Joshi.'

Two tall, broad men, clad in identical shirts, waited outside the door, not letting the Principal into his own office. Known to be a calm man otherwise, even he was flustered with the matter at hand. He walked away, cursing under his breath.

'This is uncalled for,' Kabir replied. 'I'm sure there's nothing so important that you had to call up the college principal. Besides, I do happen to have a cellphone. You guys at the Wing must really keep up with new technology.'

'Well, I wasn't getting through. And, yes, it is that urgent.'

'Does the prime minister want me to teach his daughter Shakespeare?'

'No,' Joshi replied. 'The prime minister doesn't have a daughter.'

'Exactly!' Kabir snapped. 'Please never call me again.'

'This is a matter of high importance, Kabir Anand.' Joshi was beginning to lose his cool. 'And there is a chopper at the base waiting to get you here.'

'Tell me what it is now,' Kabir said. 'I don't want to miss my favourite show on TV tonight.'

'I'm afraid this matter can't be discussed over the phone,' Joshi said. 'I will see you at the Office in a bit.'

The line went dead. Kabir turned to see the two men watching over him, blocking the door.

'You can tell Joshi to screw himself,' Kabir said. 'I'm not going anywhere.'

Kabir took a step towards the door. The men didn't budge.

'Sir, we have been instructed to bring you back. Now we either step out amicably, or . . .' The other man raised a small pistol.

'You don't have the balls to do that,' Kabir said.

'It's a dart gun,' said the man quietly. 'One shot, and you will be fast asleep in seconds. The choice is yours. The three of us walk out together like respectable gentlemen, or the two of us carry you out whilst you are unconscious.'

Kabir glared angrily at them.

'After we step out of the door and fly down to Delhi,' Kabir hissed, 'be careful never to cross my path again—both of you!'

3

29 August 2014
RAW HQ, New Delhi

It was ten minutes past ten when the chopper touched base. Kabir was reluctant to be where he was, but the little episode at the college had left him with no choice. He didn't know why he was being called back and wasn't sure if he wanted to know. He had bittersweet memories of his past life—mostly bitter, though, because of the unceremonious exit he was handed. He promised himself to hear out what they had to say now, but nothing more.

Earlier, the agents assigned with the task of bringing Kabir to Delhi had planned to take him directly to the chopper that awaited him. Kabir had insisted on going home first to shower and change before flying. The game had left him sweaty.

He had left the agents waiting outside and taken a good forty minutes to get ready. He did this more to annoy them than anything else. He combed his long hair back neatly, wore one of his standard white Arrow shirts with a pair of grey trousers, and put on his only black jacket. Even though he hated to admit it to himself, his muscles had begun to ache after playing that little bit of football.

He got into the standard-issue black Tata SUV and the two men followed in another vehicle. He recalled the last time he had travelled to the RAW HQ. It was a long time ago. Something he had wished to get out of his head over the past few years. His mentor, a father figure to him, Lieutenant General Sadiq Sheikh had led him to quit the service.

The driver got out of the car and rushed to open Kabir's door the moment they arrived at the Wing. Kabir had already opened it himself. He didn't much like ceremony. The driver then went on to flash his ID at the entrance, to a guard who unlocked the door. Once in the Wing, the driver began to instruct Kabir as to where the Chief sat. Kabir already knew, but listened anyway and then patted him on his back gently. He walked towards the Chief's cabin, and found his assistant's desk outside. Unlike those portrayed in popular culture, the chief of this intelligence agency didn't have a leggy lass with a tight shirt and skirt to welcome his guests. Instead, the assistant was a rather ordinary-looking middle-aged man, with his hair combed severely to the right, and a pencil moustache. He looked up at Kabir and acknowledged him.

He pushed a little buzzer and said into the microphone, 'He's here, sir.'

'Send him in,' the voice replied immediately. Kabir was already in the process of pushing open the Chief's door.

He entered and looked at the Chief's cabin with a sense of familiarity. Not much had changed. The same old yellow light, resembling that of a five-star hotel, illuminated the room. The wooden flooring was intact. The picture of

Mahatma Gandhi hung exactly where it had the last time Kabir had seen it. There were more books this time around and the TV was almost as large as the wooden panel on the wall. The entire office was simple yet grand, and the Chief's cabin stood testimony to this. Arun Joshi, who was watching the news, made a great show of switching the TV off. He was fifty-five, dyed his wavy hair an awkward jet black and wore a pair of silver glasses and a sharp navy blue suit. He got up swiftly and stretched his right hand out. Kabir shook it firmly.

'Please sit, Mr Anand.'

His voice was calm, but at the same time not one that you'd want to disobey. Kabir sat down.

'Would you like some tea or coffee?'

'Coffee,' Kabir replied instantly. *Never refuse coffee.*

The Chief pressed a button on his desk and asked for two cups of coffee. Almost immediately, an orderly came running in with a tray with two cups of steaming coffee. He asked Joshi if he should bring in something to eat. Joshi looked at Kabir, who declined. Joshi thanked the orderly and sent him away, and then looking towards Kabir clasped his hands together, making a let's-get-down-to-business gesture.

'I'm sorry about the little hiccups we had earlier this evening,' Joshi said.

'Let's cut to the chase already.'

He stared at Kabir's inscrutable face for a moment before he broke the news to him. *Sadiq Sheikh was shot dead last night.* Kabir closed his eyes and breathed in deeply when he heard it. His throat had gone dry all of a sudden, his stomach lurched. A slideshow of repressed memories flashed through his mind. But his face remained expressionless in the moments of silence that ensued. It is impossible to judge a person's feelings by his countenance. Joshi knew that Kabir was hurt deeply, even though his face did not betray any such emotion.

'Before dying,' Joshi continued, as he adjusted his spectacles, 'he left a message through a concealed transmitter in his wristwatch.'

He then went on to play the message by tapping a button on a small Sony recorder. Kabir listened silently to the audio. There was a lot of static throughout the recording. The voice of the killer was almost inaudible, and Sadiq's voice could just barely be deciphered.

Of all the wonders that I yet have heard,
It seems to me most strange that men should fear;
Seeing that death, a necessary end,
Will come when it will come.

And then the muffled gunshot was heard.

Act 2, Scene 2, *Julius Caesar*, Kabir recalled instantly.

'The bad sound quality is because of the scramblers present in the room,' Joshi explained. 'The killer was careful. He suspected Sadiq might have left his phone on in his pocket, which I'm glad he didn't. Had he done that instead, we wouldn't have gotten even this piece. The phone wasn't found on his body anyway. The techs are still working on the other man's voice. I'll tell you more about that when I get to know.'

'Why didn't he name his killer in the conversation, if he was transmitting,' Kabir asked, swallowing his coffee, in an attempt to do something about his dry throat.

Joshi shrugged. 'The killer would know for certain then—that he was trying to leave us a message. He knew he was going to die and didn't want to take the chance of not letting his message get to us.'

Kabir just sat silently, scratching his stubble. He couldn't quite decide on a single emotion. Joshi continued to explain.

'When the message popped up on our computers this morning, it took us a while to figure out what had happened.'

'That doesn't surprise me,' Kabir said sourly. Joshi ignored the jibe.

'When we did figure out that Sadiq was quoting Shakespeare, we realized it was because he was trying to tell us something.'

Joshi paused. He needed to be careful how he approached the subject from here.

He continued, 'It's common knowledge in the Wing that Sadiq Sheikh had a young protégé in the Military Intelligence, who was asked to leave due to certain circumstances that went out of hand. There are various versions of the tale floating around. But apparently, he now teaches Shakespeare at a college in Mumbai.'

'And why is he here now?'

'Look, Kabir. I wasn't Chief when you were serving our country. I didn't know the finer details about what happened in Balochistan until I looked up your files and your impressive track record. Rumour has it that you turned on us and that may have gotten Vikramjit Singh killed. But Sadiq didn't believe that. And I believed in Sadiq.'

Kabir cleared his throat and then looked at the clock. It was closing in on eleven.

'That still doesn't answer my question.'

'We need your assistance,' Joshi said finally. 'Four of our agents have been compromised. They were embedded in Balochistan a few years after your incident. We use them to fund the Balochistan Liberation Army and other such militia that are fighting for secession against the Pakistani government and the ISI.'

Kabir leaned in towards Joshi and spoke softly. 'This is not my life any more. You all took that away from me a while back. I don't understand why you're telling me all of this.'

'I wasn't the Chief that time, Kabir,' Joshi repeated.

'I couldn't care less,' Kabir said. 'The only thing that has hurt me is the fact that Sadiq is no more. So tell me when the funeral is, and I will be there. But that's it. I believe we're done here.'

'His death is just a piece of a larger puzzle. Don't you want to know who may have gotten him killed?'

'There's nothing I can do about it. Besides, I was told seven years ago that there are better agents than me in the game. I'm sure you can make them do something about it.'

Kabir got up, turned and began to walk towards the door.

'Mullah Omar,' Joshi said flatly. Two dreadful words.

Kabir halted in his tracks. He stood still for a few seconds. He turned to face Joshi, his arched eyebrows stitched together in a frown.

'Sit down, Kabir.'

Kabir was drawn back to the chair, his body reluctant, his mind inquisitive. He sat down.

'The last piece of information we had about Omar recently was that he was dead. But then again, he dies every two months,' Joshi spat out. 'Of course, he resides in Quetta and keeps shuffling around within Balochistan. But the last time he made an appearance was around four years back.'

Kabir ran his hand through his long hair. Joshi noticed the streaks of silver hair and the ashen temples.

'It beats me,' Kabir said. 'Omar doesn't give a hoot about India. He has other fish to fry. Even when I was in Balochistan, he was busy directing the Taliban insurgency against the US-led NATO forces and the Government of Afghanistan. When he found someone spying on him, he had him executed immediately. Then why is he holding these guys hostage?'

Joshi nodded his head understandingly.

'Mullah Omar is, for the lack of a better explanation, the ISI's puppet. His second-in-command Mullah Baradar is the one who looks after his day-to-day affairs. They fund him and so they get him to do some of their dirty work. For instance, Omar and Baradar had helped the ISI kill Balach Marri and Akbar Bugti in Balochistan. You know that, of course.'

Kabir nodded. He was there when Bugti was killed.

Balach Marri was the leader of the Balochistan Liberation Army—the BLA—a militant organization fighting for the independence of Balochistan from Pakistan and Iran. The BLA had been pronounced a terror organization, rather ironically, by the Pakistani government. And Marri had been killed by the ISI and the Pakistani military in 2007.

Akbar Bugti, too, had run a well-organized militia against the Pakistani Army. It was on the lines of the BLA, and Pakistan believed that it was the BLA itself. He fought for autonomy, something that cost him his life in 2006.

RAW believes that Mullah Omar played a big hand in assisting the ISI kill these two revolutionaries.

Kabir was posted in Quetta when Bugti and his son were killed. It was the sixth day of August. A Saturday. Kabir relived the moment day after day. He, along with Vikramjit Singh, had spied on a special camp of the Quetta Shura, set up by Omar, which trained terrorists and insurgents to attack Indian interests in Kashmir during that time. The day had started off no differently. But it ended with the death of Akbar Bugti. And Vikramjit Singh. And soon enough, that of Major Kabir Anand's career.

'Why he would keep our agents alive didn't make sense to me.' Joshi broke Kabir out of his trance. 'Until I got the demands from the Taliban spokesman, Zabiullah Mujahid.'

'Which are?'

'Mullah Omar, apparently, wants us to free four of the terrorists we have captured, in exchange for our agents.'

He held up the remote and switched the TV on. He tapped something urgently on his laptop and a grainy video filled up the screen.

It had the four Indian men kneeling next to each other. A turbaned man, with his face covered, stood with a rifle behind them. Not Mullah Omar, of course. Unlike Osama bin Laden, he didn't believe in recording his showmanship on tape.

The screen blacked out, and four names popped up: *Yasin Bhatkal, Assadullah Akhtar, Fayaz Mir, Umar Madni.* After which, there was a simple message.

Freedom in exchange for freedom. You have ten days.

As if it were that simple.

Joshi turned to face Kabir, who had a half-smile on his face.

'Freedom in exchange for freedom,' he repeated. 'Omar is clearly acting as the ISI's mouthpiece.'

Joshi nodded, poured Kabir and himself a glass of water, and gulped his down. Kabir left his untouched.

'I've had a good time catching up with you, sir. But, unfortunately, I have a class waiting to learn how Macbeth met his end.'

'Macbeth has already met his end, Kabir. But you can stop four of ours from meeting theirs.'

The words floated in the silence that ensued.

Kabir scratched some invisible lint off his jacket, and finally asked: 'What do you want me to do?'

'Clearly, there is a larger conspiracy at play. The ISI is up to no good as usual, and Sadiq's death is connected. The mole—that my predecessor mistook you to be—is still in the agency. I want you to help me connect the dots. There is a reason Sadiq asked for you before he died.'

'He didn't ask for me,' Kabir said, avoiding eye contact. 'How exactly do you want me to connect the dots?'

'I want you to meet the former Afghan head of intelligence, who is in Mumbai currently. He's dissatisfied with President Hamid Karzai's appeasement policies. Needless to say, he strongly dislikes the Pakistani government and the ISI. His bitterness led him to quit the agency, but he still wields a lot of influence amongst his supporters back in Afghanistan.'

'Arifullah Umar Saleh,' Kabir said. 'I meet him, then what?'

'He will tell you everything you need to know,' Joshi stated. 'Omar's location in Quetta. Omar's camps and their infrastructure—something Afghanistan's current director of intelligence would deny. Saleh is helping us settle a score, which kind of helps him settle his. Amongst other things, he's a good guy at heart.'

'Hard for the head of an intelligence agency to be a "good guy at heart",' Kabir said sardonically.

'*Former* head of an intelligence agency,' Joshi corrected him with a wry smile. 'After that, you meet a team of three that I will send down. And then you leave for Balochistan.'

Kabir looked up, surprised.

'And then I leave for Balochistan,' he repeated and laughed softly. 'Are there any good end-of-season sales in Quetta, Mr Joshi? Should I pick up a few RPGs for you?'

'No.' Joshi forced a slight laugh. 'Bring back my agents to me.'

'Ridiculous.' Kabir sighed. 'I'm not fit, mentally or physically, to get back in the field. And that is only if I consider it in the first place.'

'That is why you'll be leading a team of those who are physically fit,' Joshi said. 'I don't believe that you aren't mentally fit, though. Secretly, I know you're enjoying the prospect of getting back.'

Kabir couldn't place a finger on the emotion he felt. The news of Sadiq's death had shaken him. And then he was flooded with a sudden surge of information that made him feel he could do something about it. And now that Joshi had asked him too, he was confused.

'Do you have clearance for the rescue mission from our government? After all, we're no Mossad.'

'Leave that to me,' Joshi replied with a reassuring smile. 'Besides, the new prime minister is a little more open to these kinds of ideas.'

Kabir laughed and shook his head uncertainly, and was about to say something when Joshi interrupted him.

'Stop playing hard to get. Do it for Sadiq, Kabir. Do it for Vikramjit. Do it for your country,' he said as he dropped a large folder in front of Kabir. 'Dossiers with everything you need.'

Kabir lifted his glass of water and took a big gulp.

'More importantly, do it for yourself,' continued Joshi. 'In my opinion, I don't think anyone else knows as much about that part of Pakistan than you do. If you believe you were wronged, this is your way to prove it.'

Kabir stared at the folder with the dossiers for a moment. This was his chance to avenge his friend and mentor. It was also his only shot at redemption.

'It's your choice at the end of the day. You can walk out. I have a Plan B in place.'

Kabir shot one final look at Joshi's face, as he got up from his chair. He picked up the folder from the table casually and strode out of the office. Joshi smiled to himself. He didn't actually have a Plan B.

4

Akhtar Mohammad Road was crowded with chirpy adolescent boys who cared little about the oncoming traffic and walked like carefree sheep in front of the vehicles. The incessant honking didn't seem to bother them at all. It was four in the afternoon. They had just got out of the Dar-ul-Islam madrasa, which on the face of it was supposed to teach them the principles of Islam and make them learn the Quran and the Hadees by rote. What they did end up learning eventually was another story altogether. These young children wore tight skullcaps and clutched copies of the *pa'ara* (chapter of the Quran) they were being taught at the time, while being brainwashed and trained, simultaneously, to be the future faces of terror. And most of their parents were willing accomplices.

Behind the steering wheel of one such honking off-white Mercedes car was an anxious brigadier, Tanveer Shehzad. The forty-year-old Shehzad, a typical military beefcake, was the Pakistani Army's ace weapon against India. He was given the volatile area of Balochistan to take care of by the ISI chief. He was also the only ISI operative who had direct access to Mullah Omar, after the latter went entirely off the radar four years ago. He had the intelligence to match up to the task and physical prowess to boot. He was the architect of terror organizations like the Indian Mujahideen, a group based in India that was a front for the Lashkar-e-Taiba. A fact that he took great pride in was that he had trained Mohammed Ahmad Siddibaapa—or Yasin Bhatkal as India knows him.

In 2006 Bhatkal was asked by Shehzad to enter Pakistan from Dubai. Bhatkal didn't have the necessary papers, or even a visa. Shehzad had sniggered over the phone when Bhatkal voiced this concern to him. His reply was terse: *'Aa jao, bhaijaan. Dekh lenge.'*

As Bhatkal's plane touched down in Karachi, he was taken aside and greeted by a large man with a welcoming smile. The other passengers began to walk towards the airport to collect their baggage. Bhatkal was spared the trouble, and was whisked away past the immigration desk. His bags were already loaded into a large SUV, which stood a few metres from the Boeing that had just landed, with two others waiting in it. They greeted him warmly.

'Khairiyat?'

'Shukrana,' replied Bhatkal.

The next day itself, after a ten-hour journey, he found himself in a hilly province of Balochistan. He was in Quetta, being trained by Omar's Shura. Over the next fifty days, along with a few other recruits, he was taught how to handle weapons and explosives by Brigadier Shehzad and six other instructors from the Pakistani Army. Amongst the many attacks he was to carry out, the most dangerous was a plan to detonate a nuclear bomb in Ahmedabad.

After his training, Bhatkal was dropped back to the airport with a passport to return to Dubai. There were fake immigration stamps indicating he had entered and exited India. It was as if he had never been to Pakistan at all. All a part of Shehzad's master plan.

Yasin Bhatkal was also one of the reasons Bollywood superstar Shah Rukh Khan was detained at the Newark airport. Bhatkal had used the alias Shah Rukh, for reasons best known to him. He had created havoc in India, discreetly leading the Indian Mujahideen. However, his rather conspicuous alias was one of the reasons he was arrested on the India–Nepal border near Motihari, Bihar, on 28 August 2013. Superstar Shah Rukh Khan, among others, must have been immensely relieved.

Shehzad had now hurriedly entered the Dar-ul-Islam madrasa. He had someone to meet rather urgently. Shehzad was known to be fiercely loyal to his people. He saw the abduction of the four Indian agents as a chance to get Bhatkal back to him. Hell, he could even get the notorious Lashkar-e-Taiba militants Fayaz Mir and Umar Madni back. Asking for another lower-level IM operative, Assadullah Akhtar, would be like rubbing salt into the Indians' wounds.

He parked his car neatly into a corner and walked out quickly. The guards noticed the familiar burly figure with a swift but sturdy gait walk towards the door. They opened it and saluted him. He nodded at them and walked right in. Another guard met him inside and greeted him.

'Where is he?'

'In the chamber downstairs,' the guard replied, motioning towards a staircase that led to the chamber. 'He'll be here in a bit.'

The guard brought a large carpet that he laid out on the cool marble floor. Shehzad looked at his watch impatiently as he sat down. Next, the guard went in again, ordered a pot of tea, and asked Shehzad if he would like a snack as well.

'Just ask him to come here quickly,' snapped Shehzad. 'I'm not here for snacks.'

The guard shrugged and walked into another room. Even Shehzad knew he couldn't ask him to come quickly. Amir al-Mu'minin came when he wanted to.

His relationship with Mullah Omar had always been volatile. While Shehzad had a lot of respect for the Mullah, it was born out of fear and awe more than anything. And Shehzad wasn't the kind to be intimidated easily. But here was a man, he believed, who could instil fear in a nation like the United States of America. Mullah Omar, an enigma of a man, was astoundingly temperamental. There were times when one could not reason with him at all, but then all of a sudden, he would appear to become subservient. The ISI had created a Frankenstein's monster in Mullah Omar. His second-in-command, Mullah Abdul Ghani Baradar, on the other hand, had a more even temperament and stronger negotiating skills. In Mullah Omar and Mullah Baradar, the ISI had found a duo which needed skilful manipulation, and the utmost care. Another reason it couldn't quite rub them up the wrong way was because of their strong alliance with Jalaluddin Haqqani and his son, Sirajuddin. The Haqqanis were an integral part of the ISI's campaign against India and its other enemies. Together, the Haqqani Network, Mullah Omar's Shura, and of course, the ISI itself, presented an indomitable force—one that had the potential to bring the world to its knees.

Shehzad took his cellphone out and began to check something. He had a live constantly streaming video of the Indian prisoners locked up in small cells at the Shura base. He needed to ensure that they were kept alive, and that the torture meted out to them never got out of hand. He watched as one captive convulsed like a fish out of water, soon after being waterboarded.

'Salaam aleikum,' came an indistinguishable voice. It was the typical throaty baritone of a maulana, used to praying out aloud.

Shehzad got up and wished the Amir, in reply. The Amir did not have his eyepatch on, a sight that sent a shiver down his spine. It always did, even in a hardened man like Shehzad.

'Waleikum as-salaam,' he said and then continued in chaste Arabic: 'I'm here to tell you something of importance. I want this to be confidential for now, ask your guard not to come into the room.'

'I will do no such thing,' replied Mullah Omar. 'I'm an open book to my people.'

The guard entered the room with a half-smile, having eavesdropped. He left the teapot on the carpet along with one cup. Mullah Omar sat on the carpet and crossed his legs. As always, he wore a heavily embroidered black kurta over a black salwar that ended just above his ankles. It was the Taliban uniform. He looked up at his guard and nodded towards the staircase that led to the chamber. The guard nodded back obediently in response and went downstairs.

'The Indians are asking for some time to consider your request,' stated Shehzad.

'Your request,' Omar corrected him quickly.

Shehzad shook his head fervently.

'Yes, but they don't know that. They need more time to trade my men silently in exchange for theirs.'

Mullah Omar poured himself a cup of strong black tea and looked up at Shehzad with his one good eye. Shehzad didn't make the mistake of looking back into it.

'You must understand that I have other things keeping me busy, Shehzad. I have the Americans to fight. The NATO and the US are about to make a decisive move. The new Afghani presidential candidates have promised to sign pacts for the Americans to stay put! My war is about to get prolonged and tougher! And then you come along and stop me from executing those four kafirs, and get me involved in these small-time games you're playing.'

'Small-time games, Amir? These aren't games! We are battling India every day and this is one of the few instances when we have some leverage over them. If we can get Bhatkal back, it will be a victory for us. He is one of the best bomb-makers we have ever produced.'

Mullah Omar sipped his tea, trying to place Bhatkal. And then he did.

'We trained Bhatkal and those boys here, so that they die for a cause.'

'But they aren't dead. They've been arrested. And this will help me in my objective of being one step ahead of India. Bhatkal was an extremely talented bomb-maker. I will have to start from scratch and get someone to replace him and reach his calibre.'

'The current lot is certainly more talented, Shehzad.'

Shehzad knew of Omar's stubbornness. He needed Omar to know that despite him having his fingers in many pies, the ISI should never let go of an opportunity to arm-twist its favourite enemy. He sighed resignedly.

'I need your help, Amir.'

The guard had emerged from the chamber below, holding two young boys by their hands, probably thirteen or fourteen years of age. They seemed red-faced and their eyes were moist. They had been crying, clearly. Shehzad had always heard of Mullah Omar's escapades in the madrasa. He realized what

Omar had been doing in the chamber below, and it was one of those rare moments in his life when Shehzad felt pity for another human being. The boys were escorted out of the room. Omar didn't look at them, but he wore a sinister smile.

'I've helped you get Akbar Bugti and his son. I've helped you get Balach Marri. I even allow you to train your insurgents in my area. See, these are causes that I believe in myself. But I haven't got time for playing little political games with India. I want to wait till Mullah Baradar gets back to Quetta.'

Mullah Baradar, his deputy, was on his way back from Islamabad. He had been released on 21 September 2013 by the ISI. But he had been tied up with all sorts of clandestine meetings with high officials for almost a year.

'You've also helped us because we offered you refuge when you had nowhere to go. We, the ISI, have created you, trained you, and made you a force to be reckoned with. This isn't a small game,' said Shehzad, continuing in the same vein. He waited for his outburst to sink in. 'India is Pakistan's worst enemy. In fact, I want to do this so we can go ahead with our other plan, too, with your blessings. The plan to unleash al-Qaeda on India.'

Omar looked up, his right eye wide, alive with excitement. His left eye was chillingly lifeless.

'The other plan is on?'

'*Jee*, now is the best time to go ahead with it. The new prime minister has instilled a strange confidence in them. But we want to prove a point. They're a vulnerable country, way beyond their imagination! And the way things are headed, we have reason to believe that there is about to be a high-level meeting pretty soon.'

'How many days have they asked for before they can send your people back?' Omar asked, suddenly interested.

'Two weeks,' replied Shehzad. 'They are trying to buy time. But it won't be long before they realize that their only choice is to succumb to our demands.'

'What do you think?'

'I want you to compose a message approving it. Throw in a slight measure of reluctance,' answered Shehzad. 'They cannot know of the ISI's direct involvement.'

'Fine,' Omar said, 'I will order Zabiullah to do it. But remember, this better be for the greater good.'

'*Inshallah,*' Shehzad replied.

And despite trying to avoid it, Shehzad looked into Omar's deathly eye that was baying for blood.

5

31 August 2014
Pune, Maharashtra

The area around Inorbit Mall on Nagar Road in Pune was being cordoned off. There was a constant buzz on the walkie-talkies as the police rushed around in a frenzy trying to push away the herd of media persons who had gathered at the site. One of the inspectors slapped a cameraman who was following him around. The other cameras recorded this little scuffle. They had to have something to broadcast until they could get a better picture of the bomb that was supposed to be inside. A fairly jovial mood had quickly transformed into a state of helpless panic.

'The bomb squad is on its way,' shouted a stocky ATS officer, Pradeep Shinde, into his walkie-talkie. 'They should be here in a couple of minutes.'

He then fired a volley of abuses and ordered his men in Marathi to go and divert the traffic away from the area.

It was around 10.30 a.m. and the traffic was at its peak in anticipation of the year-end celebrations. The mall, it seemed, was the perfect target for a bomb—the perfect occasion to kill a large number of people. Fortunately, an alert young couple had spotted it when they decided to sit on the last seat of a mini roller-coaster and quickly informed the mall authorities.

Shinde had then barked orders to shut down the entire air-conditioning system of the mall.

'Even the lights of all the other floors, except the third. God forbid, it goes off, there will be a huge electrical problem in the entire city.'

Soon enough, two fire brigades thundered in, sirens blaring. Three Mahindra combat vehicles sped up and halted right outside the mall entrance. Four heavily armed men got out of each vehicle.

'Officer Pradeep Shinde of the ATS,' Shinde introduced himself, flashing his ID as he led the twelve men towards the mall. Six of them wore bomb-suits and carried bomb-disposal kits in their hands. 'My men have evacuated the mall. There is no threat other than the bag.'

The man in the Kevlar bomb-suit, Devraj Sinha, asked: 'Which floor is the bomb on?'

'Third floor,' Shinde replied. 'There is a small roller-coaster in the amusement park. It is kept on the last seat.'

Sinha nodded, and shouted orders to his men: 'Two of you come with me, the rest carry on and make sure there are no hostiles in the mall.'

They stormed into the mall, Shinde following them. Sinha turned to Shinde with a raised eyebrow.

'I don't think you need to come. Stay out and update RAW about the threat.'

Shinde opened his mouth in protest, but Sinha had already turned around and started running up the stairs. His men followed in pairs.

They hurried up the stairs, and began to walk cautiously towards the roller coaster in the amusement area. They passed the many gaming consoles, ready to attack anyone who might surprise them. So far, so good. The only problem at hand, then, was the bomb.

They had just about reached the roller coaster when they saw a figure bending over the open bag on the back seat. All of them raised their guns in a swift motion.

'Put your hands behind your head,' Sinha shouted. 'NOW!'

The person looked up hurriedly and cursed. Devraj Sinha was taken aback. If this were a terrorist, he would've been shot immediately. Unfortunately, they didn't make terrorists as pretty as this. She moved the hair from her brow, revealing a face with delicate features, and looked up at the men. She wore a grey tank-top, stained with sweat, and a pair of jeans. Beads of sweat trickled on her gently upturned nose.

'There's enough Semtex in here to blow the entire floor up, which would cause the building to collapse,' she said urgently. 'It's not remote-detonated, not motion-sensitive. An Improvised Explosive Device. But a crude bomb, nonetheless.'

The man raised his rifle threateningly. 'Put your hands where I can see them, now, or I will shoot.'

'Isha Khan,' she said, looking through her riotous curls as they fell over her forehead. 'Military Intelligence. Call Director-General Khanna at the Sena Bhavan in Delhi, if you need to cross-check.'

Sinha was taken aback. He nodded to one of the men, who went aside to make the call to verify. The man dialled the number. Within a few minutes, Director-General Khanna had confirmed her identity. There was a tone of relief in his voice when he realized that Isha was at the scene.

'How are you here?'

'I happened to be at the mall,' she said. 'Now get over here and help me neutralize this thing.'

Sinha walked up close to her and kneeled. The two members of the bomb squad followed suit. They admired her fair, slender yet muscular arms as she pointed towards the bomb. They were awed by her fearlessness.

'See this thin red wire here? It's connected to the energy supply of the roller coaster.'

She pointed towards the red wire that continued underneath and converged with a bigger cable at a junction.

'Had the roller coaster been activated even once after the bag was left here, it would have been the last ride those people would've ever taken. Good thing those kids noticed it in time. Unfortunately, I don't carry a bomb-disposal kit in my handbag. I had half a mind to do it with my hairpin before you stormed in.'

She looked at one of the men and pointed to the kit. The man handed it over. She dug inside and pulled out a pair of pliers. She climbed on to the rails of the roller coaster and sat right next to the bomb. In a swift motion she pushed her hair off her forehead and prayed under her breath—perhaps to the same god that the man who had left the bomb there had prayed to. She always prayed, out of habit. She held the wire between the serrated jaws of the pliers and, with a sharp burst of force, snapped it. There was a long beep. The red LED on the detonating device turned green. The bomb had been disarmed. The group of men gawked at her, jaws dropping in admiration.

She pulled out her phone from the side of her jacket, which she had left on the floor. She saw eleven missed calls. Ten from her mother and one from an unidentified number. She turned to the men as she put on her jacket.

'You're welcome,' she said as she turned to walk away. She called her mother up. Her voice was frantic. She thought her daughter worked as a doctor, attending to the injured in the military. She wasn't entirely wrong. Isha did know how to extract a bullet from a wound, among the many other things she knew.

'*Beta*, are you okay? They found a bomb at some mall in Pune.'

'Is that right? Don't worry, Ammi, I'm getting back home as promised. Should be there in a few hours.'

'Come back soon, I've made your favourite mutton biryani.'

'I will, Ammi. *Khuda hafiz.*'

'*Khuda hafiz,*' her mother said with a sigh of relief.

Isha smiled to herself as she walked out of the back door of the mall. She looked at the unidentified number and dialled it.

'Hello,' the voice on the other end was curt. 'Am I speaking to Isha Khan?'

'Yes,' Isha replied as she climbed on to her bike. 'May I know whom I'm speaking to?'

'Arun Joshi.'

And then she had to call her mother back and tell her something urgent had come up. She had to rush to Delhi. Jee, Ammi, I'm fine. Unfortunately, her favourite biryani would have to wait.

~

31 August 2014
New Delhi

A small section at the Prime Minister's Office in New Delhi went on with what was just another day. The control room was dimly lit, and one of the agents, Ivan Fernandes, had begun to play some Goan music in the background to help him maintain his sanity. Some of the others stared at their screens, typing away furiously, trying to decode some message or the other. Quite unnervingly, they were being sent hoax messages ever since the new PM took office. The agents cursed at them in contempt and pushed them into an archive of other similarly received messages.

'Another lame threat,' thirty-five-year-old Nihar Shah complained, as he quickly dragged and dropped the message into the collection of bogus threats.

Nihar was an expert hacker, amongst other things. He had previously intercepted a message being sent to Pakistan from somewhere in the North-East. Though he could never triangulate the location, he brought this to the notice of the rest of his team. Soon enough, what seemed like an innocent message discussing a Bollywood actor had led to the arrest of Indian Mujahideen leader Yasin Bhatkal.

Nihar and his team were lauded for their efforts. Besides being good with a computer, Nihar was an extremely good shot. In the basement, where all the agents trained in basic gun combat, Nihar had developed a good eye for the target. Unlike his counterparts in the control room, Nihar could fire at the heart of the paper target at least four times out of five—which was rather unusual for a desk agent. But the higher authorities, who monitored them, knew that with a little polishing Nihar could well become an all-round agent,

with abilities both on and off the field. A rarity amongst the rather uninteresting babus at the RAW office.

'I'm going out for a smoke,' Ivan tapped Nihar on the shoulder as he walked out. Nihar got up and followed him out of the door into the cold veranda. They saw the dry Delhi wind swoop the dust along the streets. Ivan and Nihar each lit a cigarette.

'It's funny,' Ivan said, 'the rest of the world is out there having a great time. And here we are, watching the fun from a fucking balcony.'

'Yeah, anything new?'

'Routine stuff. Unless something serious pops up,' he continued.

'This is the job we signed up for,' Nihar said as he exhaled the smoke. His throat was drier than before. 'I don't know any other way to earn a living.'

'Neither do I,' Ivan said. 'Anyway, how are Trisha and the little one?'

Nihar smiled to himself. Of late, his wife had been complaining about his rather irregular work pattern. He had no time to spend with her and their baby. Sometimes she would break down and behave irrational, and Nihar would sit calmly and explain to her how his job wasn't the standard nine-to-five kind. He knew that his marriage was on the brink of becoming a strained one. He could decode the toughest of messages and intercept them with ease, but a woman—he thought all men would agree—was the hardest to decipher.

'I promised Trisha we'd go out for dinner. She's with the baby now.'

'Any first words yet?' Ivan chuckled as he rubbed his shaved head. 'Apparently, I had learned to swear before I even said "Maa".'

'Well, then, you're not meeting my kid until he says "Maa".'

'It's about time you named him,' Ivan said.

Nihar's phone vibrated in his pocket. He pulled it out and saw that it was his wife calling. It was their anniversary, and he had promised to take her out to dinner.

'Hey, Trisha,' he greeted her. 'Don't worry, I'll be there at eleven. Why don't you take the little one over and reserve a table?'

'It's ten,' she replied. 'Why can't you get back home now? Is your work more important to you than me—even today?'

'I will,' Nihar said. 'Don't worry. Nothing can stop me from spending time with you and our baby.'

'I love you,' she said softly. She was in a good mood today. Ivan winked at a blushing Nihar.

'You, too,' Nihar said, smiling.

'No,' Trisha said. 'Say it. Say the three damn words.'

'I will when I meet you,' Nihar replied as he flipped the finger to a laughing Ivan.

'Fine, bye.'

She disconnected the phone. Ivan held his sides as he laughed.

'Go home now and surprise her. I'll handle the work on your computer as well.'

Nihar grinned. 'For real?'

'Yes, not like I have a wife waiting at home for me.'

Nihar smiled, and thanked Ivan as he left the veranda and walked into the control room. He picked up his bag from the desk and said goodbye to the others in the room. As he walked out of the control room, he saw Arun Joshi walk towards him.

'Aah,' Joshi said with a plastic smile. 'Just the person I was looking for.'

Nihar was confused as he smiled back at Joshi.

'Sir, I was planning to get home early. The baby is slightly unwell.'

'Oh, you had a baby? Congratulations! But I'm afraid you're going nowhere, Nihar. I have something important to discuss with you. Your expertise with all things technical will be required over the next few days.'

Nihar's heart sank. On a normal day, he would have loved to discuss something important with the Chief of RAW. But today he'd made a promise in a bid to make amends. He wondered how he would make that phone call to his wife. This might just be the end of his marriage. But then again, this was the job he had signed up for.

~

31 August 2014
Helmand Province, Afghanistan

The night hit Afghanistan earlier than usual. Helmand, located in the southern part of Afghanistan, was amongst the largest of the thirty-four provinces of the country. It was a part of the Greater Kandahar region before it was carved out into a separate province in the twentieth century. The Helmand and Kabul regions were known as 'White India' in the days of pre-Islamic Afghanistan, when the Helmand river valley had a large population of Hindus and Buddhists. Currently, it is rather well developed for a province in a country that seems to have all but lost its way. A healthy fraction of its population of 15 lakh people is tribal, with the ethnic Pashtuns forming the majority. The Balochis, Tajiks and Hazaras make up the rest. And then there are the considerable number of NATO troops, which are supposed to pull out by the end of the coming year.

'You can tell me when to take over the wheel, Farid.'

Farid Azizi nodded as he slowed down the truck and moved it to the side of the road. He left the engine running as he hopped out. He took in a lungful of the cold, dry air of the desert. His head was covered in a black turban and his face wasn't much visible behind his dense facial foliage. His companion, Abdul Samadi, took his position at the wheel. They were driving from the Lashkar Gah district into Quetta, almost 400 kilometres.

'Thank you, brother. I was beginning to feel sleepy.'

'I could tell,' Samadi replied in Pashto, as he set the truck into motion again. 'We should be at the border within an hour and a half.'

'I hope they don't trouble us too much there,' Azizi said with a tinge of fear. 'This is the first time I'm taking a truck across with so much opium.'

'Don't worry, brother. You haven't been caught all these years, have you? We just hand over a little something to the Border Police and continue. Tonight should be no different. Besides, it is well known that President Karzai turns a blind eye to our business.'

Tonight should be no different, Azizi repeated in his head.

'Yes.' Azizi sounded relieved. 'We hand the consignment over, stay the night and get back tomorrow evening.'

'Unless we get intercepted by the Americans. There is always a chance, so we cannot afford to goof up.'

'I'll take a short nap, Abdulbhai,' Azizi said as he eased himself into a more relaxed position. 'Wake me up when we approach the border.'

He shut his eyes, rested his head back and then he saw *it* again. It happened every time he tried to sleep. *There's no point in trying to block these memories out,* he thought.

I've tried. I've tried hard. And then he relived that wretched day in his head all over again. Sometimes, he felt, this was the only reason that he was still able to maintain whatever little he had of his identity. It was the only factor that helped distinguish himself, Veer Singh, from his cover, Farid Azizi.

The year was 2008, when Veer Singh, a thirty-year-old Sikh, was sent to Kabul along with Brigadier Ravi Datt Mehta on a posting for six months. Mehta had been assigned a key role as defence attaché, serving as part of India's military and logistical help to Afghanistan. He was an experienced analyst, a sea of knowledge on the counter-insurgency operations in Kashmir and the North-East.

Veer was a fresh-off-the-bench RAW agent, who had an extremely high level of endurance and a skill set to match. Being a typical Sikh, and six foot five, he was built like the side of a house. His assignment was to shadow Mehta, be his personal security guard and also serve as a link between Mehta and the HQ back in Delhi to exchange intel on a daily basis.

On 7 July 2008, when Veer drove Mehta and an Indian Foreign Service officer Venkat Rao from their hotel to the Indian embassy in the centre of Kabul, little did he know he would not see them ever again. There was a huge rush that day, as people usually lined up at the embassy gates to apply for visas to India. The meeting that day was supposed to be of high importance and Rao had politely asked Veer to wait it out. Veer decided to take the car for a spin and probably have some morning kahva from a local stall. What happened thence is etched vividly in his mind, frame by frame.

He drove the car out of the gate and he saw a Toyota Camry speeding towards them from the opposite direction, missing his car by a whisker. He spat out a Hindi expletive and didn't pay it any heed. He had driven a short distance ahead, when he heard a sound that still resonates in his ear. The ground shook, his windshield shattered and his car skidded into a barricade. He staggered out, pistol ready, as he saw plumes of smoke and dust rising from the centre of Kabul city. He was within the blast radius, but luckily enough nothing seemed to have happened to him. The explosive-laden Toyota Camry was being driven by a suicide bomber and had rammed into two vehicles in the embassy and detonated.

Veer remembered running into the smoke and seeing some people running away from it. He pulled off his turban and wrapped it around his mouth to minimize the intake of the black smoke from the bomb. He went inside, his eyes burning. He didn't have to go far to realize that both Brigadier Mehta and Officer Rao had been burnt to a crisp. However, the top floor of the embassy didn't look too badly damaged. He rushed upstairs, sidestepping the dead bodies and holding his breath to avoid the smell of smoke and burnt flesh, and found a few embassy personnel unhurt. Later that evening, he recalled this incident to Lieutenant General Sadiq Sheikh. He wished he had paid more attention to the speeding Camry and done something about it. If it had struck him early enough, there could have been an outside chance of him preventing the car from reaching its destination, even if it meant sacrificing himself for the well-being of his fellow countrymen.

'Don't fret over it. You did what you could. Anyway, we have reason to believe that the Haqqani Network and the ISI have a role to play in this,' Sadiq had said, his voice as calm as ever. 'Veer, I want you to get the rest of the ambassadors to an extraction point. After which you will await my further orders.'

Veer did as he was told in the wee hours of the next morning. And then he got his orders. He was to be posted in Afghanistan from then on. He would be on the list of the officially dead, making him the perfect spook. Non-existent and living in the shadows. He was given the choice to accept the long-term mission or return to India. He accepted the challenge.

The NATO and the American troops had cracked down hard on drug trafficking under the US Agency for International Development programme. Opium had brought in a lot of money into Afghanistan ever since the Soviet occupation. And once the Soviet Army was forced to withdraw, the locals resorted even more to poppy cultivation. However, there was even a phase when a reluctant collaboration between the US forces and Afghan warlords to hunt down drug traffickers spelt more chaos. They used it to settle scores with each other, in order to grow their own businesses. The most significant use of the money generated from the drug trade was the funding of terrorism—or jihad, as the other side chose to call it.

Mullah Omar, in early 2000, had collaborated with the United Nations to eradicate heroin production in Afghanistan. 'Allah wouldn't approve,' he had said. This phase led to one of the most successful anti-drug campaigns in the world, with almost three-fourths of the world's supply of heroin being choked out. However, as soon as the Taliban was deposed and it was discovered that funds were required for their insurgency, Allah miraculously seemed to approve.

Veer moved out of Kabul and spent time in various regions before settling in Helmand. He spent the next few years rebuilding his life. He learnt the finer nuances of Islam and studied the Hadees and the Quran, and changed his personality to blend right in with the Afghans. He was given the cover of being born to an Afghani father and a Pakistani mother, since he never quite looked entirely like an Afghan. It was easy for him to adapt, since in reality, he was an orphan, and orphans like him are quick-change artists. But even so, it took him a while to get used to. He didn't have too many people in his past, so he was lucky in that sense. The absence of emotional baggage is essential for a good spy.

So now here he was, an insider to the drug trafficking world of Afghanistan. He learnt the technicalities of converting raw opium into heroin using chemicals, but preferred the job of being the courier of the consignment. The job was of relatively lower risk and paid well, too.

'Wake up, we're here.' Samadi tapped Veer on his shoulder.

Veer got up and looked at the Afghan Border Police inspecting the truck.

'Azizi, pass the bag.'

It took a while for Veer to recall he was Azizi. It always did upon waking up.

He passed over a bag with wads of cash and a large bag with opium. The Border policeman smiled a toothless smile as he waved the truck on into Quetta.

A short distance into Balochistan, where there was no sign of other human beings being around, Veer requested Samadi to pull over. He wanted to take a leak. Samadi stopped the truck and got down to stretch his limbs. Veer went behind to the side of the road. It took Samadi a couple of minutes to realize Veer was taking unusually long to pee.

He called out: 'Farid?'

No response. And then he shouted out louder.

'FARID!?'

Still no response. He walked towards the side of the road in search of his friend. He suddenly felt a blow to his right temple. He collapsed to the ground, unconscious. Veer kneeled over his body and strangled him with his bare hands. He got up, dumped the body into the truck and drove away. He felt a tinge of remorse, but allowed himself nothing more than that.

The next morning, the truck, emitting the smell of burnt opium, was found torched in the middle of a deserted road. Abdul Samadi's body was charred beyond recognition. It was Veer's signature.

'Farid Azizi here,' said Veer into a secure line.

'I take it you're in Quetta now, Veer?'

'Yes, sir. I should be in Gwadar by tomorrow.'

Joshi had asked Veer to find a way into Balochistan the very night he had spoken to Kabir at the Office. He was instructed to meet the team at Gwadar. Veer had assured him he'd find a way and, sure enough, he had delivered on his word. Sometimes Joshi wondered if they had turned the man into a machine. Even Kabir, at the height of his career, had lacked the ruthlessness Veer possessed. In many senses, Veer was Kabir without a conscience—except taller and stronger. But he needed Kabir's experience and brains to oversee the team he had assembled. It was the best he could muster at such short notice.

'Your team will arrive shortly.'

'Give me a date. And remember, sir, that I follow the Islamic calendar.'

6

It is difficult for anyone to look at the Taj Mahal Palace in Colaba without associating it with the horrific attack of 26 November 2008. The hotel always stood proudly in the most elegant area of Mumbai, where the most influential in society mingled over their champagne and slightly supercilious smiles. It was a symbol of power, a power that was primarily born out of one's wealth. But those few terrorists had wreaked havoc overnight. They had killed with ease, unflinchingly. Some even smiled as they gunned down helpless women and children. The country had been brought to a standstill, and the repercussions were long-lasting. The memory of it was difficult for someone like Kabir Anand, as he thought of the glaring lacunae in the national security infrastructure he had once worked within.

He walked past the memorial that had been set up for the victims, glancing momentarily at it. In his mind he'd sworn revenge every time he thought of the attacks. At that point there had been absolutely nothing he could have done about it. *But now, I will.*

He still recalled vividly the night when it had all happened. He had been asleep, ready to go to work the next day when his cellphone began to buzz constantly with chain messages warning the recipient from stepping out. He had half a mind to call Sadiq, wanting to understand the bigger picture. But he held himself back. Instead, he drove down the next morning and watched the drama unfold from where the news reporters stood. In a reckless moment, he even tried to make a breach past the police barrier claiming to be from an intelligence unit. But he had no proof to back his identity.

'The Presidential Suite on the fourth floor,' he said to the receptionist. He gazed nonchalantly at his cellphone, while the receptionist called to confirm. He smoothed his hair with his hand and adjusted his tie. He decided to button up his blazer. *Must be a media person here to interview that Afghani guy,* the receptionist thought. The Afghani guy, on the face of it, was in town to conduct a seminar on terrorism and how to deal with it. The truth, however, was that the RAW chief, Arun Joshi, had requested him to come down to Mumbai for some rather urgently needed assistance. She nodded to him a few seconds later and directed him to the elevator. Kabir thanked her and took the stairs instead.

Following his brisk climb up, he knocked at the door of the Presidential Suite. A large man, with a set jaw and a crew cut, opened it. *Personal security. Afghani, without doubt.* He directed him into the room, and asked him to sit on the sofa. The suite was, needless to say, luxurious. There were two pots, one with coffee and one with tea, already waiting on the little wooden centre-table. The large man nodded, and went into another room to inform the person Kabir had come to meet about his arrival.

Soon enough, a man roughly Kabir's height and stature walked out, sporting a polite, formal smile. He had mousy features, a receding hairline, and sloping eyebrows set above droopy eyes. He was in his mid-forties, not much older than Kabir. He wore an expensive suit, probably Savile Row, judging by the cut. Kabir got up from the sofa, with his version of a formal smile. They shook hands firmly, one intelligence agent with another.

He got right to the point. 'Mr Joshi told me about the current situation, Mr Anand. I wouldn't say I'm surprised.'

He pronounced his Ts flat, with the tongue touching the roof of his mouth. He spoke slowly, as Kabir took the seat opposite him.

'Yes, Mr Saleh,' Kabir replied. 'He's asked me to meet you to get a better understanding of what I'm getting into.'

Arifullah Umar Saleh had last served as the head of the Afghan intelligence service—the National Directorate of Security or NDS. Earlier, while in his twenties, he had caught Afghan political and military leader Ahmad Shah Massoud's eye for his uncanny knack of gathering intelligence. The charismatic Massoud—'The Lion of Panjshir'—appointed Saleh to lead the Northern Alliance liaison and intelligence outfit. At a young age, Saleh had had the weight of responsibility thrust upon his sturdy shoulders, as he led the Northern Alliance against the Taliban. Massoud had strongly opposed the Taliban's fundamentalist interpretation of Islam. He was assassinated in a suicide bombing by al-Qaeda two days before the September 11 attacks in 2001.

Saleh had been broken to see someone he admired so much meet such a tragic end. But that only encouraged him to grow even more upright and committed to his cause. Soon enough, after the fall of the Taliban regime in 2004, he was appointed the head of the NDS by President Hamid

Karzai. However, a spate of differences that arose during Karzai's re-election and in the days that followed, led Saleh to quit his position in 2010. Soon, Karzai and Saleh couldn't stand each other. Saleh was a man reputed to be upright and honest, who loved his country to a fault. He went on to create the strongest pro-democracy and anti-Taliban movement soon after, mobilizing more than 20,000 supporters. Kabir admired few men, but Arifullah Saleh was everything that epitomized nationalism and patriotism. And this appealed to Kabir the most.

'What you're getting into is certainly not an easy task, Mr Anand. But then, again, that is what men like us are used to.' He got up swiftly and went over to the large flat-screen television, proceeding to pull out a pen-drive from the breast-pocket of his coat and plug it in. He switched it on and fiddled with the remote a bit, before a large flow-chart appeared on the screen. He then shuffled back to the sofa opposite Kabir and sat down.

'The Quetta Shura is nothing but the Afghan Taliban that has set itself up in Balochistan, Mr Anand. It should not be confused with the Pakistani Tehreek-e-Taliban. You do know what the word *talib* means, don't you?'

'Student,' said Kabir. He felt slightly insulted. But then he realized Saleh wouldn't be expected to know much about his past either. He must be assuming that this was the first time Kabir was entering Pakistan on a mission and therefore was explaining everything like he would to a newbie. But Kabir respected Saleh too much to interrupt him and nudged him on. Besides, Saleh would definitely have a better read of the situation than the entire machinery within the Indian intelligence.

'Exactly. They both have common traits and common interests at times, but they are separate entities. And, of course, they are primarily funded, directly or indirectly, by those bloodhounds, the ISI.'

Saleh let the words linger as he poured a cup of coffee for Kabir and a cup of tea for himself.

He smiled, and answered the question before Kabir asked. 'You're a coffee person, I can tell. Your eyes look tired, but your mind and body seem alert.'

Kabir smiled as he thanked him and took his cup.

Saleh continued on to the more important topic. 'As I said earlier, it came as no surprise to me when Mullah Omar made his demands to you. I like to call Omar the one-eyed puppet of the ISI. He dances at their whim, and even though he'd like to project it otherwise, he is no spring chicken. At roughly fifty-seven, his reflexes have died down and he isn't the capable warrior he once was. He requires constant health care, which the ISI provides.'

'He is their spiritual leader,' Kabir contributed. 'Even though he may not be physically able any more, he is highly capable of destruction.'

'Yes,' Saleh conceded. 'But his day-to-day activities are overseen by his rumoured brother-in-law and great friend, Mullah Abdul Ghani, popularly known as Mullah Baradar.'

'Mullah Brother.' Kabir shook his head, and sipped the coffee. Saleh was right. While Mullah Omar was certainly still the figurehead and spiritual leader of the Quetta Shura Taliban, his operational expertise, as it stood now, was limited. Moreover, his relative isolation due to fear of capture and his advanced age made it difficult for him to be actively involved in operational work.

'Baradar and Omar fought side by side against the Soviets,' Saleh went on, as he took a large gulp of tea. He waited as the warmth spread along his throat and continued, 'But you cannot discount Mullah Omar. All enemy groups operating in the country have sworn their allegiance, in varying degrees, to him.'

'Amir al-Mu'minin,' Kabir scoffed.

Saleh flinched as he heard the words. 'He is trying to represent a religion as pure as Islam.' The Sunni Muslim in him overpowered Saleh. His voice rose substantially. 'Does Islam promote sodomy? Does Islam support child abuse? Does Islam ask its followers to kill each other? Or kill anyone at all? That bastard is misrepresenting an institution that has its very basis in the purity of one's soul.'

He waited, his face turned a veritable red from his otherwise distinctly pink Afghan complexion. The rage made his cup tremble in his hand. He kept it down and folded his arms.

'Take a moment,' Kabir said with a smile. 'We have fifteen days to get my colleagues back.'

Saleh let out a slight laugh. Kabir refilled his cup of coffee, and poured Saleh another cup of tea. Despite the air conditioning, beads of sweat had formed on Saleh's hairline.

'The post-9/11 Taliban, in a nutshell, is largely supported by the Pakistani Army and the ISI,' Kabir said. 'And then, of course, there is the booming narcotics trade.'

'Having said that, they gain a large amount of money through taxes on livestock and agriculture as well.'

Kabir raised an eyebrow. He knew of the money they made through narcotics from regions like Helmand and Kandahar, but taxation on livestock and agriculture was rather new to him.

'Taxation?'

'Yes.' Saleh smiled disappointedly. He waited a brief while, the smile still on his face. 'This is the part nobody understands, my friend. The West, especially. The Taliban is still in Afghanistan. It's just that it doesn't have Mullah

Omar in Afghanistan. The Taliban has its elements inside the government itself. We are a poor Third World country. A country which has been fucked over again and again. First, by the Russians. Then the Americans, too. And then by our own people. And to crown it all, by Pakistan.'

Kabir began to understand. 'Is this why you quit? Because Karzai is spineless?'

'Spineless would be an understatement. Don't even get me started on Karzai,' he spluttered sardonically. 'Yes, one of the innumerable reasons I quit is that I didn't want to be working under the Taliban indirectly. And I didn't want to be looked upon as a fool for working under a man who faked the existence of ballots, which got him more votes than the turnout itself!'

Kabir scratched his beard thoughtfully on hearing this sadly amusing piece of news. It was true, the actual voter turnout in some regions like the Pashtun south was around 5 to 10 per cent. But the ballot stuffing done for Karzai at some polling stations, which didn't even exist as such, recorded more than a 100 per cent turnout!

'So Karzai's presidency has run its course now,' Kabir replied. 'Will you go back?'

'If Abdullah Abdullah wins, I might. He was a friend of Ahmad Shah Massoud. He believes in fighting fire with fire and won't hesitate to take action against the Taliban,' Saleh said. 'I don't agree with some of Ashraf Ghani Ahmadzai's policies, on the other hand. With Abdullah there's still a ray of hope for Afghanistan. He might just be the saviour we need. Having said that, Ghani is a smart man, too.'

Saleh paused. And then as if remembering something important, he spoke again. 'Karzai had very smartly asked Omar to run for presidency too! He made a public announcement of the same just recently. He made it look as though he's asking Omar to leave the gun and run Afghanistan peacefully. Omar obviously declined. He wasn't going to fall for this. He has his aims, both short and long term, in place. And he wants to achieve them violently.'

'What you're saying is the Taliban initially wanted fragmentation in a government they wanted to overthrow eventually anyway,' he said.

Saleh nodded, adding, 'In many ways, this situation is similar to the Hezbollah in Lebanon. And to top it all, since Mullah Omar and bin Laden had forged forces early on, a government with the Taliban at its helm will mean a government with elements of al-Qaeda itself.'

Kabir took a while to process this. He let out a deep breath. It had been so long since he had been part of a discussion as heavy as this. He instantly recalled an apt Shakespearean line. *Hell is empty, and all the devils are here.*

'I thought Karzai was anti-Taliban, and that they weren't too particularly fond of him either,' Kabir said. 'But he's played a smart political game thus far. President Obama had made it clear through his actions that he wanted little to do with Karzai on the personal front, unlike Bush. I believe Bush and Karzai used to chat regularly over videoconferencing.'

'The rest of the world thought Karzai is anti-Taliban too. Till he started his slimy appeasement policies. He tried to keep America happy. He tried to keep India happy. He tried to keep Pakistan happy. And to top it all, he tried to keep the Taliban happy! I don't know about the others, but he succeeded in keeping the Taliban happy. And since he's kept them happy, Pakistan seems content. As for me, I'm happy there will be a change soon.'

Kabir countered, 'But then there are innocent Pakistanis being killed in the tribal regions, the Federally Administered

Tribal Areas! What's worse is that the Pakistani government encourages it.'

'Yes, but let me explain it this way. The tribal areas are the servants' quarters of a palace. If a fire breaks out in the servants' quarters, the rest of the palace will take notice of it for certain, but be thankful that the fire didn't break out under their asses. The FATA are the servants' quarters. Islamabad, Rawalpindi, Lahore, Karachi are the royal quarters of the palace.'

'Hardly, if the palace is a place like Pakistan,' Kabir said sarcastically.

A pregnant silence followed. Both men lost in deep thoughts of their own. Kabir had learnt more by looking at the situation from Saleh's point of view. Saleh, himself, began to reminisce about how his short-lived dream of a perfect Afghanistan had been realized under Ahmad Shah Massoud and then subsequently shattered after his assassination. Their thoughts converged simultaneously to the point that had triggered off this discussion. The four Indian agents held captive in Quetta.

'Now see this,' Saleh continued, pointing to the TV screen that had had a static image on it for the past half hour.

Kabir looked at the screen and saw the hierarchy, in the form of a flow chart, of the Quetta Shura that Saleh had produced. It was an image that he had used consistently even during his days at the NDS.

'The Quetta Shura leadership structure has two main bodies . . .' he began. Kabir completed his sentence for him, 'The Rahbari Shura and the Majlis-al-Shura. The Rahbari Shura, which translates to "leadership gathering", is where Omar feeds his ideological spiel from. The latter is based more on the strategy of the Taliban.'

'The Quetta Shura is the intellectual underpinning of the

Taliban insurgency in Afghanistan' read a caption, as Saleh flipped to the next screen with the remote. It had maps, obtained through drone imagery, tiled up along with photographs.

'This is the Madrasa Fayyaz-ul-Uloom that Mullah Baradar has set up. It's nothing short of a fortress, but then it does have entry and exit points that are unguarded.' He then flipped to another image. It was a large compound with high walls, with the hills around it forming natural barriers on three sides. Impossible had just gotten tougher.

'This is where Omar's training camp, where he operates from, is,' Saleh said. 'He resides here as well. If by any chance your compatriots are held captive here, you can forget about rescuing them.'

Kabir took in a deep breath. There were four of them in all, he recalled. To infiltrate this and get his people out would be a tactical nightmare. In a Hollywood film, the four of them would've come out unscathed with their spoils, but in reality, Saleh was right. This was mission impossible.

Saleh then flipped to another image. Another madrasa. 'Dar-ul-Islam', the caption below the picture read. 'This one is where Omar works his magic with young boys,' Saleh said, spewing contempt. 'It is run by the Haqqani Network.'

The Haqqani Network, which, rather unsurprisingly, has the backing of the ISI and the Pakistani Army, was undoubtedly Afghanistan's most sophisticated insurgency organization and terror syndicate. Needless to say, it's now the most dreaded outfit in the world, since the death of Osama bin Laden. The Haqqani Network operates from their safe haven in North Waziristan. It is run by Sirajuddin Haqqani, the son of the famous anti-Soviet fighter Jalaluddin Haqqani. Siraj is more ruthless than his father, and openly supports anti-India operations. Kabir wouldn't be surprised if the captives were held in this madrasa, since Siraj would openly support and take responsibility for the ISI's nefarious and extremist anti-India activities.

'Technically, the Haqqani Network falls under the Quetta Shura umbrella,' Saleh chipped in. 'But they maintain a distinct command and control.'

Kabir swallowed. His throat had gone dry. So many elements, all coalescing to disrupt the peace amongst humanity. The coffee was over, even in the pot. Kabir got up to stretch, and walked up to the refrigerator. 'Can I have a Coke?'

'Of course,' Saleh said with a chiding smile. 'Too much caffeine, Mr Anand?'

Kabir smiled and glugged down a mouthful. He enjoyed the slight bite of the drink in his dry throat.

'The Haqqanis,' Saleh continued, 'are the most vicious sons of bitches you're ever likely to find. The Shura is relatively weaker than them at this stage. And with their momentum building and the Shura's power diminishing, they may begin to co-opt the Shura.'

Kabir finished the Coke and crushed the can, Saleh moved to the next slide.

'Should Omar die,' Kabir said solemnly, 'the Haqqanis will seize the overall leadership of the Quetta Shura. Omar, all said and done, was ideologically driven—unlike the Haqqanis, who are just power-hungry. Afghanistan will then be left to a terror network at the height of its power.'

Saleh shut his eyes and nodded. The thought always sent a chill down his spine. The inevitability of it seemed to trouble him even more.

He pointed at the screen that showed a vast expanse of relatively less hilly terrain. 'The HQ of the Shura training camp,' he said simply. He pulled out the pen-drive and tossed it to Kabir.

'This is a relatively new training camp. The previous

one was in another large madrasa,' Kabir said, pocketing the pen-drive.

'Yes, the one the ISI blew up themselves.'

Kabir was impressed at Saleh's knowledge on this point. Kabir himself had been at the site when it had happened. It was where he had lost his friend Vikramjit Singh.

'There is a lot more useful information in there.' Saleh pointed at the pen-drive, indicating that he was done talking for a while. 'I hope I've been of help to you.'

Kabir thanked him. They began walking out towards the door.

'I have spoken to my friends at Al Jazeera,' Saleh said. 'I hold seminars at Doha often, and they're well-wishers. Once you're in Balochistan, your team will have the official cover of being reporters. And remember, the local Balochis tend to be a hostile bunch. There is a lot of infighting. But play your cards right, and they can be of help to you.'

'This means a lot, Mr Saleh.'

'People like you and I are few, Mr Anand. We need to make each one count,' Saleh replied matter-of-factly.

'I don't know what Mr Joshi has told you about me, Mr Saleh, but I was in Balochistan myself when India was a part of the Northern Alliance. In many ways, I fought for the same cause as you and Ahmad Shah Massoud. That is one honour I'll take to my grave.'

'I remember my interactions with Lieutenant General Sadiq Sheikh. He was a good man. I'm told he's the only reason you're willing to go to Balochistan.' Saleh smiled, as he opened the door for Kabir.

'How much did Mr Joshi tell you?'

'Not much,' he replied. 'But if there's anyone who understands your situation, it's me. For you, the driving force is Sadiq Sheikh. For me, it's Ahmad Shah Massoud.'

7

1 September 2014
Quetta, Balochistan

'It is very simple, my friends. I will not ask you any questions.'

Mullah Abdul Ghani Baradar's voice echoed as he entered the dark cell. A blinding white light came on and two of the four prisoners looked up. They had their hands chained to their legs in an awkward position that limited their movement. They blinked hard as they saw an unfamiliar silhouette walk towards them. The other two were reeling between consciousness and unconsciousness.

The cell where the four prisoners were holed up wasn't the typical dark dungeon with rats and cockroaches scampering all around the place. On the contrary, it was a surprisingly neat underground structure. It looked well-thought-out, and it was. Mullah Omar had insisted that they model their interrogation techniques on those of the United States, where the surroundings permitted them to. He had enough men who had experienced torture at the hands of the US to tell him what it was like, and he quickly issued orders to his men to construct similar cells in every madrasa and camp he ran in Quetta. Even though they lacked the infrastructure, they came as close to recreating the torturous experiences the US meted out. His directive was simple. *We break them the way they break us—except much harder.*

These series of cells had one solitary commode, to which the prisoner was given access after every nine hours. The commode wasn't flushed through the day and the stench was unbearable. They were given a scanty meal once a day, which was just about enough to make them revive the ravenous hunger they had learned to ignore after a point. It usually consisted of a few morsels of extremely dry rice and a spare part of a goat or cow. Since these particular prisoners were Indian, and primarily Hindus, they were tauntingly given small morsels of undercooked beef or other unsavoury entrails of a cow. None of the four Indians touched these and just ate the bland, dry rice instead.

Besides this, the torturers had learned to exhaust their prisoners mentally before carrying out a gruesome physical assault. They played with the prisoners' natural biological cycles and sleep patterns. The prisoners had no clue as to what time of day it was. The tormentors would switch on a blinding white light for hours together—something that would make a man lose his mind if exposed to it even for twenty minutes. To add to that, they would simultaneously play a constant buzzing sound at a deafening volume, in the background. They would do this for hours at a stretch, and then suddenly switch the lights off along with the sound. Instead of this having even a remotely soothing effect on the prisoners, it would begin to play on the mind even more, leaving the prisoners fighting to maintain their sanity. They recorded all of this on a camera that was strategically placed to watch every move the prisoner made. The Taliban had learned to combine modern techniques along with their traditional brutality.

'Rajveer Bharadwaj,' Mullah Baradar read as he held up an Indian's identification card and walked over to the sweaty man who lay on the floor. 'Case attaché at the Indian embassy in Kabul. It is really worrying to know how negligent you Indians can be.'

Mullah Baradar was a tall man of about six feet two, and had a wild, black beard on his long face. His eyes were unforgiving, and he had prominent cheekbones that were set above a small mouth.

He grabbed a handful of the fifty-year-old Bharadwaj's grey woolly hair, making him look directly at him. Bharadwaj's eyes were bloodshot, his face gaunt. His breath smelled foul. He opened his mouth to say something, but words failed to find their way out.

'You should be extremely sorry that the ISI wants to keep you and these men alive,' Baradar continued. 'Our Amir was more than happy to grant you kafirs an easy death. A lot easier than you deserve for trying to spy on us.'

On 25 July 2014, a senior Taliban member had received a call from an Indian source that four Indian intelligence agents, headed by the attaché of the Indian embassy in Kabul, were on their way to Quetta. The same source informed them that they were about to set up shop in a safe house that was being managed by the Americans to spy on the Quetta Shura. However, the reality was slightly different. The Indians had arrived in Quetta to fund the local Baloch rebels in their civil war against the Pakistani government and the ISI.

Balochistan, being a poor and neglected province, has been home to a radical insurgency orchestrated by ethnic Baloch leaders demanding separation from Pakistan. So far the Baloch tribes have rebelled at least five times since 1947. But each time their insurgency had been crushed brutally. Baloch militants have targeted the security forces with assassinations, ambushes, and landmines or 'flowers', but this led to large-scale collateral damage, that has also robbed non-Baloch settlers of their lives. The security forces retaliate by detaining, torturing and killing ordinary Baloch civilians and students. The assassination of Nawab Akbar Bugti and thirty of his men in 2006 by the ISI and the Pakistani Army triggered a wider spread of insurgency. The counter-insurgency in response, led by Pakistan, was and still is barbaric. However, Mullah Omar's Taliban has been careful to maintain fairly decent relations with the Balochis, refusing to get involved in their civil war. But there have been instances, as in Bugti's assassination, where the ISI used them as a silent force to get at the Balochis.

Soon enough, the four Indian agents who had arrived at the safe house had been compromised. After being tailed, they were picked up at gunpoint by Mullah Omar's men. Omar had a simple policy: *Immediate death to spies.* But the ISI thought otherwise, and planned to use the Indians for leverage. And that is how the four RAW agents—Rajveer Bharadwaj, Suraj Agnihotri, Karan Bhatt and Tarun Singh—wound up here. Hanging in an abyss of uncertainty between life and death, fearing that their own country, in all likelihood, was about to disown them.

'I feel surprisingly generous,' Baradar said, smiling at Bharadwaj. 'I am going to allow you to choose the way you want to die.'

'F-fuck you,' a frail voice came from behind. It was Suraj Agnihotri's voice. He was still half unconscious and completely disoriented. 'We will die for our country if that is what it takes.'

Baradar stormed up to him and punched him on the nose. Suraj's face was already caked with blood, and the punch opened an old gash again. Blood dripped out and Suraj fell back into unconsciousness.

'When the time comes, I'm not so sure we'll be making such an offer. You'll die a painful death.' This time it was another agent, Karan Bhatt. He couldn't seem to open his swollen eyes.

Mullah Baradar turned around and fixed his gimlet eye on Bhatt. He strode across to him and kneeled down. He punched him hard. Bhatt felt his tooth loosen, over the taste of blood. Baradar was about to launch another punch into his face when the door opened.

'Enough!'

Mullah Baradar glanced slowly over his shoulder to see a tall man clad in a black salwar-kameez. He smiled.

'*Salaam aleikum*, Amir al-Mu'minin. It has been a while.'

~

They found their way back to the large hall they had usually held their discussions in: the Fayyaz-ul-Uloom madrasa. This madrasa was primarily run by Mullah Baradar, before he was arrested by the ISI in 2010. He had begun to talk covertly to Hamid Karzai's brother in Kandahar—Ahmad Wali Karzai, who had a local corrupt government running. In fact, the Karzais and Baradar both belonged to the Popalzai tribe of Afghanistan.

The ISI didn't like the idea of the Taliban speaking to the Afghan President's people, much less his brother, without notifying them. The ISI wanted to have control over all the meetings that took place between the Taliban and other groups that were willing to engage with them. The Taliban were their trump card. Therefore, when Mullah Baradar did speak to Karzai's brother, they arrested him on accusations of being a spy for the Americans by taking five million dollars from the Central Intelligence Agency—the CIA. This, despite knowing that Abdul Ghani Baradar would never double-cross the man he loved like an elder brother, Maulana Mohammed Omar.

Baradar's arrest infuriated Mullah Omar. They had fought together, serving in the Afghan mujahideen against the Soviet-backed Afghan government in the 1980s. After driving the Russians out, Baradar and Omar jointly founded the Taliban in 1994.

In November 2001, the US pounded Kandahar with drones, killing almost all of Omar's men. While the others were escaping, trying to save their lives first, Baradar ran directly into the line of fire and seized a motorbike. He zipped past the cloud of smoke and dust, towards Mullah Omar's hideout, risking his life. He found a weakened Omar, who was in a state of asphyxiation, helped him sit pillion on the bike, and fearlessly drove him safely into the mountains. After this, they rebuilt the infrastructure of the Afghan Taliban in Quetta, where they now hide in plain sight.

Baradar had portrayed himself to the world as a loyal lieutenant to Omar, but the reality was slightly different. He was almost as influential in the Taliban's decision-making as Omar himself. Being Omar's deputy, Baradar had a more modern and efficient way of handling matters. This didn't mean that he came down softly on his enemies or avoided bloodshed, but he put in the extra effort to figure out the alternatives. It wouldn't be a far cry to say that Baradar, with Omar's blessings, had made the Taliban the resurgent force that it is.

After his arrest in 2010, Omar made it clear that he still had access to Baradar when he needed it. The ISI realized that they couldn't afford to rub Omar up the wrong way if they wanted to maintain their stronghold in the covert operations. They agreed, and even gave Baradar a comfortable safe-house with all amenities. After his release in September 2013, the ISI sent Baradar to the Gulf to lie low for a while. But he could sense that Omar needed him back, as his movements were anyway limited, owing to the ten-million-dollar bounty on his head.

'It is good to have you back,' Mullah Omar said in Pashto as he embraced Baradar tightly and planted a brotherly kiss on his cheek. 'I hope the ISI hasn't misbehaved with you. Words cannot explain how much we have all missed your presence.'

Mullah Baradar smiled as he embraced his Amir. Mullah Baradar was the only one who could look into Mullah Omar's dead eye without flinching. They sat down together on the plush carpet. Omar ordered one of his men to bring in some food.

'It is good to be back. I see not much has changed here, Amir.'

'Quetta is safe as ever for me, Baradar. But it was rather difficult for me to operate without you. And with all that's going on now, I need you to help me more with my cause.'

A young Hazara boy walked in with a large dish and left it in front of Mullah Omar. Omar pushed it towards Baradar. There was a large chunk of charred beef, with sliced lemon. Another boy came in with a large glass of sherbet. Omar asked them to leave and close the door behind them, after they served his loyal deputy.

'It depends on the new President, Amir. Both of them have agreed, in principle, to let the Americans keep their troops in Afghanistan. Our battle has been in vain.'

'The battle has only begun, Baradar. You know that as well as I do.'

'We have to be very careful about your movements this year, Amir. Just because they move out doesn't mean that they won't try to capture you.'

Mullah Omar breathed in deeply. He stroked his wiry beard.

'That is exactly what I have told the ISI. But these are going to be testing times for us. The ISI is nobody's ally.'

'Yes,' Baradar consented. 'Especially now that the Americans have stopped donating money to them, they might resort to ill means, such as handing you over to get into the good books of the Americans, and even collect the bounty.'

'The Haqqanis are well aware of this, too. It is good to have them on our side.'

'Indeed it is,' Baradar said, wolfing down a piece of the meat. There was a sharp knock at the door. Omar looked over his shoulder and asked the person to come in. It was Brigadier Tanveer Shehzad.

'I'm afraid we don't have time for this now, Shehzad,' Baradar spat out, annoyed.

After his arrest, Mullah Baradar naturally loathed the ISI.

'You need not hold a grudge against me, Mullah Baradar. We did what we had to. We were pressurized into arresting you. If you ask me, it was hardly even an arrest. You were treated rather wonderfully at our hands.'

Baradar's eyes widened in anger. Mullah Omar raised his hand, indicating him to calm down. He gestured Shehzad to sit down.

'To what do we owe the pleasure, Shehzad?' Omar said.

'I'm here about the Indians,' Shehzad replied.

Baradar had finished eating, and had lit up a cigarette rolled up with *afeem*—opium. He was still in the process of calming down when Shehzad said these words. 'I cannot believe this, Amir. Since when have we begun to let go of our principles? We kill the spies who are a threat to us! We do not use them to negotiate for our purposes, let alone the purposes of the ISI! If you ask me, we ought to behead them right away, before it's too late!'

Omar nodded and then fixed his eye upon Shehzad.

'We have had this discussion before,' Shehzad said haughtily. 'And Mullah Baradar, I have nothing but the deepest respect for you. But it ought to benefit us all, if you keep in mind the larger picture.'

'What larger picture? You want Bhatkal and some silly nobodies back in exchange for spies who have seen where and how we operate?'

'You're being naive, Mullah Baradar. The Indians can't touch us here. Neither can the Americans. This is Balochistan.'

'Why are you here, Shehzad?' Mullah Omar spoke up.

'To discuss the other plan that we will carry out after the Indians send Bhatkal and the others back.'

'And if they don't?'

'We go ahead with it anyway,' Shehzad replied. 'This is a mere distraction for the Indians. I'm here to tell you that Sirajuddin Haqqani has agreed to provide us logistical support, as long as you approve of it.'

Baradar was getting confused about the conversation that was going on. Omar read the puzzled look on his face and smiled.

'I was about to tell you, Baradar. This is surely going to put your mind at ease.'

Shehzad looked at Baradar's baffled countenance as Omar spoke to him.

'I don't understand, Amir. I hope they haven't coaxed you into something you don't need to do.'

'They haven't, Baradar. But I will ask Shehzad here to relay the plan to you. If you do not like it, say so. I will not give my go-ahead, and you can go down and castrate those kafirs right away.'

Shehzad got agitated at what Mullah Omar had just said, but tried to look sanguine. He had always believed that

Baradar was given a lot of leeway and authority by Omar. This was again one of those instances where he witnessed it. He didn't like pitching the idea to Baradar for his approval. Baradar always did have a strong viewpoint and suggestions. Brigadier Tanveer Shehzad breathed in deeply, and explained the plan in brief to Mullah Abdul Ghani Baradar.

Baradar raised one eyebrow after listening to it. His gaze, behind a curtain of opium smoke, shifted from Shehzad to Omar. Omar shrugged as if to ask: What do you think?

Baradar spoke, his voice calculatedly low. 'What if the meeting doesn't happen?'

'I have an insider who knows for certain that it will happen later this month. It's on the itinerary. Besides, the conflict in Ladakh is escalating. A meeting of this kind is definitely on the cards.'

'Who will take the eventual responsibility?'

'The attack will be orchestrated by Ayman al-Zawahiri. This will be al-Qaeda's first attack in India. After which, keeping in mind the situation, we will take a call on the final plan. I have a skilled operative in tow, waiting for a chance to get back at India.'

'And all Mullah Omar has to do is give the nod, right?'

'Yes,' Shehzad replied. 'We will use a few of your camps to train the militants. And, of course, you will have to keep the prisoners alive until India sends back its reply to Mullah Omar's message.'

'How many days have the Indians asked for?'

'Fifteen.'

'And how many are left before we know for certain?'

'Thirteen.'

Baradar smiled as he took a drag of the afeem joint again.

'Let's go ahead with it, Shehzad. This ought to cripple that country for good.'

8

One minute to make it to the exit. One minute to jump into the car and drive the hell out of there. A figure of average height, clad in a black kurta, ran out of the madrasa frenziedly. He had an assault rifle, which he fired in the direction from which bullets were spraying at him. Around six large, bearded men, chased him. They were hot on his heels, abusing in Pashto and firing indiscriminately. The man ran in a zigzag pattern, making it difficult for them to get him. He ran like a gazelle towards his jeep. A bullet hit him in the back of his right thigh. The man lost his footing and collapsed to the ground. The men were closing in on him. He was going to die. He was certain of that. He raised his rifle and fired. He managed to hit one man.

About thirty seconds before they got to him.

He crawled towards the jeep. The attackers were closing in, equidistant from their prey and the beautifully constructed madrasa.

Twenty seconds.

The man was almost there. He mustered all his strength and got into the jeep. A pang of pain shot through his body. He was losing blood at an alarming rate.

Ten seconds.

The man saw another jeep with reinforcements driving in through the entry of the madrasa. He had to make it out of there. He started the car after fumbling for the keys in his pocket. He rammed the accelerator.

Five seconds.

As he drove out of the madrasa, a bullet hit his tyre. The car skidded, but he managed to control it.

Three seconds.

He was now on the road, making his escape.

One second.

A large, deafening explosion shook the ground. The man turned to look. Black smoke enveloped the entire compound of the madrasa. The structure itself was ablaze. The man looked on for another few seconds. Then he turned and drove away. The smell of burnt flesh wafted distinctly from the smoke that enveloped the vicinity. Amongst those dead, the man thought, is one of ours. He closed his eyes and yelled in pain. He still had work to do.

Later, when he recounted what had happened to the person he reported to, this was all he got back in reply: 'I want you to come back, Adonis.'

He knew what they thought. They thought Adonis had killed Ares and the Afghani defector. They thought Adonis had sold them out. That's exactly how it looked.

~

2 September 2014
Indira Gandhi International Airport, New Delhi

The terminal in the Indira Gandhi International Airport was a little less crowded than usual, considering the time. It was two in the morning, and there were many businessmen, both Indian and foreign, and a few families. They wore tired smiles, the kind you usually see at airports. Some relieved to get back home, others in anticipation to reach their destination. A few energetic children ran around chasing each other, as their parents chided them meekly. One of them ran in the direction of the 'Restricted Area' meant for 'staff', when an airport policeman stopped him gently. *Even I'm not allowed there,* the man thought.

Inside the Restricted Area was a rather large lounge. The four walls of this lounge had been witness to matters of high importance. This sector of the airport was reserved by the government for its intelligence activities. This is where the families of many agents had spoken to them for the last time. Or the first time after a successful mission or assignment. This is where embassy members or attachés waited before they were whisked into a small private jet. This is where the prime minister waited when he had to fly out of the country. But today, the guard who manned the post outside the lounge had been provided three names. Two were here already. They were waiting for the third. Their flight was scheduled to take off at three in the morning.

'How much do you know about the mission?' Isha Khan inquired of Nihar Shah, in an attempt to break the ice.

'As much as you do,' Nihar replied, avoiding looking at her for more than a split second. Once he saw her, he knew he couldn't take his eyes off her. 'There are three of us. You, me, and a certain Veer Singh, who's crossing over from Helmand. Our team is led by a former major by the name of Kabir Anand. All I know about him is that he teaches some kids Shakespeare at a college in Mumbai.'

Isha nodded slowly. That's all Joshi had told her, too.

'When I pulled out the files on Balochistan, I read about an incident concerning a certain agent code-named Adonis. Who is he?'

Nihar scratched his shaved chin and allowed himself to look into her inquisitive brown eyes.

'Adonis was the code name for an ex-Military Intelligence agent who was posted in Balochistan until 2006. He had a colleague in RAW who died in an explosion when they had covertly infiltrated a madrasa in Quetta. Some say Adonis blew it up, or indirectly set Ares up, because he was close to unravelling something serious, but Lieutenant General Sadiq Sheikh believed otherwise.'

'From what I have heard, Adonis was Sadiq's protégé. The RAW chief at the time felt that Adonis disregarded his authority and recklessly blew up the op. Some even branded him a traitor. But Sheikh came to his rescue and asked him to leave the job, pushing away the case for good.'

Nihar shrugged. *Sheikh was dead now.*

Isha echoed his thoughts and said with a gentle laugh: 'What kind of a code name is Adonis?'

'I'm sorry about the delay.' Kabir entered, closing the door behind him. 'I was figuring out some last-minute stuff with Joshi. I am Kabir Anand.'

Isha and Nihar both looked at Kabir. He wore a blazer and a white T-shirt on a pair of faded jeans. He hadn't combed his wild hair nor had he trimmed his unruly beard. Kabir wasn't conventionally good-looking, thought Isha, but there was a magnetic aura about him. He acknowledged both of them with a nod of his head, shook hands as they stood up to greet him, and then sat beside them, pulling out an iPad from its case.

'We fly to the Konarak airport in Chabahar first,' he said, pointing to a port in the Iranian part of Balochistan. 'Once we're there, we can assume our fake identities and drive to Gwadar.'

'I thought we'd fly to Gwadar directly,' Isha said.

'It's a decision Joshi and I took,' said Kabir. 'If we were to be questioned upon landing by the authorities in Gwadar, our cover would most likely be blown. I met Arifullah Saleh yesterday. He has asked an Al Jazeera journalist to receive us outside the airport.'

They nodded their heads in understanding.

'And if we go by ship to Gwadar,' Nihar added unnecessarily, 'we risk being gunned down almost immediately by the tight security forces manning the port. That, and it would take a day or two by sea.'

'Since India has investments in the port of Chabahar in Iran, that would provide us a valid reason, if we are questioned in Iran. We can simply state that we are part of an Indian committee creating a report on the development of the port. That is the same story Joshi has sent the Iranians. They have no qualms about it.'

Kabir looked at both of them with the gaze of a professor. They nodded understandingly, the way students do.

'The real challenge is getting to Quetta,' Kabir said. 'But we'll cross that bridge once we get to it.'

Kabir ran his fingers through his hair, and looked at Isha. He noticed her properly for the first time. A few women managed to catch his fancy, but there was something about her eyes. He looked at them, a delicate hazel-brown. Her hair tied up in a bun. Her fair skin glistening with sweat, even though the room was air-conditioned.

'You have ample reason to be worried,' Kabir addressed her. 'It's not going to be easy. And that is an understatement.'

He got up from the couch and then leaned against the door.

'If you want out, now is the time. Developing cold feet at the last moment is not an option.'

He looked at Nihar, who loosened his tie. He was nervous. Isha and Nihar shot a glance at each other. Neither of them wanted out.

'I want to clear up one thing. This is a rescue mission. We attack only if attacked.'

He opened the door. He knew what he said at the end wasn't true. There *was* going to be blood. Kabir never waited to be attacked first. And then he turned and looked back at Isha and Nihar.

'Make your calls to your family now,' he told them bluntly. 'You never know when you'll speak to them next.'

He stepped out of the room with his luggage and walked towards the runway towards the small plane waiting for them. He took his place next to a window. It was a good ten minutes before he saw Isha and Nihar begin their walk towards the plane. He shut his eyes, trying to put himself to sleep. A long journey lay ahead. Unlike his young colleagues, Kabir did not make any calls.

As Shakespeare put it in *King Henry VI*: *Having nothing, nothing can he lose.*

~

2 September 2014
Chabahar, Iran

The flight landed at the Konarak airport in the wee hours of the morning, at ten past five. It had been a three-hour flight. The weather was pleasantly cool and the wind was soothing. The salty smell of the sea lingered over Chabahar. Kabir met the pilot briefly, asking him to rest for an hour before leaving for India again. He asked him not to hang around too long and not to talk to too many people. If asked, he should stick to the brief: *I have flown in some Indians who are here to inspect the infrastructure of the Chabahar port.*

Chabahar is a city situated on the Makran coast of the Sistan and Balochistan provinces of Iran. On being declared a free trade zone by the Iranian government, this city, facing the Gulf of Oman, immediately gained significance in international trade. India is in the process of helping with the development of the Chabahar port, with a view to gaining direct access to the oil and gas exported out of Iran. This is India's counter-bid to China's pre-emptive access to the port of Gwadar in Pakistani Balochistan.

Nihar and Isha collected their luggage along with Kabir's and found their way out to the lobby. They were checked briefly and, after a momentary glance at their passports, allowed to exit the airport. Kabir strode out soon after. He had taken a brief nap and so had Isha. Only Nihar seemed a little ruffled.

'What's the matter?' Kabir asked him as they walked out of the airport. 'It's still not too late. You can get back on the flight.'

'It's not that.' Nihar shook his head.

'Then?'

'My wife,' Nihar said simply, unwilling to elaborate further.

'It's okay,' Isha told him. 'We women have the habit of blowing things out of proportion. Once you're back home, just be there for her.'

'And your son,' Kabir reminded him. 'Yes, Joshi told me about him. What's his name?'

Nihar was slightly uncomfortable discussing his family with people he had met only a few hours ago. 'Haven't named him yet.'

'Then that's the first thing you ought to do, once you're back,' Isha said, and motioned towards the only car waiting outside the airport. Kabir lifted his bags.

'Be careful of your luggage,' Nihar added, shifting the attention from himself. 'Don't let anybody else touch it. All our dossiers are in there.'

The dossiers, if found by anyone else, could never be explained away. So they held them close to their person and walked towards a red Peugeot sedan. As they came closer they realized that the driver was asleep in his seat. Kabir knocked lightly at his car window. The driver woke up with a start and stared out of his daze at Kabir. Then he nodded with familiarity and stepped out of the car.

'Zain Hussain?' Kabir checked.

Zain was a little rotund, and as tall as Kabir. He had a bushy moustache and his hair was greying and smoothed to one side. He looked like a tough guy. He wore a checked shirt on a pair of well-pressed trousers. He was Al Jazeera's top correspondent in Iran. A thorough journalist, with a hunger for knowledge, Zain had grown to become one of the most influential names in his profession in this part of the world. He had fearlessly documented the Northern Alliance's war under Ahmad Shah Massoud. Despite being a Shia himself, Hussain never missed an opportunity to write scathing articles on the religious–political leadership in Iran.

'Yes,' he replied, and shook Kabir's extended hand. 'Mr Saleh told me about you, Mr Anand. Let's put your luggage in the boot. We will drive to a cafe nearby and talk.'

Kabir took his seat next to Hussain. Isha and Nihar sat behind, after putting their bags in the boot. They rolled down their windows and Hussain drove them to a cafe ten minutes away.

'I don't know what you're getting into, Mr Anand, but I'm sure Mr Saleh wouldn't come into the picture unless it was extremely dangerous.'

He handed Kabir a sealed brown-paper envelope. Kabir looked in and saw fake documents and ID cards that showed his team as representatives of Al Jazeera, with false names. Hussain ordered some local Iranian tea with omelettes for his guests. Kabir passed the bag on to Isha, who slipped it into her handbag. Hussain noticed that a gentle breeze blew her curls across her face.

'The Taliban don't take too well to women,' Hussain said. 'You need to make sure she's always in hijab. In fact, some of the local Balochis may not like it either.'

'Don't worry, Mr Hussain. I've brought my hijab along.'

'I don't need to tell you guys this,' continued Hussain, 'but to blend in, you must look like them. You need to grow their kind of beard and wear their kind of clothes.' Nihar knew this was meant for him. He had shaved out of habit the previous night.

'Chabahar is a beautiful city,' Isha chimed in as she sipped her tea.

'It is, indeed. But then the geography is always beautiful. I agree that Chabahar is now much less turbulent, but there is always the chance of some conflict between the Shias and the Sunnis that could lead to instances of violence. The majority of the Muslims here are the local Balochis.'

'Does Khamenei crack down hard on them?' Kabir asked.

'Khamenei is an archetypal hypocrite,' Hussain scoffed. 'He claims to be supportive of them, but since they're mostly Sunnis he encourages violence against them. Similarly, on the global stage, he condemns terrorism, but there is something contrary to his messiah-like image that not everyone knows of.' He lowered his voice before continuing, 'I have reason to believe he funds al-Qaeda.'

Nihar and Isha gasped collectively.

'His true wealth is estimated to be in tens of billions of dollars,' Hussain continued. 'The old crook has even managed to finagle his way into being the only representative of the German automobile giant BMW in Iran. He got a charity organization of his affiliated with the company's dealers, pretending to be promoters of a noble cause. Gradually, he took over the reins. I haven't seen anyone as corrupt as this man. It disturbs me to see people placing their faith blindly in this mere mortal!'

Kabir's face remained sphinx-like.

'What about Iran's alliance with India?' he asked. 'I guess that is beneficial to both parties.'

'Yes, it is an important alliance, politically. Currently, the governments are planning a collaboration to build a gas pipeline between the two countries along the bed of the Arabian Sea. Strategically, it would be on much firmer ground than the proposed Iran–Pakistan–India pipeline. We all know why.' Kabir smiled as he wolfed down his omelette with a loaf of buttered bread.

'How far is Gwadar from here?'

'A couple of hours,' Hussain replied. 'I suggest you get moving as soon as possible. You are less likely to be seen by the security forces now than during the middle of the day.'

Kabir and his team thanked him. They offered to pay for the breakfast, but Hussain refused to let them, appearing somewhat offended at the suggestion. They walked towards the Peugeot, and Hussain handed Kabir the keys. Kabir shot him a questioning look.

'Saleh asked me to hand a car over to you.' He shrugged. 'It is much safer that you drive than have someone else drive for you. In the trunk are the cameras and tripods.' He smiled sheepishly as he said this. The content in the trunk was essential to their cover.

'This car is a little too conspicuous to be driving around in,' Kabir said.

'I agree with you,' Hussain replied. 'But it's all I could manage at such short notice.'

'I can't thank you and Mr Saleh enough,' Kabir said as his team settled into the car.

Hussain leaned into Kabir's window. 'Remember, if anyone needs a reference, just ask them to call me. I will say you're from Al Jazeera. Let's hope you succeed in your quest, no matter how dangerous.'

'Inshallah,' said Kabir.

The rest of the team thanked him, and Kabir put his foot to the pedal and eased the car out on to the highway.

~

2 September 2014
Gwadar, Balochistan

A rush of memories flashed through Kabir's mind as he sat behind the wheel. He had never imagined returning to the land that had changed everything for him. The roads, the people he passed by, all of it felt so familiar, as if he had been there just the previous week. He tried hard to forget everything that had happened in his past, especially in Balochistan. He had managed to turn over a new leaf. He had repressed all his memories of the province. But destiny has its own way with people.

They reached Zaveri Hotel in Koh-e-Batil at eight in the morning and checked into the best suites the hotel had to offer. It was a two-hour drive, but Kabir drove the Peugeot hard, so they reached a little earlier. He liked the feel of the car. Isha had offered to drive, but Kabir had declined. He asked them to rest. There was still a long way to travel. They needed to be in Quetta the following day itself, according to the plan. A healthy recce was needed before any covert operation could be undertaken. Especially an operation where you're messing with the Taliban!

Gwadar was in many ways a mirror image of Chabahar. The Pakistanis had planned the city well, recognizing the value of the port. In 2013, port operations were officially handed over to the Chinese. With an initial investment of 750 million dollars, the Pakistani contract with China envisioned the port to be developed into a full-scale commercial port. India, not surprisingly, was not allowed anywhere near Gwadar, given its rivalry with both Pakistan and China.

The port is a key strategic resource for the Chinese, enabling it to import oil and gas without much ado. Currently, 60 per cent of China's oil needs to be transported by sea from the Persian Gulf to the commercial port of Shanghai, a distance of more than 16,000 kilometres. The journey is rather risky, and takes a couple of months, making it vulnerable to pirates off the coast of East Africa as well as inclement weather. The Gwadar port facility will reduce the distance these ships travel as well as enable oil transfers to be made all year round.

'Get all the rest you can. We need to leave for Quetta first thing tomorrow,' Kabir said, looking out of the window at the scenic view Gwadar had to offer. He looked on as the gentle waves kissed the shore, reminding him of Mumbai's Juhu Beach.

Isha went in straight for a bath. Kabir and Nihar unpacked their communication equipment in the hall, so that they could send a quick message to HQ.

'The secure line,' Kabir reminded Nihar. 'Remember, only a select few in India know of our mission. Joshi wants to keep it that way.'

Nihar sent a coded message through the secure iPad to Delhi. They had to be doubly sure that none of their messages were intercepted. The ISI always kept a lookout for messages exchanged between Indians and Pakistanis, even if they were frequent phone calls between family members who lived across the border.

'I want you to check the equipment again,' Kabir said. 'We are bound to be stopped at a few checkpoints before Quetta.'

Nihar agreed and opened the bag with the equipment. The tripods of the camera, when unscrewed, had little pieces of metal and a smaller barrel. Kabir had insisted that they wouldn't need a gun until they reached their destination. He had got the little pieces put in the bags as random pieces of metal, so he could assemble them when the need arose. There was no place for carrying a weapon larger than a semi-automatic Glock.

Isha stepped out of the bathroom, her hair wet. She was dressed in a black tank top and a pair of jeans. Nihar looked at her from the corner of his eye as she entered the hall. Kabir got up to go shower.

'I suggest you put on your hijab now,' said Nihar as she walked in.

There was a soft knock at the door. Nihar quickly zipped the suitcases and looked through the peephole.

He saw a tall, bearded, turbaned man standing in a Pathani suit.

He turned to Isha. 'Are we expecting the Taliban already?'

'I think that's Veer in character.'

Nihar opened the door and moved away. The man walked in slowly and turned around. He looked at Isha and Nihar, who looked curiously back at him.

'Veer Singh?' she asked, observing him. He looked very different in the file pictures.

The man didn't reply. His eyes widened in horror as he saw how Isha was dressed. He put his hand in his suit and pulled out a pistol instinctively. He pointed it towards Isha. Nihar was dumbfounded. Kabir was still in the toilet.

'Who are you?' Isha shouted loud enough for Kabir to hear. Kabir realized something was wrong. He had finished showering and was towelling his wet body when he heard Isha's voice. He picked up a small pair of scissors near the washbasin, preparing to use the sharp end as a weapon. It was the only option he had. He put on his boxers quickly and stormed out of the room.

The turbaned man was caught unawares as Kabir charged into him from behind. Pinning him to the ground, Kabir stabbed the man in his thigh with the scissors. The man shrieked in pain and let go of the gun. Nihar picked it up and aimed it at him.

As a network of veins throbbed furiously through his shirtless body, Kabir said through gritted teeth: 'Who are you?'

'Nawabzada Nusrat Marri has sent me to bring you to him,' he said finally. Kabir pulled out the scissors from the man's bleeding thigh. The man let out another shout in pain. His salwar was stained with blood.

Nusrat Marri was the brother of Balach Marri, the creator of the Baloch Liberation Army, which fought for autonomy against Pakistan.

Isha chided the man. 'You could've just said that, instead of waving your gun around.'

'In this part of the world, we wave our guns first before talking. I just wanted to make sure it was the same bunch of Indians that Nawabzada Marri was expecting.'

'How did Marri know we were here?' Nihar questioned him.

'Zain Hussain informed him. Besides, he has a stake in this hotel,' the man replied. 'Whenever there is a guest from another country, we alert him first.'

'And then wave your gun at him?'

The man decided not to explain why he had acted so impulsively. He simply shrugged.

'What's your name?'

'Irfan Baloch Khan.'

'We're documentary film-makers, Irfan Baloch Khan, if that puts you at ease,' Isha lied with a smile. 'Certainly not Pakistanis.'

Kabir threw a bandage to the man. There was a knock at the door again. Kabir pulled on a pair of trousers and put on a linen shirt hurriedly. Kabir sensed it was Veer Singh, the fourth team member, but he took the gun from Nihar as a precaution and walked up to the door.

'Let me get the door this time.'

Kabir looked through the peephole and then opened the door. He looked at Veer, who, at six foot five, towered over him.

'Veer Singh.' The man stretched out a large hand.

Kabir shook it firmly.

'Welcome back to Balochistan, Adonis.'

There was a moment of silence from Nihar and Isha. *Kabir Anand was the infamous Adonis.*

'Well,' Isha added finally, 'we don't call him that any more.'

Kabir shot a glance over his shoulder. He sensed an uneasiness in Nihar's manner.

'Joshi has given him a more poetic sobriquet,' she continued with a half-smile. 'He calls him The Bard.'

9

2 September 2014
Gwadar, Balochistan

The sun shone brightly over the port city of Gwadar in the afternoon. A strong wind swept the dusty streets, as both men and women protected their faces with scarves. The sea breeze kept the city cool through the year, except for a couple of months in the summer when the hot and dry shamal winds from the north reminded its residents of their barren and dusty neighbourhood. The winters were cold, continuing through most of January, and it even rained a bit. Almost everyone needed more layers of clothing. Except Kabir, who stepped out in just a shirt and linen pants. The trio, along with Veer, were off to meet Nusrat Marri, the leader of the local Balochi militia.

Kabir and his team had followed Irfan Baloch Khan's white SUV in their red Peugeot. The porter at the hotel porch had noticed Khan's bloodstained pyjama, but decided against poking his nose into the matter. He simply loaded their bags in the trunk and walked away.

There was an elephant in the room. The team hadn't had a chance to interact with him directly, and could only etch a sketch of him from the backgrounder. Veer, on his part, spoke very little. It seemed as though he did not want to get to know his fellow Indians any more than necessary. He took the keys from Kabir, started the ignition and revved it up a bit before following the SUV closely through a marketplace, as the rest of the team sat in silence, each lost in their own thoughts. The smell of kebabs wafted through the air, as they saw several stalls with men skewering and grilling marinated morsels of meat over earthen hearths. Veer clucked his tongue irritably, and rolled up the windows and started the air conditioning.

'Don't like kebabs?' Isha asked him.

'I'll ask you the same question in a week,' Veer said. 'After you've eaten them every day, at every meal.'

Isha shrugged. Nihar wasn't too fond of meat either. As if the mission wasn't hard enough already, it looked like there wasn't going to be much to look forward to in terms of food either.

'The only good thing about Gwadar is that you get some fish from the sea as well,' Veer continued. 'When I was in Afghanistan, the only food we got was coarse, charred beef. Pakistan has a lot more variety, I'd say.'

The next ten minutes went by without any conversation. The SUV in front of them took a sharp turn and came to a halt outside a white bungalow. Irfan Baloch Khan limped out and motioned them to park behind his car. Khan's limp was rather exaggerated as he led Kabir and his team through the wrought-iron gates of the bungalow. The bungalow itself was small. It was white, two storeys high, with a large flag pinned to the front wall. The combination of green, white, red and blue stood out rather conspicuously against the white backdrop of the bungalow. The flag of Balochistan.

Khan gestured to Kabir to stop. He walked on, knocked at the door and said something into the ear of a servant. The servant nodded, went inside, and after about a minute returned to let them in through the door. Khan motioned Kabir and his team to enter.

'Remove your shoes,' he whispered, untying his own laces. Kabir and the rest followed suit and entered the house. The dining area welcomed them with the smell of kebabs, again. Isha smiled at Veer, who remained expressionless, however.

The house was well decorated with local Balochi artefacts: large, colourful embroidered dhurries, and little glass-and-crystal curios that reflected the sunlight that streamed in through an open window. There was a European tinge to the house that blended in interestingly with the vibrant Balochi flavour. Kabir wasn't surprised—the sophisticated Marri family had spent a lot of time in England and the Soviet Union, and so had inculcated their tastes appropriately. Nusrat Marri himself had studied in the former USSR and then settled down in England. He frequented his homeland regularly.

'Sit down,' Khan said, motioning to a sofa. 'Nawabzada will be with you in a moment.'

And almost as soon as he said it, Nusrat Marri walked in. He was almost Veer's height, but not as well built. He had droopy eyes, and a long, angular face. He wore a waistcoat over a light-blue shirt, and a pair of formal pants. Except Kabir and Veer, who had seen him before, the others had a slightly different image of Marri in their minds. They expected him to have a long mullah-like beard, and a typical air of the rural tribal about him. Instead, they found Marri to be clean-shaven, with a neat haircut. He patted Khan on the shoulder, shot a fleeting glance at his bleeding thigh and asked him to close the door behind him as he went.

'*Salaam aleikum*,' he said in a slight British accent, as his guests stood up to greet him. 'Please sit down. I must start by apologizing about my man.'

'*Waleikum as-salaam*,' Kabir replied. 'On the contrary, we must apologize to him.'

'You must understand,' Marri said, 'there was this one instance, not too long ago, when the ISI followed me around in a Peugeot just like yours. They thought driving a car brought from Iran would not raise any suspicions. Peugeots are not common around here. After a brief gunfight, we managed to kill all of them.'

He said this with an air of calculated nonchalance. The forty-six-year-old Nusrat Marri, a Baloch nationalist, was the sixth son of nationalist leader Khair Bakhsh Marri, who now calls the shots from Britain. Khair Bakhsh Marri, known as the 'Tiger of Balochistan', has been leading the ongoing insurgency against the Pakistani government for over four decades. However, as age caught up with him, his sons shifted him to England, and combined forces, making them hard to contend with. Balach Marri, the second son, was the more radical of the lot. His solution to every problem involved violence, and that proved to be his downfall. Unlike the other remaining members of the Marri tribe, Balach made it a habit to fight alongside his tribesmen.

In 2007, on 21 November, Balach was asked by the family doctor to come over to see his father in south Quetta. Balach, who was hiding on the Afghan side of the border, took two of his men and drove recklessly into Balochistan. He was forced to stop at a checkpoint by a posse of officers of the ISI and soldiers of the Pakistani Army. Balach immediately understood what was about to transpire, and tried to drive his way out of the ambush. They knew his car would be armoured, so they shot at his tyres first. Finally, Balach and his two men were left with no choice but to come out and fight. The instant they stepped out of the car, they were peppered with bullets. The great Balach Marri had met a premature end. And it was none other than Brigadier Tanveer Shehzad of the ISI who had pumped the bullets into his chest. Needless to say, the family doctor, who tried to flee, was taken captive. Nusrat Marri flew down from England the very next day, and mercilessly killed him. The doctor's severed head was kept on display to serve as an example to others lest they try and betray the Marri tribe.

'I'm sorry,' he said suddenly. 'I forgot to introduce myself. I'm Nusrat Marri. And you?'

They told him their cover names. He shook his head.

'Real names,' he said softly. 'We both know that no Indian would have the balls to come to Balochistan to make a documentary. Besides, I think I've seen you before.'

He looked at Veer. Veer nodded.

'I've delivered money to you in Quetta once,' Veer said. 'We aren't going to beat around the bush, Mr Marri. We're Indian spies.'

'That wasn't so hard now, was it?' Marri smiled.

Without any warning, the door opened and a trolley of dishes came in, pushed by a young boy. The aroma of food filled the room.

'I hope you are hungry,' Marri said. 'A lavish spread awaits you.'

Kabir smiled at his team. Veer didn't seem too fascinated. In every training session they had attended, they were usually told never to give up the chance to eat or sleep. When in the field, you never know when you might get to eat, drink water or sleep next. The food that Marri had arranged for them was elaborate indeed. There were a variety of kebabs and koftas, and a local speciality known as sajji. One of the highlights of Balochi cuisine, sajji consists of an entire skewered lamb, marinated in papaya paste and stuffed with fine rice. Marri had even organized a few bottles of Pepsi. Kabir personally didn't like Pepsi, but he needed something fizzy to help him ease down the rich spread. They discussed the current scenario in Balochistan. And then, suddenly, Marri felt the need to move on from the small talk.

'This is all very good, Kabir, but tell me why you're here, really.'

There was a pregnant pause. Kabir chewed silently on a succulent lamb kofta, thinking of a way to answer. *The truth. Tell him the truth.*

'Four of our agents are being held hostage in Quetta,' he replied. 'We're here to rescue them.'

'How did they get captured? You guys are pretty cautious about how you go about your stuff.'

'We were compromised by someone within the agency itself,' Kabir said. 'They were captured by the Taliban.'

'The Taliban? How can you be certain they aren't dead already? Omar's men behead captives the moment they sense even a sliver of suspicion.'

'We have reason to believe that the ISI is holding him back,' Kabir replied. 'They are calling the shots, using Omar as their front. They've made certain demands.'

'And what might those be?'

'They want four terrorists of theirs that we have holed up in India in exchange for these four agents of ours. We have managed to buy some time, hoping we'd be able to manage to rescue our agents in the meanwhile.'

Marri breathed in deeply. The rest of the team had paused eating, in wait for a reaction. Kabir gulped down his cola.

'If they indeed are with Mullah Omar,' he said finally, 'there is no way you can get to them. It's a Herculean task.'

'And the four of us are up for it,' Veer interjected with a smile. 'Nusrat Sahab, we are well aware of what we are getting into.'

'Omar and us, Baloch nationalists, don't really interact much, nor do we interfere in each other's business. But there have been instances when he's aided the ISI against us. He's a slithery snake of a man. He and Mullah Baradar.'

It wasn't breaking news to Kabir and his team.

'And the ISI,' Kabir said.

'I'm sure it's that bastard Tanveer Shehzad who has come up with such a scheme.'

'Tanveer Shehzad?' Isha asked.

'He's the man ISI has assigned to be in charge of their operations in Balochistan. He shot my brother Balach dead.'

He said this without flinching, but his voice had an undertone that betrayed him. Kabir knew the feeling. Sadiq Sheikh's death was still fresh in his mind.

'I would want to kill him in the worst way possible, too, if he had killed my brother. I know of Shehzad. He's the one who's hiding Omar in Quetta,' Kabir said.

'In plain sight,' Marri added. 'So basically, yes, that is what you're up against.'

It was never going to be easy. Everyone told them that repeatedly.

'Once the US pulls out of Afghanistan later this year,' Kabir said, 'there will be chaos, Nusrat Sahab. Balochistan stands to lose a lot. The Pakistanis will get even more reckless with you rebels.'

'I'm entirely aware of that, Kabir. But I don't know what we can do. I flew down from the UK last week to meet my brother-in-law, Nabil, to discuss what our strategy should be.'

Nabil Bugti was Akbar Bugti's son. The Marri and Bugti tribes had set up the Baloch Liberation Army together.

'And?'

Nusrat Marri sighed deeply. He looked profoundly discontented.

'We might dissolve the BLA and give up the idea of autonomy. There is a bit of infighting because of the impatience amongst us. The Pakistanis will crush us if we continue like this.'

There was a deafening silence. Kabir could not believe his ears. The rest of the team looked at Marri, who avoided eye contact. After half a century, they were going to give up their fight for an independent Balochistan!

'This isn't the right decision, Marri Sahab.' Veer's voice punctured the quiet. 'You stand to lose everything you've ever stood for. Everything your illustrious family has ever stood for!'

'You think I don't know that!' Marri raised his voice. 'You think Nabil and I are happy about it? We have come to learn what is better for us. We don't want our people dying helplessly at the hands of those hounds. We can't have any more widows, any more children without their fathers!'

'You know what,' Kabir said, 'I think there's a sudden element of fear that has crept into you, Marri Sahab.'

Isha's jaw dropped at this. Nihar's eyes widened. Veer looked on with interest. He knew very well what Kabir was up to. He was recruiting an asset. Someone who could play an important part in carrying out an operation, and there were few better men than Marri for this particular mission.

'I don't give a fuck about what you think, Kabir. You haven't lost a brother or a father in this war.'

'You all aren't playing to your strengths,' Kabir replied, his face reddening with anger. 'After you lost Bugti and Balach, you have stayed low-key. Attacking a few Pakistani soldiers here and there doesn't cut it any more.'

'Yes?' Marri said caustically. 'And what is your grand plan?'

'How many fighters do you have in the BLA?'

'Five, maybe six hundred.'

'And the fighters from the Bugti tribe?'

'They're relatively bigger than us in size. I'd estimate around a thousand to twelve hundred.'

'Add them together, Marri. Add them together. You have seventeen hundred people.'

Marri nodded, still missing the point.

'You have seventeen hundred people willing to die for a cause! And better still, kill for it too!'

Marri poured himself a glass of water. A lump formed in his throat.

'What you lack is initiative,' Veer interrupted. 'Let me be extremely honest. We Indians are looking at maiming Pakistan covertly by funding you. But the numbers are not big enough, and once NATO pulls out, it won't be long before our government stops giving a shit about some little tribe in Pakistan. Not unless there is something larger at hand.'

Marri put his glass down and shifted his gaze from Kabir to Veer and then back again.

'What are you suggesting, Kabir?'

The same question lingered in Isha's and Nihar's minds. Veer had already understood.

'We hurt them where they least expect it,' Kabir said. The use of the word 'we' didn't go unnoticed.

'How?'

'We capture Mullah Omar and claim the ten-million bounty. We expose the Pakistani hypocrisy to the world. They can't afford to have another Abbottabad situation all over again.'

Nihar choked on his water. Isha's eyes bulged out of their sockets. Veer smiled.

'You're fucking insane,' Marri scoffed.

'Think about it. The world will applaud the true Balochis. The ISI will have lost their main trump card. The Haqqanis will lie low for a while. The Americans will support you against Pakistan. In all likelihood, Balochistan will be on its own after that.'

Marri shook his head furiously and got up. He picked up his plate and stormed out of the room.

'What was all that about?' Isha asked Kabir sternly. 'We are still trying to figure out how to get our own people back and you're talking about abducting Mullah Omar? '

Kabir didn't answer her. Marri walked back into the room.

'I'll be leaving for England tomorrow,' he said, sitting down on the chair opposite Kabir. 'Which is when you should get moving too. What you have suggested is extremely difficult, but not impossible. I will speak to my father about it.'

Kabir nodded in understanding.

'Your father is a respected man,' Kabir said. 'Much of the respect he has gained is through his fight against Pakistani injustice. You can't let that go to waste is all I'm saying.'

Kabir stood up, and on cue, so did his team. They felt like they wouldn't need to eat for the next three days. Nusrat Marri led them to a basin, where they washed their hands.

Kabir walked back to the hall, and looked the tall Nusrat Marri in the eye.

'You should meet Nabil once you're in Quetta,' Marri told him. 'I'm sure he will help you in some way to get your friends back.'

Kabir smiled politely at him. 'I certainly will,' Kabir said.

Nusrat took Kabir's hand and shook it warmly. 'Don't get into trouble, Kabir. We need more people like you and your friends in the world.'

'I agree,' Kabir smiled. 'Think about what I've said.'

Marri nodded and then wished all the members of the team luck in their endeavour.

'Oh,' Marri said before Kabir stepped out of the house. 'Please don't take that red car around. You'll stick out like a sore thumb. You can take my car instead.'

Their plan, as it stood, was to take the rest of the day off. They would set out for Quetta early the next morning. It was a twelve-hour drive, and the team wasn't quite ready to embark on a journey that long the same day.

'I insist you take Irfan along,' Marri said. 'He is well versed with the route. And it won't hurt to have an extra pair of hands at the wheel.'

Kabir and his team agreed. They needed someone to guide them along.

Marri followed them out and pointed at a silver Toyota Land Cruiser. He walked up to it and opened the boot. Isha and Nihar gasped at what they saw. It had guns of various shapes and sizes. Kabir and Veer exchanged smiles. Guns seemed to help strengthen some bonds.

'Trust me,' said Marri, looking at Isha, 'you will need them.'

10

The team hit the sack early that night. After their meeting with Nusrat Marri, they drove back to the hotel and checked into their suite. Kabir and Isha decided to sleep in the room, and Veer and Nihar in the adjacent hall. Kabir had asked Isha if she was comfortable sharing a room with him, else he could get another one for himself. She rolled her eyes and told him not to be silly.

'Just remember,' she said with a friendly laugh, 'try anything funny and you'll find out I'm stronger than you are.'

The room was small and Kabir ordered a mattress for himself. He laid it out on the floor and lay down after changing into a white kurta, which he wore over a pair of Adidas trackpants. Isha giggled at this curious combination. Kabir just smiled back at her.

'Why did you choose this line of work, Isha?'

She paused before responding. She climbed on to the bed and crossed her legs, looking down at Kabir. He had tried not to look into her eyes, but this time he had no choice.

'It chose me,' she said. 'I had an uncle in the army. I remember spending a lot of time with him when he was home. I guess he inspired me to become what I am. He was martyred in Kargil.'

Kabir remained silent. He knew saying anything would break Isha's stream of thought.

'What about you, Major Anand?'

'My father was in the air force. I lost him at a very early age,' Kabir replied. 'I wasn't inclined towards the forces, though. One thing led to another and one fine day I was inducted into the Military Intelligence.'

Isha probed further. 'Elaborate, please!'

'Maybe another time, Isha. Maybe another time.'

'I understand,' Isha said. 'There are things you may not want to talk about. Things that we all would like to keep secret, Adonis.'

Kabir was a little taken aback by the way she brought up his old code-name without a smidgeon of propriety. *Surely, she's heard some version of the stories doing the rounds.*

'Are you hinting at my shrouded past?' Kabir asked. 'I will tell you all about that when the time is right. We have too much on our plate right now to bother about the past. Rest assured, it is not what you guys have been told.'

Isha leaned towards him, unwilling to press further. The lamp that lit the room dimly enhanced the colour of her curls. Her eyes, though tired from lack of sleep, still showed interest.

'So, are you married?'

'No.' Kabir smiled. 'What about you?'

'I'm still young,' she chuckled. Kabir laughed at her jibe. 'But you never intended to marry?'

Kabir remained silent. His lips curled into a sad smile. She saw his deep dimples, behind his fuzzy beard, but his smile didn't reach his eyes.

'I did intend to,' he said. 'She was the one who forced me to teach Shakespeare. Initially, studying literature was only a hobby. A refreshing change from the gore I had witnessed and inflicted. '

'And then?'

'I woke up one morning,' Kabir said, 'and didn't find her next to me any more. Not that that hadn't happened before. But I knew that day that she was gone.'

Isha didn't speak. He stroked his beard, still looking confused.

'I'm sorry,' she said finally. 'Didn't you ever bother finding out where she was? I mean, you're a spy after all.'

Kabir laughed softly, and nodded.

'As a matter of fact, I did. To get some form of closure, I did.'

'And?'

'I wish I hadn't,' he said, laughing. 'She got married to some other guy a year later. Rich, maybe. A banker, perhaps.'

Isha raised an eyebrow at him.

'Perhaps?'

'Yeah, all right. A banker. But I was angry, naturally. She could've told me and then left. What could I have done anyway?'

'That bitch.' Isha smiled. She reached out and touched his shoulder. 'If it's any consolation, I'm sure you're a better agent than he is a banker.'

'The thought never crossed my mind.' Kabir laughed. 'But I'm certainly better-looking than him.'

'He must be really ugly, then.' Isha laughed. Kabir joined her.

'Anyway, this was a while ago. I don't think about it any more. Not much, anyway.'

He had reluctantly come to the realization that when you love someone, there may come a time when you need to let go.

Isha nodded understandingly. *Maybe that's why he's always brooding.*

'And now if you're done invading my privacy, let's catch some sleep? We need to get to Quetta tomorrow. It's a twelve-hour journey.'

It was well past midnight. Irfan Baloch Khan, the man Nusrat Marri had assigned to the team, had told them he'd pick them up at five in the morning. They needed those few hours of sleep now.

'Goodnight, Kabir,' she said, smiling.

She switched off the dim light and fell asleep almost immediately. Kabir, however, stayed awake long after. Today was the first time he had opened up to someone about that aspect of his past. It was just a couple of days since he had known Isha, but she seemed like someone he didn't mind speaking his mind to. He was beginning to like his team.

In the adjacent hall, however, Nihar was voicing his concern to Veer in a low tone.

'Is what they say about him true?' he asked. 'The sketchy Adonis story?'

'It's not up to me to decide what is true and what isn't.' Veer shrugged.

~

3 September 2014
Pakistan

They had driven for five hours straight, taking turns at the wheel of the Toyota Land Cruiser. Irfan Baloch Khan had arrived, as promised, at five in the morning. They had had a light breakfast of toast and scrambled eggs. Kabir looked extremely alert, though his eyes were red owing to lack of sleep. He tried to take a nap in the car, but kept waking up now and again, volunteering to take over the wheel.

Veer and Nihar seemed adequately refreshed. Isha, though, was the chirpiest of the lot. She kept the driver engaged throughout with small talk. Before leaving the hotel, Irfan had insisted they all wear traditional clothes to blend in. It was rather warm and dry outside, and their clothes stuck to their bodies because of the sweat.

They had reached halfway along the 650-kilometre Makran Coastal Highway that ran parallel to the coastline of the Arabian Sea. The highway primarily connects various parts of Balochistan, linking them with Karachi on the other side. National Highway 10, the official designation, was a combination of well-paved roads and rough dirt-tracks. They had traversed most of the section that ran along the sea and would soon take a sharp left towards the heart of Balochistan. They had been checked once at a toll gate, but had no difficulty getting past. The guard looked into the car, eyeballed Isha for a bit, assumed they were local Balochis and let them pass.

'I can take over now, Irfanbhai. You've been driving for a while.'

Irfan Baloch Khan parked the car on the shoulder, and Veer took his place at the wheel. Khan sat in the third row of the SUV, along with Nihar, rubbing his eyes. Nihar was playing a game on his iPad. Khan looked interestedly at it. He had seen one of those with Nawabzada Marri, but had never had the chance to touch one. Nihar looked at him and smiled.

'It is like a computer,' he explained. 'Here, see this. You can even watch movies. You like movies?'

Khan grinned and exclaimed he did. Kabir looked on, out of the window. His throat had begun to ache because of the cold. Isha had headphones plugged in, listening to something with her eyes shut. Veer was clocking over a 110, and at the pace they were going, they were likely to make it within twelve hours. He whistled lightly to himself.

'You guys mind if I put the radio on?'

'Go ahead,' Kabir said. Veer fidgeted with the deck, and after a while he put on some local Afghani music and hummed along. Kabir and Isha shot confused looks at each other. Nihar looked rather surprised. And then they all realized: Veer was more Pashtun than Indian now.

'Here, take my iPod,' Isha said, handing the gadget over to Veer. 'Plug it in, so we can play some music we all can appreciate.'

She went on to play an album by Nusrat Fateh Ali Khan. Except Irfan Baloch Khan, who was busy watching a Bollywood movie on Nihar's iPad, all of them were enchanted by the singer's majestic voice. Kabir watched Isha sway her head delicately to the rhythm from the corner of his eye.

'In another four hours,' Veer said as he parked the car so that Kabir could take on as driver, 'we should be at Kalat. Just follow the road.'

Kabir enjoyed driving on these roads that ascended in height. He had always admired the stark natural beauty of the rugged terrain of Balochistan. The large mountains, the pristine lakes, the wild Zayaki Jangal bypass.

A little while later, Kabir pulled up near a little dhaba.

'This is a largely Shia Hazara area. They are the local Balochis,' Khan informed the team as they walked into the little shanty. They were welcomed by three Hazara men, with almost indistinguishable Mongolian features. The oldest was probably the grandfather of the youngest. He patted the boy lovingly on his back, and nudged him forward to take the order.

Khan spoke to them in their native language, ordering large glasses of buttermilk. After they had their salty but surprisingly refreshing drink, they left the dhaba, leaving a large tip for the man.

'I will drive now,' Khan said. 'We are likely to face a few checkpoints here. It's better if they interact with me.'

~

The car had been stopped at a checkpoint before Kalat. Three heavyset guards with rifles walked towards them. One heavily moustached guard knocked at Khan's tinted window, which he rolled down. He looked into the car, at all the passengers. He smiled sickly at Isha, exposing a yellow set of teeth. *These Balochis are bastards, but their women are so pretty.*

'What is the purpose of your visit to Kalat?'

'None of your business,' Khan replied curtly.

The man looked enraged. 'How dare you talk to me like that, you fucking Balochi!'

'Calm down, sir. We are here merely as visitors,' Kabir intervened. 'We have no real agenda. I apologize for my man's insolent behaviour.'

Kabir pulled out a few Pakistani notes and pressed them into the guard's hand, who nodded and motioned the car ahead.

'What the hell was that, Khan?' Kabir frowned.

'We should never show we fear them,' Khan spat out. 'Did you see how he was looking at the lady? These guys are rapists. They have been known to rape Balochi women. It infuriates me.'

Nihar looked warily over his shoulder at the guards. They were still looking at the vehicle, speaking into a walkie-talkie. It looked suspicious, but he chose not to say anything about it. They had passed that hurdle anyway. The highway continued for a short while before breaking into a fork. Khan took a left and slowed down a bit. The road was narrow and dusty. And then he saw something.

'Hell!' he exclaimed. 'They are following us.'

Kabir and his team turned abruptly and looked. There were two SUVs following them. Veer reached for the bag with the weapons. There were at least six firearms. He picked up a Glock pistol and passed it to Kabir. Kabir always insisted on a pistol. The Glock was his favourite. It was light and discharged bullets without too much of a delay. Moreover, it was highly accurate, if the shooter was skilled enough. Veer picked up an MG18 light machine gun for himself. Khan stepped on the gas. Swirls of dust made it difficult to see what was directly ahead of him.

Isha picked up an SAF Carbine sub-machine gun and loaded it. She passed it to Nihar, who seemed rather frightened. He wasn't ready to fire a gun anywhere else other than target practice. Not yet, anyway. He held it reluctantly. Isha picked up another SAF Carbine for herself.

'There is one for you as well, Khan!' she said. 'If the need arises . . .'

The rest of her sentence was drowned in a deafening noise. The car was thrown off its wheels. Another Pakistani car, waiting ahead down the road, had rammed into them.

The Toyota turned upside down. The glass shattered. Everyone closed their eyes, to prevent the shards from entering. They were thrown off their seats. Kabir held his head in his hands, protecting it from damage, as he had been taught in training many years ago. After somersaulting twice, the car came to a halt upside down.

The three Pakistani cars parked around a hundred metres away. They got out of the car. Kabir opened his eyes and saw the rest of the passengers. Veer was struggling to open the door.

'Wait,' Kabir told him as he picked up his Glock. 'We have to be quick about this. We open fire immediately.'

They clutched on to their guns. They were a tangled mess, and it took a while for them to extricate themselves from it. Khan was bleeding profusely from a cut on his head. Little shards of glass and mangled metal were everywhere. Nihar's expression was one of sheer bewilderment. He had never been in such a situation before.

'On my count,' Kabir said to Veer, as he saw the attackers approaching. 'Three, two, one.'

And with a start, Kabir sprang up from his seat and fired three bullets continuously. He found his way out of the car and took cover behind the upturned roof. Veer had jumped out, too, spraying bullets wildly, taking cover next to Kabir. This made the attackers retreat as they were taken aback. They thought they had done the job. Kabir opened the door, leading Isha, Nihar and Khan out. There was a round of gunshots and all of them lay prone.

'Isha and Nihar,' Veer said, 'switch positions with me and Kabir. Let us do the shooting. You provide fire to distract them.'

Kabir threw aside his Glock and grabbed the Carbine from Nihar, who looked too shaken to do anything. Kabir moved aside and opened fire. He managed to gun down two of the attackers with a short outburst of bullets.

'There are eight of them,' Kabir said. 'I got two.'

Khan picked up the gun and stood up, exposing himself. He shot bullet after bullet that missed its target. The attackers began to aim at Khan. Veer got on to his knees and shuffled to the side of the car. He fired with his light machine gun, taking out two others. He shot one square in the head, the other in his stomach.

'Four more,' Veer said. Isha had moved aside herself, opening fire recklessly. 'Be careful, Isha! Aim and shoot!'

She didn't pay attention, and continued to spray bullets recklessly in the direction of the cars. The four attackers began to shoot back, towards her. She didn't have adequate cover. Kabir ran and pulled her back. A bullet grazed his arm.

'Are you insane?' he said through gritted teeth. Blood drenched the left sleeve of his kurta. They could smell gas.

'Fuck,' Nihar said. 'They've hit the gas. If another bullet hits the tank, the car will explode!'

They got to their feet and began to run away from the car. The dust and smoke filled their lungs, as they moved clumsily to find cover. Nihar hid behind a large rock. Seeing them run away, the attackers began to shoot at them. They closed in towards the battered Land Cruiser, hoping to get a better shot. That was exactly what Kabir wanted.

'Shoot at the car!' Kabir bellowed. His team began to fire at the vehicle. Within a few seconds, the car exploded. The two attackers who were close to it got completely engulfed in the flames. The two who remained retreated backwards to their own car. They scampered in hurriedly and drove off.

'Come back here, you fucking cowards!' Irfan Baloch Khan yelled, thumping his chest. The car drove away, leaving a large cloudy trail of dust. Then he fell to his knees.

'W-who were they?' Nihar asked, gasping for breath.

'The ISI or the Army,' Khan said. 'This was possibly an attempted assassination on Nawabzada Marri's life. They must've recognized his car.'

Kabir helped Isha up. Little shards of glass still clung to her skin. He moved them aside delicately. She supported his arm on her shoulder as they walked to the car that the attackers had abandoned. In hindsight, they would've regretted leaving it behind. Veer realized there were no keys. He smashed the plastic beneath the steering wheel and tugged out two wires. He tore them apart and hot-wired the car. Within five minutes, the engine was running.

'We must wait in Kalat,' Kabir said, recovering from the adrenalin rush. 'We need to lie low for a while.'

'I will contact Nawabzada Nabil Bugti,' Khan said. 'We will get some backup. Then we can proceed to Mastung to meet him.'

Mastung was a short distance from Quetta. It was where the Bugtis had settled.

Kabir grimaced as he clutched his bleeding arm. Isha pulled out a gauze bandage and wrapped it around his arm.

Nihar had had the presence of mind to grab the bag with their equipment and the Pakistani currency when they had exited the car. In those few moments of firing, only one face appeared before his eyes—that of his newborn son.

'I think we need to tell Delhi what just happened.' Nihar sounded shaken up. He pulled out his iPad and began to type a message. 'Once we get a network, I'll check in.'

Veer remained silent throughout, concentrating on the road, blood dripping from a gash on his forehead. Nihar sat silently, perturbed. Isha held Kabir's hand firmly. They understood what Marri had said about them needing firepower. And he hadn't even anticipated this.

This little battle may not have meant much in the way of their cause, but it had already announced their arrival. They needed to lie low. There was a lot more blood to be shed.

11

3 September 2014
RAW HQ, New Delhi

'The nation deserves to know!'

RAW chief Arun Joshi watched a debate amusedly on his office television, as an uptight anchor spluttered forth uncontrollably with his words. He shot out one question after another, not allowing the people he had invited on the panel to respond. Trussed up in a suit like the head prefect of a school, he portrayed himself as a crusader for some popular, noble cause. He failed to realize that his theatrics had no visible effect on the audience at large, except for generating a few spikes in viewership. Joshi looked at the clock and decided to go home early. Nothing of note seemed to be happening today. He picked up some files and pushed them into the drawer, thinking about the entire Balochistan affair and how it could possibly be connected to Sadiq Sheikh's death, when his intercom rang. He lifted the remote to mute the television.

'Sir,' his assistant said, 'Major Narayan is here to see you.'

'Send him in,' Joshi replied. Within a minute, the door opened and Major Ashwin Narayan stepped in. He was tall, dark and wore a neat off-white shirt over black trousers. Narayan was a military officer whom Sadiq had had transferred to RAW. He was exceptionally skilled in tactical support and preferred handling matters from a cabin rather than on the ground.

'Yes, Ashwin.' Joshi motioned him to sit. 'I trust all's well.'

Ashwin scratched his wiry hair and looked disturbed.

'Sir,' he started. 'Of late we are feeling the pinch in our technical department. We need to update both the hardware and the software. It is getting easier for people to bypass our security system and we don't even have the resources to track them down.'

'What do you suggest, Ashwin?'

'We need to revamp the entire system, sir.'

Joshi nodded in agreement and was about to say something when his secure phone rang. He picked it up, squinted at the display, and looked at Ashwin.

'I'll look into it, certainly. Now I must take this call. Thanks, Ashwin.'

Ashwin got up, still looking worried and stepped out of the door. Joshi answered the phone.

'It's us,' Nihar said from the other line. 'Are we secure?'

'Of course we are,' Joshi said. 'You've called the HQ from a satphone for God's sake! What's the matter?'

'We are in a safe house in Kalat now,' Nihar replied. 'We had a bit of a hiccup along the way.'

'Elaborate.'

Nihar told him about the attack on their car. Joshi nodded his head intensely, while assessing the situation. He flipped open his laptop and clicked on the 3D imagery of a map of Balochistan. He switched the TV on to the AV mode, which allowed what was on his laptop to be projected on to the screen. He zoomed into Kalat. He traced the route they took with his finger, while Nihar explained. He had expected problems to crop up, but not this soon.

'They don't know you all are Indians, right?'

'I don't think so. They suspect we're Marri's men,' Nihar said. 'But I believe they'll be on the lookout. I'm sure it's alerted them. What do you suggest?'

'Split up for the time being,' Joshi replied. 'Two of you stay in the safe house, the other two find some accommodation. Staying as a group might make it easier for them to identify you. I suggest you spend another day or two in Kalat before leaving for Quetta.'

Joshi heard a distinct voice in the background, addressing Nihar. It was Kabir.

'Have you made any progress on Sadiq Sheikh's killer?'

Joshi rubbed the bridge of his nose hesitantly.

'No,' he said. 'We've hit a dead end. The voice isn't distinguishable enough.'

Joshi squinted at the door, noticing there was a slight gap left open. He grew suspicious. He closed the call and stood up. He walked quickly towards the door and opened it. He saw Ashwin leaning against it, tying his shoelaces and speaking on his phone simultaneously. Ashwin ended his call and looked up.

'Anything you want to tell me, Ashwin?' Joshi asked sternly.

'Actually, yes, sir. I was waiting to talk to you about something else,' Ashwin said nervously. 'I had applied for leave three days ago, citing personal issues. I wish to move to the South for a bit.'

Joshi nodded irritably. Ashwin had expected him to ask him the reason, but Joshi didn't bother. Ashwin told him anyway.

'My mother is really unwell.' Ashwin's voice trailed away. 'I fear the worst. I was just speaking to her on the phone.'

Joshi's stance softened. He knew Ashwin was a man of integrity and that he wasn't the kind who would malinger on the pretext of his mother's illness.

'I'm sorry,' he said, 'but I expect you to be there for the ceremony we've organized in honour of Lieutenant General Sadiq Sheikh tomorrow. After that you can leave until you find it fit to come back, Major Narayan.'

Ashwin nodded quickly.

'Of course, sir,' he said in an attempt to please. 'I wouldn't miss that for the world.'

Joshi walked into his office and shut the door behind him.

~

3 September 2014
Kalat, Balochistan

Until August 1947, Kalat was a self-governing state in a subsidiary alliance with British India. In the eight-month interim between August 1947 and April 1948, Kalat was entirely independent until the ruler, referred to as the 'Khan of Kalat', ceded power to Pakistan, despite being given the choice of remaining independent. The offer, of course, had little credibility, coming from a government like Pakistan's. So when they were given the choice, the majority of the people were opposed to being governed from Islamabad, but the Khan of Kalat,

Mir Ahmad Yar Khan, felt a moral obligation to join
his Muslim brethren and become a part of Pakistan.
He came to an understanding with Islamabad, which
was supposed to allow Kalat to maintain some form of
autonomy. Islamabad readily agreed and made Kalat the
capital of the Balochistan States Union, along with three
neighbouring states, in October 1952. Mir Ahmad Yar
Khan was the last Khan of Kalat, as the Khanate ceased
to exist in 1955, when the province of West Pakistan was
formed. And with that, Quetta became the provincial
capital of modern-day Balochistan.

The historical town of Kalat is located slightly to the
west of Quetta. The majority of the population is Muslim,
but there is a small minority, 2 per cent, that is Hindu. This
segment of Hindus are primarily Hindkowan merchants.
The Hindkowans are an Indo-Aryan group native to the
Khyber–Pakhtunkhwa and Kashmir regions. In fact, these
Hindus lived near a Hindu temple dedicated to the goddess
Kali. That is also where the Indian team had strategically set
up their safe house.

Kabir's team had entered Kalat with the attacker's car
and driven straight to a marketplace. The mercury was
dropping low as night approached. They abandoned the
car in a deserted lane and then proceeded to an area near
their safe house by cab, from where they walked down to
the small seedy-looking flat in an inconspicuous, three-
storeyed building, Barkat Manzil. They had split up, taken
every precaution. Kabir had put on a jacket, so that his
bloodied shirt wasn't entirely visible to those who cared to
look. With his scraggy beard and long hair that he covered
with a skullcap, Kabir didn't have any problem fitting
in. Isha had her burkha on, so there was no real question
of her attracting attention. Veer and Nihar didn't draw

much attention either. Veer looked Pashtun anyway, and a stubbled Nihar looked more like his younger sibling who may have just finished college. After a while, everyone met up at the safe house, washed up and put on a new set of clothes. Irfan Baloch Khan had decided to go on and meet Nabil Bugti at his residence to inform him of the situation at hand.

The safe house wasn't anything elaborate. It was a few hundred square feet, and had a small partition that divided the hall into a tiny room and a kitchen. It lay bare, and a musty smell seemed to linger. From the window you could see the noisy main road, which lay beyond the lane that led to the shaky gates of the compound. This was helpful, since the team would always be able to keep an eye on who entered and exited the building. In the corner of the room rested a small cupboard that had a few mattresses, some scruffy blankets and worn-out pillows. There weren't too many occupants in the building apart from them, and it was believed that this flat belonged to a small-time businessman in Karachi. Nobody seemed to inquire any further, nor did anyone care to find out.

'Hold on,' Isha said as she poured a generous amount of antiseptic solution on to a piece of cotton. 'It's a shallow wound, shouldn't be that bad. Just a graze.'

Kabir twitched. Unlike what's shown in the movies, a bullet, even if it only grazes an arm, does cause a world of pain. Isha made Kabir remove his shirt. She noticed many scars, and even a bullet wound below his right shoulder-blade. She folded a scarf and put it in Kabir's mouth, lest he bite his tongue on impulse when she applied the solution. Nihar was making a call to Joshi. Veer was tidying up the little room of its cobwebs and little mounds of dust. Isha applied the solution and patted Kabir's back gently.

'There.' She smiled, speaking as if to a child who has taken his first tetanus shot. 'Looks like our professor here is quite a brave man.'

'I'm not ten.' Kabir scowled. 'Nihar, ask Joshi if he's got any leads on Sadiq's killer.'

Nihar repeated the question into the phone, and completed the conversation. He turned to Kabir and said, 'They haven't got anything on him. They've hit a dead end.'

'What else did he say?'

'He asked us to split up till we get to Quetta,' Nihar said.

Kabir sighed and sat up, nursing his bandaged arm. Isha handed him a shirt. Nihar looked thoughtfully out of the window and lit a cigarette. So much had happened. He was in this godforsaken place with people he didn't trust entirely. If only he could speak to his wife. If only he could hear his baby gurgle over the phone, it would put him at ease. Then he turned and opened his mouth as if to say something, and stopped halfway again. He knew it was a silly thing to ask, but he wasn't thinking clearly. He realized it was still worth a shot.

'Something bothering you?' Veer asked.

'I was wondering if . . .'

'If what?' Isha raised an eyebrow at him.

'Can I go to the marketplace and make a call back home?'

Kabir's face remained expressionless. Veer smiled sourly, waiting for a reaction.

'Say that again and see if it makes sense to you this time,' Kabir said sardonically.

'It'll just be one phone call,' Nihar persisted. 'To tell my wife how I'm doing. To find out how she is. How my son is.'

'I can't believe we're having this conversation. I'm pretty sure they're doing well. But if you continue asking I'm not so sure you will share their fortune.'

Nihar frowned angrily. He looked back out of the window and mumbled something.

'Say that louder.' Kabir growled in a low voice.

'You wouldn't understand,' Nihar repeated defiantly. 'You have nobody of your own.'

Isha looked at Kabir's sphinx-like expression from the corner of her eye. He always maintained a calm exterior, and he knew Nihar was shaken up after the attack.

'I know you're a bit flustered, Nihar.' Isha broke the silence. 'But you need to think rationally during times like these.'

Nihar exhaled a lungful of smoke.

'You may be comfortable around this killer.' He pointed at Kabir. 'I sure as hell am not. How much do we even know about him?'

Kabir's face was deadpan. Veer watched on, sitting cross-legged, as the drama unfolded. Nihar had referred to the only killing Kabir hadn't committed. Isha shot a glance at Kabir, to look for a reaction. Nothing, except for a vein in his forehead which was throbbing.

'Calm down, Nihar.'

'Or what?' Nihar raised his voice. 'He'll kill me, too?'

Kabir remained impassive.

'You're overreacting,' Isha said sternly.

'Let him try to kill me.' Nihar grew hysterical. 'This time that old bastard can't even save him!'

There was a moment of dead silence. Nihar's words lingered in the air. Both Veer and Isha couldn't believe what they had just heard. Kabir's face reddened with fury. He got to his feet and ran towards Nihar, enraged. He rammed his shoulder into Nihar's chest, and pushed him to the wall. He grabbed his collar and looked him in the eye.

'Never insult Sadiq Sheikh again,' Kabir said through gritted teeth, lifting Nihar off his feet with his collar. 'You aren't half the man he was.'

Kabir released the collar and punched Nihar hard in the stomach. Veer got up and intervened. Nihar slumped to the ground. Veer helped him back to his feet and put his finger to his lips, gesturing him to remain silent. Isha saw that Kabir's shoulder had begun to bleed again. She took him aside and asked him to calm down.

'I don't even understand what he's creating such a fuss about,' Kabir fumed. 'He didn't do shit when we were getting attacked. I'm pretty sure we can do without him if he's here just to make phone calls.'

Nihar was about to open his mouth again in retaliation, but Veer stifled his mouth with his hand. Veer found this entire situation rather comical. Isha led Kabir away to the only available room in the flat and asked him to rest. She stormed out and brought him and Nihar a glass of water each. On her way to what was an apology for a kitchen, she heard Veer speak: 'You better watch your glib tongue, mister. Otherwise, the next time, we won't stop him from dislocating your jaw.'

Later that night, when the team reunited in the small hall for a little meal, there was an awkward silence. Nihar didn't seem too interested in the dry kebabs Veer had brought from a little shop in the vicinity. Kabir noticed that Nihar was still sulking and turned to Isha. She shrugged. She was getting tired of these grown men behaving like college kids.

'I don't owe you or anyone here an explanation,' Kabir said in a low voice, pushing his long hair away from his forehead.

Nihar avoided looking at him. Veer was about to light a cigarette, but Isha frowned at him. He lit it anyway.

'Let us get done with our dinner,' she said.

'But if it's going to interfere with the mission,' Kabir continued, 'I'm going to get this out of the way once and for all.'

Nihar looked up at him, his eyes wary. Isha and Veer set their gaze upon him, too. Kabir stroked his beard and avoided their stares.

'I'm going to tell you what went down in Quetta that day.'

12

24 August 2006
Quetta, Balochistan

'The bastard doesn't want it to happen,' Sadiq Sheikh spoke softly into the phone. Kabir—then 'Adonis'—could tell he was enraged.

'What did he say exactly?'

'He says if the shit hits the fan, all the blame will be thrown upon him. I told him that being the Chief of RAW isn't about keeping a clean reputation, it's about doing what has to be done. But he's busy licking the Americans' asses.'

'So we don't have the go-ahead from Rao?' Kabir asked again.

Viraj Rao was the Chief of RAW. Sadiq and he never got along well. As is the case with most organizations, in most professions, interdepartmental rivalry prevailed even in India's premier spy agency. Rao was insecure about the fact that Sheikh, a soldierly man, had received more accolades than he had. Sadiq was a dynamic leader, a man willing to put his life on the line for the greater good. People in the organization respected Sadiq more than they did Rao, and this used to gnaw on Rao's mind. As a result, he would downplay Sadiq's contribution and try to throw a spanner in the works of operations that Sadiq had planned. The current situation was one such instance. Rao didn't want Sadiq to go ahead with this plan because it was a highly risky one, for starters, but also because if Sadiq succeeded in achieving what he wanted, he would emerge a greater hero than he already was.

'You know what, Adonis,' Sadiq said confidently, 'go ahead with it. If something happens, I'll take the blame. But don't forget to get the Afghani defector to the Americans.'

Kabir remained silent on the other end of the phone. He knew it could be disastrous for Sadiq's career if the mission went awry. Initially, the plan was simple. All they had planned to do was take an Afghani defector Asghar Malek to the Americans located in Shamsi without getting caught. Malek was willing to help the Americans if they ensured the safety of his wife and two daughters. He had been forced into the Taliban at a young age, but killing was not for him. The brutish and barbaric murders that he knew the Taliban was responsible for made him want to escape and start life afresh.

'I will get him to the Americans only after we are done,' Kabir said. 'Is that all right?'

'Yes. I haven't planted you all there to sit like spectators and watch shit go down anyway. I'll talk to you later.'

Sadiq put the phone down abruptly. Kabir still held it to his ear, wondering what would happen if a mission that wasn't even sanctioned went wrong. Suddenly the door of the safe house opened. A man in a white kurta and pyjama walked in. He was taller than Kabir by a couple of inches, had a strong jawline and a long beard. He was stocky as opposed to Kabir's lithe but muscular figure. He clutched a copy of the Holy Quran, which he lay down respectfully on the table.

'Salaam, Maulana Ares.' Kabir smiled. 'Ares' was the code name Vikramjit Singh was assigned. Kabir and Vikramjit both found their respective code-names rather funny, and pulled each other's legs about it.

Vikramjit Singh had been working undercover as a teacher at the Madrasa Ashraf-ul-Madaris. Over the years, Vikramjit had grown so well versed with the nuances of Islamic teaching that he felt he was as Muslim as anyone else in Balochistan. He had always wanted to be a field agent, despite not being very physically capable of combat. But his big break came when he managed to get a Lashkar operative, Haneef Sayyed, arrested, after tailing him fearlessly for over a month. Sadiq was impressed by Vikramjit's guile, and decided to post him to the conflict-ridden area of Balochistan. After the necessary training, Sadiq deemed him fit enough to be assigned the job. He had been posted in Quetta way before Major Kabir Anand. Kabir was sent later on for his corporeal strength and mental dexterity.

'Did you speak to Sheikh about the mission?'

'Yes,' Kabir said. He paused. He knew Vikramjit wasn't too keen on infiltrating the madrasa because of the high risk involved.

'What did he say? Do we have the necessary clearance?'

Kabir scratched his head and fiddled with his short-cropped hair.

'Yes,' Kabir said matter-of-factly. 'He told us to go ahead with it.'

'And what about Asghar and his family?'

'We take him to the Americans at Shamsi tomorrow,' Kabir replied.

If we live to see another day, Vikramjit thought.

~

25 August 2006
Shamsi, Balochistan

'This is all I can give you guys,' Michael Porter said over the phone. 'I'm way ahead of myself already, so I guess you all can thank me now.'

Michael Porter, a man in his early fifties, was an American working for the CIA, in charge of the agency's operations in Shamsi. The Shamsi airfield was located around 300 kilometres southwest of Quetta. It was nestled in a barren desert valley between two ridges of the rugged Central Makran Range. In 2001, Pakistan under Pervez Musharraf had leased the airstrip to the United States to use as a base. The CIA ran their operations jointly with the US Air Force in order to carry out their surveillance and drone operations against militants in the FATA at the time.

'Thanks, Mike,' Kabir replied. 'I appreciate it.'

'Cheers,' Porter replied. 'Don't get into trouble. And remember, Asghar has to be here tomorrow morning.'

'Yes, we'll bring him.'

Kabir had picked up an armoured jeep laden with munitions that Porter had organized for him at short notice. The United States and India had worked in tandem in Balochistan, mainly to fund the rebel groups. But Porter knew something larger was at play this time. Sadiq Sheikh had personally called him up earlier that day and requested that he help a couple of agents out with a few amenities. Porter was reluctant and wanted to know why. That is when Sadiq reminded him, via videoconference.

'You had told me about the information the CIA had intercepted about the ISI planning a possible attack on

India.' Sadiq adjusted his glasses. 'I have an agent placed as a teacher in the very madrasa that you suspect to be a front for ISI's activities.'

'Go on,' Porter said, rubbing his bare sunburnt head. 'It was all conjecture at that point of time, but if what you have is helpful, I'm all ears.'

'Yes and no,' Sadiq said. 'Apparently, within the madrasa there is a large chamber that the ISI operates out of. They lock that room up securely. My men think that they can get their hands on their data if they infiltrate the madrasa.'

'That's ballsy,' Porter said. 'I'm sure there's a lot in those files that could help us, too.'

Sadiq raised an eyebrow. Porter understood that expression even over the grainy footage. He regretted thinking out aloud.

'It's a win-win situation for you, Porter. We get our hands on that information, we share it with you. But you must give them what they need.'

Porter scratched his chin. It wasn't a hard call to make. He didn't have to send in anyone of his own and, having laid hands on the intel, he would have scored a great deal with the CIA. Plus, of course, he would have the Afghani defector at his behest as well.

'I'll see what I can do,' Porter replied. 'I'll get in touch with your guys. What are they called, once again?'

'Adonis and Ares,' Sadiq said wryly. 'Don't laugh, it's not like you give your guys better code-names.'

Sadiq disconnected the line and got up from his seat. He looked through his spectacles at his accomplice.

'Narayan,' he said. 'Nobody should know about this conversation. We are going to need the control room tomorrow for the entire day. Just organize some smart techies to be in there. And more importantly, Rao cannot have an inkling about this op.'

~

26 August 2006
Quetta, Balochistan

It was early morning and the children had Saturday off at the Ashraf-ul-Madaris madrasa. Vikramjit and Kabir kept watch through the windshield of the armed jeep at the locked and abandoned gates. The madrasa, built over a vast expanse of land, looked deserted. It seemed a perfect time to sneak in and out with the information. Vikramjit and Kabir had initially chalked out a plan to get in there covertly: scaling the high wall and getting out the same way. Stealth, they had decided, was the way to approach this operation. But then Sadiq seemed to think differently. He wanted them to have a solid getaway vehicle and at least a rifle each, just in case.

'There's no need to be subtle about it,' Sadiq said, stubbing his cigarette as he spoke on the phone. 'In case there is security in there, you'll need to engage them in a gunfight as you escape.'

Kabir had agreed. Vikramjit didn't quite feel the same way.

'I've been teaching at that madrasa, sir. The chamber below has only three guards waiting outside. There's no elaborate backup. We can take them out without attracting any attention.'

But Sadiq was adamant. So now here they were, parked a few hundred feet away from the gates.

'Are you ready?' Kabir narrowed his eyes at Vikramjit, the adrenalin pumping through his body. They call it the fight-or-flight syndrome. When there is an excessive flow of adrenalin in one's body, you either fight or run away. And Kabir wasn't the kind who ran away.

'Let's do this quickly,' Vikramjit said, slightly nervous as he tightened his Kevlar vest.

Kabir took a deep breath and kicked the accelerator hard. The jeep roared and jerked ahead and then picked up speed as it approached the gates of the madrasa. A few onlookers stared, wide-eyed, at the jeep when it rammed into the gates, taking one half down as it continued into the interiors of the seemingly harmless school. Kabir dropped the speed a few notches before approaching the main building of the madrasa. He parked the car and leapt out with his rifle. Vikramjit followed suit.

Kabir noticed a large guard staring at them incredulously. The guard reached for the rifle slung around his shoulder. Before he could get a hold of it, there was a bullet hole in his head. Kabir ran ahead of Vikramjit and kicked the main door open.

Five men were already waiting with their guns, which they fired the moment they caught a glimpse of the intruders. Kabir pushed Vikramjit to the ground swiftly and somersaulted aside. Bullets flew through the half-open door. Kabir looked up and saw a small glass window. He shot at it and then raised his rifle through the gap, firing blindly. He was certain he got at least one of the five. He dared to look up and saw he had been luckier than that. He had got two. The other three began shooting at him. Vikramjit lay prone and moved to get a better sight of the guards. He managed to shoot one in his leg. Kabir pushed the door open and ran in bravely, shooting all three guards dead in one quick, fluid motion.

'They were expecting us,' Vikramjit gasped. Kabir nodded and put a finger to his lips.

'Lead the way,' he whispered. Vikramjit staggered ahead of him. Kabir followed him, scanning all directions for any other incumbents that might shoot at them.

'The staircase to the chamber below is on the other side of the building,' Vikramjit whispered back. 'What if there are more of them?'

'We take them all out,' Kabir replied, gesturing to Vikramjit to continue. They held their rifles up, ready to fire, as they walked into the next room. It was clear. There was a dreadful silence.

'Go on,' Kabir said. 'Let's make this quick.'

Vikramjit started walking hurriedly and opened the door of the next room. He looked through the crack and saw nothing. He was about to push it open, when Kabir held him back. Kabir pointed at the ground. The small distance between the door and the floor betrayed a shadow. Someone was waiting behind the door to shoot them.

'Looks like this room is clear, too,' spoke Kabir clearly, in Urdu, as he walked ahead. He saw the shadow flicker a bit on hearing this. 'Let's go in.'

In one swift motion, Kabir kicked the door open and stuck his rifle through it, shooting behind the door. He heard a body slump to the ground and the metal thud of a gun falling. He stepped in and saw a large bearded man, covered in blood.

'Just one more door,' Vikramjit said. 'Then we go down the staircase.'

Kabir reloaded his weapon with a fresh round of bullets. Vikramjit checked his gun, too. His face twitched as he saw the man's disfigured face and his flesh splattered all over the wall. A rust-like smell of blood diffused the room.

'Let me go first.' Kabir narrowed his eyes. 'If you'd walked in without looking, you'd have been in his place.'

Suddenly they heard footsteps. Someone was walking in through the door ahead of them. Kabir moved to the side and got down to his knees, his gun propped. The door opened and an elderly man stepped out. Kabir shot at him without demur.

'Oh no!' Vikramjit cried in anguish. 'That's the headmaster! He is an old man!'

Kabir didn't feel any regret. 'So what?' he hissed. 'He's in on it, too.'

Vikramjit quivered. He respected the elderly maulana a great deal. He seemed locked in his position as he watched the old man's lifeless body on the ground.

Kabir coaxed him ahead and walked on. He gave a cursory glance through the door and saw three men, their guns cocked, running towards him. They began to fire, and Kabir ran backwards trying to take cover behind a desk. He took a grenade out of Vikramjit's belt, pulled the pin and hurled it into the other room, precisely through the narrow gap in the door. He closed his ears and Vikramjit followed suit. There was a loud bang. Their ears still rang as they stood up and walked warily into the room full of smoke. All three men lay dismembered, various parts of their body scattered across the room. Blood splattered all over the wall. Bits of bone crunched under Kabir's feet as he saw the staircase below. Vikramjit covered his nose with a scarf as he tried to walk around the pools of blood. The stench of the sour, coppery blood was getting to him.

'Stay close,' Kabir said as he walked ahead. 'Remember, you wanted to be posted to this part of the world, when you could've sat behind a desk in Delhi and let blokes like me do the job.'

Vikramjit let out an expletive and motioned Kabir to continue. Kabir led the way downstairs. The area seemed empty. Vikramjit followed him and pointed at a locked door on the right. Kabir walked towards it. He turned around with his gun and pointed it into the shadows.

'We're clear!' Kabir shouted.

Vikramjit was exhausted. He sat on his haunches, trying to catch his breath.

'Come on, Vikramjit. We have to do this now.' Kabir helped him up. Vikramjit wiped the sweat pouring down his forehead, and then moved ahead with new zeal. Kabir heard another set of footsteps rushing down the stairs.

'Breach the lock and get into the room!' Kabir bellowed. 'Get the hard drives! I'll cover you!'

Kabir held up his rifle and ran towards the stairs. As soon as the three large bearded men approached, a sudden volley of bullets welcomed them. All fell to the ground, lifeless, in an instant. Kabir was now shaking with nervous energy. He took the butt of his rifle and smashed it ferociously into the head of one of the dead men. A feral madness seemed to have overpowered him. The man's blood splattered all over Kabir's trousers. He turned around, having vented his anger, and walked back down to see Vikramjit still at the door, clutching the knob.

'What the fuck are you trying?' Kabir roared. 'I thought I told you to get inside and get the hard disks!'

Vikramjit swallowed, and stood still like a statue. He clutched the knob without moving, the door open just a crack.

'Cla-Claymore!' he stuttered.

Kabir's eyes opened wide in horror. He understood why Vikramjit was frozen in his position. Behind the door was an M18 Claymore mine. It was an anti-personnel mine with a directional charge. It had been rigged to detonate when the door was opened. Had Vikramjit opened the door even a fraction of an inch more, there would have been a colossal explosion. Kabir felt numb for the first time.

'If I leave the door, we die. It could probably take the entire building down, if several blocks of C4 are rigged to it.'

Kabir walked cautiously towards the door and looked through the slight crack. The mine was far away, but directed towards them. Had Vikramjit opened the door, the trigger attached to the mine would have fallen face forward and sent a bunch of explosive projectiles at them, killing them instantly and detonating the C4. Behind the mine was a large bag of C4 primed to explode. Kabir didn't know what to do. He dug his chin into his shoulder, trying to think around the dilemma. They had not considered such a situation. It was supposed to be a clean getaway. For the first time in his life, Kabir Anand did not have a solution.

Vikramjit said in a hoarse voice, 'There's no way I live, Kabir.'

'What do you mean by "I"?' Kabir asked shakily.

'You can get out,' Vikramjit said. 'I'll hold this for another few minutes, till you escape.'

'I'm not going anywhere,' Kabir said through gritted teeth. 'We're in this together. We die together.'

Vikramjit nodded frantically, still clutching the door.

'Please, Kabir Anand!' Vikramjit said, his voice quivering. 'I want you to live. I want you to find the person who sold us out and tear him apart, piece by piece.'

'I'm not going anywhere,' Kabir said stubbornly.

'He sold out our operation, Kabir. There's a traitor in our midst. Nobody was supposed to be expecting us. And if there's anyone who can find him, it's you and Sadiq. He needs to know about this. Please, Kabir. Please get out of here.'

'But . . .'

'No! Besides, you have to get Asghar and his family from his house now and rush them to the Americans! You must rescue them! If the ISI knew about us, they definitely know about him!'

A lump formed in Kabir's throat. His eyes welled up, despite him trying to hold back. There was little he could do. Vikramjit was right, though. Sadiq needed to know. And Asghar and his family needed to be saved. They also needed to find the person responsible for giving the Pakistanis a heads-up. If both of them died here, there would be more questions than answers. There was simply no choice, though Kabir had no qualms about sacrificing his life. Absolutely none. He pondered the possibilities for a few seconds, then stood upright and saluted Vikramjit.

'*Jai Hind*, Vikramjit Singh! You shall not die in vain.'

'*Jai Hind*, Major Anand! *Jai Hind!*'

Kabir shot one last look at Vikramjit, who had squeezed his eyes shut by then, swerved around and scrambled upstairs, his rifle at the ready.

13

4 September 2014
Kalat, Balochistan

There was a heavy silence as the sun peeped over the horizon. Kabir looked at the floor, his uneasy toes tapping away. Isha felt a great rush of sympathy towards him. Veer nurtured a deep admiration for his team leader. Nihar felt unsettled after listening intently to Kabir's narration, by the disturbing death of a brave comrade. He could not even imagine what he would have done had he been in Kabir's shoes.

'What happened then?' Nihar probed.

'I got to Asghar's house as fast as I could,' Kabir said. 'I found the door ajar. I feared the worst. As soon as I limped in, I saw Asghar and his family lying dead. The bastards had come to know of his intention to defect. Their bodies were peppered with bullets. It's the worst thing I've seen.'

Isha closed her eyes, a pained expression on her face, visualizing the scene. Nihar and Veer were surprised. They hadn't known of the Afghani-defector angle before.

'How did the Americans react?' Veer asked.

'I got out of the house, tied a tourniquet around my bleeding leg, and drove to Shamsi. It took me a couple of hours. Upon my arrival, the Americans raised their weapons at me,' Kabir said. 'Luckily, Porter took me in. They provided all the aid I required. He was pissed off about the defector's death. He got me through to Sadiq, who asked me to sit tight while he made arrangements to bring me back. It took three days before I was sent for.'

'What did the Americans think about the entire situation?'

'They suspected foul play, naturally. And since I was the one who got out alive, they thought I might have had something to do with it. But they waited till Sadiq sent for me.'

'Is the base in Shamsi still there?' Nihar inquired.

'No,' Veer said. 'The Americans were made to leave after they killed bin Laden in Abbottabad. Rumour has it that they had strategized that mission while in Shamsi.'

'Yes,' Kabir agreed, and then continued. 'So when I got back to Delhi, I described to Sadiq in great detail everything that transpired in Balochistan. He was appalled to know that someone was expecting us at the madrasa. Worse still, Asghar's death added to his woes. The suspects, as he saw it, could've been the Americans, who were known to play a double game with Pakistan, or someone within RAW itself. But the Americans were ruled out because they stood to gain a lot from the op and Asghar's defection.'

'Someone within RAW?' Isha gasped, recoiling. 'How many people knew about it within RAW?'

'Sadiq and his squad of three in the control room,' Kabir said. 'But he was adamant that they didn't know enough before the operation, or about Asghar, to have forewarned the Pakistanis. Nevertheless, that bastard Rao summoned us to his office.'

Kabir's voice trailed away as he recalled the moment. He poured some water into a steel tumbler and quaffed it down.

'Before getting into the meeting,' Kabir said, 'Sadiq asked me to blame the fiasco on him, and to tell Rao that I didn't know the mission was not sanctioned. But when I went in I could tell Rao was elated by the fact that he could now kick Sadiq out, and with perfect reason. And I couldn't bear that.'

'What did you do?' Isha asked, wide-eyed.

'I told Rao that Sadiq had told me the mission wasn't to be carried out, but that I chose to go through with it anyway. I could see Rao's face fall as I took the blame upon myself.'

'And Sadiq didn't deny this?'

'I was half hoping he would,' Kabir stroked his beard. 'I always considered Sadiq Sheikh to be a father—someone more than just a superior. And I'm sure he felt the same way about me. But that day, his silence meant something else. It meant he valued his reputation more.'

There was another long silence. And then Kabir spoke with an air of finality.

'Rao lost his temper at me. Branded me a traitor. Said I was the one who set Vikramjit up. Besides, the Americans had already called him and cribbed about Asghar. He wasn't willing to reason at all,' Kabir said. 'And then he asked Sadiq to throw me out right then—in front of him.'

A pregnant pause ensued.

'Which he did,' Kabir continued. 'He asked me to leave. I had chosen to dedicate my life to the country, and it enraged me to be termed a traitor! I kicked the chair over and stormed out. But later on I realized something: I may have stopped talking to Sadiq, but my respect for him hadn't lessened at all. I realized that he may have had his reasons not to take the axe for me.'

Kabir swallowed, his throat went dry. He had lived those few days over and over again since he had left the service.

'What about the talks doing the rounds of you being a traitor?' Isha asked.

'That was the story Rao circulated,' Kabir said. 'He projected it as though Sadiq's beloved protégé was, in real life, the Judas in his ranks. The fact that RAW didn't know about the op left only Vikramjit and me in the know. And guess who made it out alive.'

'Good thing he's retired now,' Veer said. 'Even though my interactions with him were brief, I never liked the chap.'

The others muttered words of agreement.

'We never knew anything about Asghar before,' Isha added.

'Asghar was never a part of our problem—until he died,' Kabir said. 'The fact that he was killed only made it easier for people to believe that I was responsible for everything that happened that day. Too many deaths with plausible motives, and I was a convenient culprit. Suddenly I had a lot of blood on my hands.'

It all added up now. After all, Kabir's survival could not have been the only indication that he was a traitor. There were instances in the past where the survivor had been hailed as a hero. But the person who sold this operation out had managed to set Kabir up perfectly.

'I hope I've cleared every doubt in your minds,' Kabir said, addressing Nihar in particular.

'I'm sorry,' Nihar mustered an apology. He held out his hand feebly towards Kabir, who shook it firmly. Both realized the unspoken importance of unity in the ranks.

'I hope we can work together as a team after this,' Veer said. 'If not for ourselves, then for our country.'

Later, the team recapitulated the incident the way Kabir had narrated it. There were loose ends that neither Kabir nor Sadiq could tie up. Who was the mole? How did he communicate across enemy lines from right under their noses? How did he manage to outsmart Sadiq and Kabir? Blowing up the madrasa, and arranging to eliminate the Afghani defector?

They mulled over the injustice meted out to Kabir. They wondered why Sadiq did not try to save Kabir's career. They thought about the chain of events that followed that had brought Kabir back into the game he was unceremoniously forced out of. They thought about Sadiq's last message. They figured that in his last moments Sadiq wanted Kabir to be the one to avenge him. That was how Sadiq brought Kabir honourably back into the fold, they realized.

It is a wise father that knows his own child.
—Act 2, Scene 2, *The Merchant of Venice*

~

4 September 2014
Miranshah, North Waziristan

It took a while for the large clouds of dust to settle before the Alouette III was finally discernible. The French-made helicopter, deployed by Pakistani forces, had just landed a few minutes ago on a barren tract of land a few kilometres from the town of Miranshah. Miranshah was the administrative headquarters of the North Waziristan Agency in the FATA. A small group of three looked on as their two guests alighted from the chopper. The men greeted each other cordially before getting into the SUVs waiting for them. It was a fifteen-minute drive towards the foothills of the Hindu Kush mountains, and there was not much by way of conversation in the car.

'*Salaam aleikum*,' a man of about forty said as he welcomed his two guests into his small, makeshift household. He wore a large black turban with a black kurta and an ankle-length salwar. His eyes were lined with kohl, and his thick beard was dyed almost maroon. He wore a thick sweater, as the temperature was just a few degrees above zero. He stretched his hand out to one of his guests, who he felt was more important, and embraced him warmly. 'Mullah Baradar, it's been a while.'

He turned to his other guest: 'As for you, Brigadier Shehzad, it's always a pleasure.'

'The pleasure is mine, Khalifa.'

Khalifa, the deputy of God. The Caliph, as his people believed him to be, was none other than Sirajuddin Haqqani—the ruler of the notorious Haqqani Network, established by his now aged father, Jalaluddin Haqqani. Jalaluddin had realized it was time to hand over the reins of the network to his son, whose ruthless zeal pumped his chest with pride.

The Haqqanis' relationship with the ISI had always been steady since the Afghan–Soviet war. Back then, Jalaluddin had been a favourite of not only the ISI and the Saudis but also the CIA. They funded him, and backed him during the movement against the Soviets. Some even say Haqqani had been invited by, and perhaps even visited, Ronald Reagan at the White House. This was also the time when Haqqani was supporting one of his brothers-in-arms in building their own militia, the al-Qaeda. This comrade was none other than Osama bin Laden.

Until 1995, Jalaluddin Haqqani hadn't been a part of the Afghan Taliban. However, once he joined, the Americans and other factions in Afghanistan shuddered at the implications of having both Mullah Omar and Jalaluddin Haqqani at the helm. The US tried to woo Haqqani over with offers of astronomical sums of money to go against Omar. But Haqqani wouldn't budge. They had Karzai offer him a post in the cabinet, but even that didn't seem to be enough. They kidnapped members of his family and tribe and tortured them brazenly, but this didn't do the trick either. If it did anything, it added to his growing resentment for those against Omar's Taliban. Moreover, Haqqani had the ISI's unwavering support. This was something Pakistan denied vehemently, but every shred of evidence—both concrete and circumstantial—suggested this was the case.

The Americans realized there was no point pursuing Haqqani any further. They counted him in with the rest of their enemies, especially after 9/11. In 2010, when Sirajuddin agreed to merge formally with Mullah Omar's Quetta Shura, the Americans began to target the Haqqanis to eliminate Jalaluddin and Sirajuddin in particular. They mostly failed, until 2012, when they managed to get the other son, Badruddin, in a drone attack. The following year, unidentified assailants killed another of Jalaluddin's sons, Nasiruddin, from his Arab wife, in Islamabad. Jalaluddin suspected it to be a joint operation between the Indians and the Afghans. That was when his thirst for vendetta deepened and he made his son promise he would make every kafir pay.

Ever since, along with bin Laden's al-Qaeda, the Haqqani Network has reared numerous other terror outfits such as the Jaish-e-Mohammad, the Lashkar-e-Taiba, the Lashkar-e-Jhangvi—even the Indian Mujahideen. Some of these units were created especially to target India. They attacked Indians and their embassies on a regular basis.

After seating his guests down comfortably and dismissing everyone else from the room, Sirajuddin spoke in a low, raspy voice: 'I believe we are going ahead with our plan, Mullah Baradar.'

'Inshallah.' Baradar smiled. 'Mullah Omar has consented wholeheartedly.'

'How many people are needed?' Sirajuddin turned to Shehzad.

'As many as were sent the last time around. Maybe fewer,' Shehzad replied. He picked up his bag and pulled out a hard disk. He placed it carefully in front of Sirajuddin.

'Is this what I think it is?' Sirajuddin asked, his eyes lighting up with a devilish smile.

'Yes.' Shehzad smiled back. 'The layout, in detail, pictures from inside the compound, everything you need is in that little chunk of metal. All this information has been very hard to gather. I'm sure you're aware of that.'

Sirajuddin nodded thoughtfully, stretched forward and picked up the hard disk. He raised it and smiled at Baradar. 'If only we had had access to technology this advanced when Abbu was fighting his war,' he said.

'Speaking of whom, how is Jalaluddin Sahab?' Baradar asked. 'It's been a while since I heard from him.'

'*Mashallah*, he's doing well. Old age may have weakened his bones, but his spirit is unflagging. He will be elated when he realizes our plans for Mumbai. The last time Abbu laughed was when we pulled off 26/11.'

Shehzad smiled, feeling an inexplicable conviction that this time it was going to be much better. And it was his brainchild, entirely. Sirajuddin picked up a wooden box and opened it. It had five fat Cuban cigars. He offered them to his guests, who picked them up gladly. He got up and went to the stove in the adjacent room and lit his. Shehzad and Baradar fiddled with theirs without speaking. Sirajuddin came back, puffing smoke in quick bursts, and with the lit end of his cigar, he lit Baradar's and then Shehzad's.

'Nothing like a Cuban,' he said, smiling. 'Yes, so where were we?'

'Manpower,' Shehzad said as he blew out a puff of smoke. 'I think we'll need to activate a sleeper cell. Gunmen. They will serve as a distraction—before the main deed is done.'

'Where do you plan to send them?'

'New Delhi first. They will blow themselves up in the most densely crowded area. The country will be in a frenzy. After that, we leave the best for the last.'

'Sounds good, so far.' Sirajuddin shrugged. 'Suicide bombers and gunmen are not the problem, Shehzad. You know I'm more worried about the subsequent attack. It has to be flawless. Are you sure we can still trust your guy?'

'He has been waiting for this for years, Khalifa. There is nobody more driven than him to do this.' Shehzad clenched his fist, knocking the table as he said the words.

'And are you sure he's ready? Have you spoken to him about green-lighting the plan?'

'Not yet,' Shehzad said. 'But I will, as soon as you are absolutely certain that we can finalize this.'

'I don't know why you think I wouldn't want this to happen,' Sirajuddin said, taking in a lungful of his cigar. 'You have my blessings. And I'm certain you have my Abbu's *dua*s, too. Besides, if Amir al-Mu'minin and Mullah Baradar have agreed, then what weight does my decision hold?'

Baradar shook his head with a disappointed smile. 'Siraj, so far, all our decisions have always been taken with mutual consent. It is because of the high regard in which we hold you and Jalaluddin Sahab.'

'We have many more victories before Allah welcomes us to heaven, then, Mullah Baradar. Let this be one of the smaller ones.' Sirajuddin smiled. 'As far as we are concerned, we are ready to go ahead with this, Shehzad. You tell us when and what you expect of us, and we'll do our best to deliver. Inshallah, Allah will guide us through.'

Sirajuddin stood up and embraced his guests again. He walked them out, escorting them to their cars that were to drive them back to their helipad.

'*Khuda hafiz,*' he said, and turned back and walked into the house.

I must go and tell Abbu this right away. He picked up the hard disk and jumped into his own vehicle. His father lived in the town of Miranshah, whereas Sirajuddin kept shuffling between the foothills of the mountains and the town itself. He was never sure when the next drone would drop on his head and take his father's entire life's work out of play.

Later that evening, the wizened Jalaluddin and his son crouched over a laptop, maniacal grins plastered across their faces. They opened each of the myriad documents and photographs that Shehzad had passed on to them.

'The Indians will never be able to recover from this attack, Abbu. 26/11 would be a petty case of murder compared to this. This is much more. This means the total annihilation of the country itself. The Chinese will wipe them off the map! There will be mass destruction. A crashed economy. Crippled newborn babies. Diseased future generations. And above all, a large step towards jannat for all of us.'

Jalaluddin Haqqani nodded in agreement. In pure rapture, he went over the layout of the Delhi Metro and the draft agenda of an important meeting.

14

5 September 2014
Mastung, Balochistan

The three stumps stood erect, more or less, as the barefoot batsman took guard. He wrapped a scarf around his face so that no dust could enter his nose and mouth. He lightly tapped the bat on the ground, and waited for the bowler to hurl the ball at him. The bowler, a young boy of fifteen, tossed the ball from one hand to the other, and looked around, surveying his field placement. He took himself rather seriously as he motioned the bearded fielders to move around. They humoured him. He ran a hand through his hair, jogged a few paces and delivered the rubber ball to the burly batsman. The batsman took a wild swing at the ball and missed, resulting in two of the stumps being uprooted. The bowler stretched his arms out like an albatross and jubilantly ran around the rocky ground.

As if on cue, there were a series of large explosions in the air. The boy didn't pay heed to them; he stood theatrically, in pose, after getting the prize wicket. The other men on the field, however, ran in the direction of the explosions and then stood upright. Cocking their rifles, they fired in the air. Another set of rocket-propelled grenades went up and blasted in the air. This was the tradition among Balochi rebels, when welcoming their leader. The leader of their tribe and militia, Nawab Nabil Bugti, had arrived.

A large frame, bursting at its seams, got out of a sedan and walked up to the boy. His skin was pink, a dense stubble covered his jaw, and his hair was cropped close. He raised his hand to the men looking on from atop a low hill, and waved to them to carry on with their work. Then he tapped the young boy on his head, and lowered his sunglasses.

'Salaam, Chachu,' the boy said, looking at Nabil Bugti's sombre eyes. 'I got Faraz Miyaan out!'

'Salaam, Azaan,' Bugti addressed his fifteen-year-old nephew with a smile. 'I saw it. You shattered his stumps just like Shoaib Akhtar used to.'

The kid looked elated at being compared to his favourite pacer. And then his uncle's face grew serious. He put his arm on the boy's shoulder and walked up towards the stumps on the ground.

'I have decided it is time for you to play a new sport, Azaan.'

He lifted his kurta and pulled out a pistol that he had tucked under the cummerbund of his salwar. He handed the firearm over to the confused boy. He called out to one of his men and instructed him to set up a target.

'What is this, Chachu?' The boy felt a sudden surge of excitement mingled with nervousness, now that he had a gun at his disposal.

'Your grandfather, Akbar Bugti, first took a life at the tender age of twelve. In many ways, after your father and grandfather died, I have shielded you from their way of life,

Azaan. But now I'm afraid I can't keep you away from it any more.'

The boy's eyes welled up on hearing his uncle mention his late father and grandfather.

'Don't shed a tear, my boy. You are the grandson of the respected Tiger of Balochistan! You are destined to complete what your grandfather began. I am merely here to guide you.'

The boy looked at the gun and felt the cool metal against his fingers. He had expected it to be lighter.

'The target is ready.' Nabil Bugti pointed to a goat's head at the end of a long rod. 'Take your time. But you will not leave until you shoot it.'

Suddenly, there was the humming of an engine behind him. An SUV had pulled up near Nabil's sedan. All of Bugti's men collectively raised their rifles at the car. Nabil turned and looked quizzically through the dust that the car had kicked up. Irfan Baloch Khan stepped out of the car. Nabil looked up at his men, and gestured to them to lower their weapons.

'Salaam, Nawab Bugti,' Khan greeted him.

Bugti nodded back in acknowledgement. 'Salaam,' he replied, looking into the car. 'Are they here?'

Khan nodded and turned around, looking at the four passengers in the car. He asked them to step out with a gesture of his hand. They got out.

'These are the people I told you about,' Khan said. Nabil scanned the three men and the solitary woman with a sharp look. Kabir walked up to him and stuck out his hand.

'Kabir Anand,' he said. 'I believe we may have met fleetingly many years ago. But I'm sure you don't recall.'

'No, I'm sorry. Anyway, I've heard of your plans from Nusrat Marri, Mr Anand.'

'Call me Kabir. And before I get to that, I should let you know whom I'm working with. These are my comrades.'

He introduced Veer, Nihar and Isha to him. Isha sensed condescension when Nabil shook her hand and smiled.

'I'm afraid she's far more capable than any of us,' Veer said, sensing the patronizing look Nabil shot Isha. 'You'd be surprised.'

Nabil shrugged and leaned against the bonnet of the SUV. Behind him, the boy had started firing the pistol at the goat's severed head. He missed, naturally.

'So there is a slight glitch in your plan, Kabir. We know Omar stays in northern Quetta, but there are very few instances of him being spotted by even his own men. How do you propose we go about abducting him?'

'We have a plan.' Kabir smiled. 'But before that, I'd like to know how thirsty you are to avenge the deaths of your father, your brother and so many of your Baloch brethren?'

'I can't put that into words.' Nabil's face reddened.

'Then don't,' Veer spoke up. 'Show it to us in your actions. If we work together this one time, we have a fairly good chance of pulling this off.'

When turning someone into an asset, you have to get to know him. His frustrations, his aspirations, how he spends his time, how he spends his resources. You need to understand his dreams. You need to appeal to them. And that is what Kabir and his team were doing. They had managed to get Marri to agree, and now co-opting Nabil would be of game-changing import.

The boy turned and looked at his uncle dejectedly. He had finished another round of bullets, but the goat's head stayed where it was. Kabir walked up to the boy and said something into his ear. The boy looked at him, trembling with anger. Kabir reloaded the gun with another round and handed it over to him. The boy took a deep breath and lifted the gun up. His forearm was rock-steady. He breathed in deeply. He took his time to aim and then pulled the trigger.

The goat's head exploded as the bullet crashed through its cranium. Kabir smiled as he walked back to Nabil, who looked surprised, like everyone else.

'What did you tell him?'

'Imagine the goat is your father's murderer.'

~

Beware the ides of March.

It was the fifteenth day of March in 44 BC. Julius Caesar had been stabbed to death twenty-three times before his meeting at the Senate in Rome. His body lay in a bloody heap, on display for the bewildered crowd outside the Capitol. Two men spoke over his dead body. Brutus, Caesar's trusted aide who stabbed him last, and Mark Antony, who remained faithful to his leader, despite their differences. Brutus was given a chance to explain his actions. He addressed the large crowd, who waited for him to speak. Now, Brutus was a noble man who respected Caesar, but who believed that once Caesar became a ruler he would assume dictatorial powers that would lead the country to its downfall. And he explained all of this to his countrymen, over Caesar's lifeless form. This was the first scene that came to Kabir's mind as he saw Nabil Bugti asking his people to gather around a large metal crate with a large lock on it.

'This shameful metal crate is what Musharraf had sent us after killing my father, my beloved Balochis!'

Nabil's statement made everyone look at the rusty metal crate. This was the very crate that the Pakistani Army had sent to the Bugti family after killing Akbar Bugti and thirty-two of his men in a cave in Kohlu, Dera Bugti. It was an operation headed by none other than Brigadier Tanveer Shehzad of the ISI. A note was attached to the crate. It read: 'The respected Nawab Akbar Bugti's body lies in this metal coffin. *Inshallah*, he'll find his way to heaven.'

In Islam, dead bodies are buried in the ground, but not placed in a coffin. The Pakistanis responsible for killing Bugti had deprived his family of the centuries-old tradition of burying a dear departed in accordance with the teachings of Islam. Bugti's mangled body was thrown into the crate on Shehzad's orders. He had then had the coffin locked securely, with a victorious smile, and thrown away the key from the top of a nearby hill.

'I'm sure all of you remember my respected father for his efforts,' Nabil continued to his army. 'And I'm sure seeing this crate frustrates you. God knows if it's his body in it or not!'

His Balochi fighters, leaning against their rifles, nodded sadly.

'But my father was a brave man. I had asked him not to hide in those caves. And this is what he had told me: "Instead of a slow death in bed, I'd rather that death come to me while I'm fighting for our cause!" So my question to you is: If this is what my father wanted, did the Pakistanis succeed at all?'

The fighters enthusiastically replied in the negative. Their gaze then shifted to the three men who stood beside Nabil Bugti. Isha was asked by Kabir to wait in the car.

'These men here are Indians,' said Nabil, pointing at Kabir and his team. 'And even if they don't follow our religion, they have shown that they stand to be more credible than the Pakistanis!'

The Balochis looked at the Indians admiringly. Nabil looked at Kabir, and gestured to him to say a few words.

'Friends,' Kabir started, 'this might sound unusual for you. But, yes, I'm an Indian who understands your plight fully.'

He pictured this slightly differently. In his mind, he was Mark Antony talking to the Roman plebeians. And just like him, he was going to appeal to their hearts and not their heads, as Brutus did. And the crate that lay before him, regardless of the fact that it may not even have carried the real Akbar Bugti's body in it, held, in his mind, the dead body of Julius Caesar.

'What is Pakistan?' Kabir asked. He proceeded to answer the question himself. 'It's not purely ethnic like Balochistan! Its people aren't humane to the sufferings of you Balochis, like we Indians are! Granted, you may think I'm saying this because India and Pakistan are constantly at war and I may have vested interests. But then, you know as well as I do, that the guns you are holding and the houses that you are living in, inadequate as they are, were at some point bought by money that my country provided to the Balochi cause!'

The Balochis shifted uneasily. They didn't like being told they owed India a favour.

'Balochistan is rich in minerals, gems, gas, petroleum and other such resources.' Kabir raised his voice. 'And these are enough to provide you a comfortable life. But do you like this uncertain life, this spectre of constant fear? Do you like taking the life of another human being just so that you can live? I'm certain that you don't. But if the need arises, you must. And that is why we are here today.'

Kabir paused for breath and to see if the crowd was on the same wavelength as him. He quite enjoyed playing Mark Antony.

'Enough with killing the odd soldier or two! Enough with wrecking small Pakistani properties that can be replaced in the blink of an eye! Enough of cutting the water supply and electricity! You, my friends, are going to hit them where it hurts. And I am going to guide you through it.'

The Balochis shot confused glances at each other.

'Nawab Nabil Bugti has agreed to be a part of my mission,' Kabir said. 'And if you agree with Nabil Bugti—and I'm sure, with Nawab Akbar Bugti as well, who is here with us in spirit—then you will be under my command for the next few days. We will, together, show the Pakistanis the real might of you Balochis! And this will maim them in a way that they've never experienced before!'

Kabir paused dramatically.

A voice cried out. 'How can we trust you? What are your motives?'

'What do I stand to gain out of it, you may think. Let me clear that up for you. I have four of my fellow Indians in their clutches. And I am here to free them. Would you not do the same for your men? Together, you and the Marri tribe will fight the toughest fight you've ever fought to get what you want . . . Revenge!'

The fighters seemed to stir up.

Nabil Bugti stepped beside Kabir and opened his mouth to speak. 'I agree with this man's words,' he said. 'And you must understand that this mission could play a very important role in our revolution if we execute it according to the plan. What the mission is, I will tell you only if you all are willing participants! So tell me now, my friends, will you do this for your leader, who lay down his life for you? For your wives and sisters whose modesty was outraged, who were humiliated by the Pakistanis? For your integrity, and for the honour of Balochistan?'

The Balochis stood up, roaring their support for the Indian man who stood next to their leader. They lifted their rifles and began firing in the air to show their appreciation. Isha, hearing the gunshots and fearing something unforeseen had happened, got out of the car and walked a few steps. She was greeted with the sight of the Balochis firing in the air and hugging each other.

Later that night, at Nabil Bugti's residence, Kabir and his team, along with Irfan Baloch Khan, sat over a lush Persian *dastarkhwan*, a feast, and discussed the full plan of action, over dishes of beef nihari, yakhni pulao and eggplant on lavash.

'One last thing,' Kabir said to Bugti, steely-eyed, 'I want you to find me a metal coffin like this one.'

Everyone looked at him, uncertain of the direction he was headed. But by now they were familiar with Kabir Anand's way of doling out his message.

'I will bring Tanveer Shehzad to you in that coffin. And then you can do to him what he did to your father.'

PART II

The Twelfth Night

15

12 September 2014
Islamabad, Pakistan

The Director General of the ISI, Lieutenant General Azhar-ul-Islam Tayyab, was seated upright at the desk in his study. It was three in the morning. He recalled everything Brigadier Tanveer Shehzad had relayed to him. It played in his mind on a loop. *It would spell disaster for India,* he thought as he worked on his proposal for the Army chief. His job was going to get a whole lot more difficult after the plan was executed. But he was ready to take it on. It had to be done.

His chain of thought was broken by the faint buzz of his phone. He had kept the phone on silent, lest his wife, in the adjacent room, wake up. To most, that buzz wouldn't even be audible, but for him it was the loudest sound at the time. He opened his drawer cautiously, picked up the phone and squinted at the number as it gently vibrated in his hand. He stood up with some urgency and walked over to the window before answering it.

'It's three in the morning,' he said through gritted teeth. 'This better be worth it!'

'I haven't called to discuss the weather, *janaab*! I have something important to tell you.'

Tayyab lit his seventh cigarette of the night. 'Well, go on, then.'

'The Wing is up to something, and it doesn't look good.'

Tayyab felt a sudden shot of fear rush through his veins. *Could RAW know about the planned attack? Could they know about al-Qaeda?*

'What do you mean by "something" for God's sake?!'

'I don't know,' the reply came. 'I'm sure there's something about to happen in Balochistan. I thought I'd give you a heads-up. Do what you can, ASAP.'

'Are you a hundred per cent certain?'

'Of course I am!' the man on the other end of the line spluttered. 'I popped Sadiq for you, I got those Indians captured for you. The least you owe me is a bit of trust, janaab.'

'I trust nobody,' Tayyab replied. 'But if what you say is true, then you know I owe you the price you name.'

'Yes, we'll get to that later. I'm leaving the country. Will contact you once I'm out of here. Will need help. Goodnight.'

Tayyab leaned against the table and picked up his glass thoughtfully. *What could they possibly know? The plan of the attack is too high-level a secret for them to get wind of. Maybe it could be something related to the prisoners. Could they be coming to get them? Of course not. They've got no backbone. Even if they do, they'll never make it out alive. But one can never be too sure.*

Tayyab lifted his phone and dialled a number quickly. Precautions had to be taken. If things were about to happen in Balochistan, Shehzad needed to know.

'*Salaam aleikum,*' Shehzad said instantly. 'Is everything okay, janaab?'

Even in the wee hours of the morning, Tanveer Shehzad sounded alert as ever.

'Are you still with him?'

Tayyab was referring to Ayman al-Zawahiri, the successor to Osama bin Laden, who had meticulously engineered a plan, in cahoots with the ISI, to set India on fire, and to sit back and watch it burn.

'Yes,' Shehzad replied. 'Fleshing out the details of the celebrations.'

'I need you to get back to Quetta. Take the chopper and get Omar and Baradar out of there. That's top priority. After that, move the Indians out, too, if you can. If they die, so be it.'

Shehzad remained silent for a while. The sudden developments confused him.

'Where do I take them?'

'Back to Swat,' Tayyab replied. 'Keep them in one of the Haqqani safe houses.'

'May I ask why, janaab?'

'The Indians are up to something in Balochistan,' Tayyab said urgently. 'I want to play it safe, in case this is something serious.'

'All right. By tomorrow evening, I'll fly them back to Waziristan.'

'Go, get some rest,' Tayyab ordered. 'You have a long day ahead.'

Tayyab poured himself a glass of water, looked at the time and shook his head. He was tired, but there was no way he was going to be able to sleep. Not now, in any case. He walked back to his table and continued to type away, robotically, on his laptop.

~

12 September 2014
Quetta, Balochistan

It was noon, and the children were ready to offer their *zohr namaz*, before they resumed their studies at the Fayyaz-ul-Uloom madrasa. They lined up next to each other, chatting animatedly while they went about the process of wudu, a ritual ablution performed before each prayer session. Their headmaster, a stout man dressed in a white kurta-pyjama that fell just short of his ankles, waited for them to assemble in the prayer hall. He sported a neatly trimmed beard, but no moustache. Beads of sweat formed along his hairline as he adjusted the microphone at his collar. He checked it lightly by tapping on it. He needed the speaker to be loud enough, to lead the children through the namaz. It also needed to be audible to the Amir and Mullah Baradar in the chamber below.

The prayers started soon enough. The headmaster's baritone boomed through the speakers. A few hundred students genuflected, pressing their foreheads to the woven-straw prayer mat. In the chamber below, Mullah Omar and Mullah Baradar performed their prayers on their strongly incensed velvet *ja'namaz*. The adjacent chamber, however, had four semi-conscious men, gagged and tied up, hoping to be put out of their misery soon. But in their minds, they prayed to their god for a miracle. They wanted the bright light that shone directly on their faces to be switched off.

They wanted that excruciatingly painful buzzing noise to stop. They couldn't take it any longer. They wished they had been executed instead. And then, all of a sudden, the light and the sound went off. Maybe their prayers had been heard?

One storey above, in the prayer hall, the speaker had abruptly gone silent, too. The children and the headmaster remained on their haunches, completing the namaz anyway. There is a strict rule in Islam that forbids distraction during prayer, no matter how extreme the circumstances. After wrapping up, the headmaster hurried to check on the speaker that had gone dead, kaput, halfway through his prayers.

'No electricity,' the peon said. 'The entire area is suffering from a power failure.'

'Use the generator, then,' the headmaster barked.

'The last time there was a power cut, our generator stopped working as well, due to a short circuit.'

The headmaster cursed under his breath and marched towards the chamber downstairs. He would need to inform the Amir and Mullah Baradar. He knocked at their door lightly. Baradar opened it.

'I'm afraid we've lost electricity in the entire area,' the headmaster told a sweaty Baradar. The chamber was dark and stuffy. There were no windows in their subterranean hideout.

'Fucking Balochis.' The Amir's voice came from behind. 'It must be them again.'

He was accurate in his assessment. The Balochis often cut off the power to annoy the Pakistanis.

'Get a trusted electrician,' Baradar instructed the headmaster. 'Until then, send all the students back home. We will sit upstairs.'

The headmaster turned and walked away obediently.

Baradar turned to Omar. 'What about the prisoners?'

'Leave a door open for them,' Omar replied. 'They need some ventilation.'

~

'Yes, janaab,' Wahab Ali the electrician said into the phone. 'I'll be there in exactly twenty minutes. *Khuda hafiz.*'

He turned and looked at his wife. She knew he had to get to work, so she helped him pack his tools and handed him his bag.

'I'll be back soon,' he told her. 'I'm going to the madrasa, so I'll bring Iqbal back home, too. They're sending the kids home early today.'

This piece of news brought a smile to his wife's face. Ali stepped out and walked towards his bike. A few metres away, two men and a woman watched him from their SUV.

'Are you sure this is the guy?' Kabir asked Irfan Baloch Khan.

'Yes,' Khan replied. 'We've noticed him at the madrasa many times before. He's the only guy who does their electrical work. His name is Wahab Ali.'

'It would never have struck me that you guys are so thorough with your work,' Isha said from the back seat.

'We may not have fancy gadgets, but do you think you people are the only ones with a spy ring?' Khan shot back.

So far, the Balochis had done a good job. The first step of the plan was set in motion. They had done the needful: cutting off the power lines.

'Isha.' Kabir turned and looked at her. 'You know what to do.'

Isha nodded, and covered her face with a veil. She got out of the car and walked towards the electrician's house. Khan started the car and followed the electrician as he started out on his bike. The electrician, naturally oblivious to the people on his trail, continued towards the madrasa. After a while, the bike stopped at a signal. Khan stopped the SUV right beside the bike. Kabir turned and looked to see if there were many cars around him—just a couple, the drivers of which did not look interested enough. He got out of the SUV, covered his face with a scarf and walked towards the electrician. The electrician looked at him confusedly. Kabir went ahead and sat pillion on his bike. The electrician froze.

'Remain silent,' Kabir whispered as he pressed the end of his pistol to the electrician's hip. The signal turned green. 'Take the next right and stop.'

The electrician's hands began to tremble and his heart thumped against his ribcage. He did as he was instructed to. He brought the bike to a halt at the next turning. Kabir got off and helped Ali off the bike as well. Irfan Baloch Khan parked the SUV a short distance ahead. If everything went according to plan, he would be able to knock the electrician unconscious and then leave him back home after Kabir had achieved what he had set out to do.

'I'm not here to hurt you, Ali.'

'W-what do you want?'

'Not much,' Kabir replied. 'Your toolkit and your bike. I want to know what it feels like to be an electrician for the next few hours.'

Ali looked flustered. He couldn't understand what was happening. *Why did the man have a gun? Why does he want to be an electrician for the next few hours? Why me?*

'I will be going to the madrasa instead of you,' Kabir clarified. 'I believe you're the most trusted electrician in that part of town. Well, let's just say I want to share your fame for a while. I want to pay the Amir a visit too.'

Ali was petrified. *Fuck. This guy knows about the Amir.*

'There's no way I'm letting you go there,' Ali mustered up the words, trembling as he said them.

'So be it,' Kabir said casually. 'I won't take up too much of your time. But I'd like to show you a picture.'

He drew out his satphone and texted Isha. Within seconds, she had sent him a photo. Kabir smiled as he held out his phone to the electrician.

'N-no way!' Ali's eyes bulged out of his sockets as he struggled to find his voice. 'L-leave her alone!'

The photo showed Ali's wife tied to a chair, her mouth taped up, tears flowing down her cheeks.

'Rest assured,' Kabir continued, 'if you carry on to the madrasa now, you won't find her like this at home. There'll be a lot to clean up.'

Ali broke down. He tried to punch Kabir, who caught him by the fist and twisted his arm.

'As I said, I'm not here to hurt you. Or your wife,' Kabir repeated, and then, as an afterthought, added, 'or your son.'

Ali went weak in the knees and collapsed to the ground, sobbing away. Kabir bent down to speak to him.

Ali looked into Kabir's fierce eyes. He couldn't see the rest of Kabir's face, since it was covered with a scarf. He didn't want to.

'J-just leave them alone,' Ali replied, finally. 'Take whatever you want. But just leave them alone.'

'That's better,' Kabir said. 'Now you're going to make a call to the headmaster saying that you won't be able to make it because your wife is unwell, but that you're sending a trusted cousin instead. Let's call him Yusuf.'

'You'll never make it out of there.'

'Let me worry about that. Make the damn call.'

Ali shook as he pulled out his phone.

'One wrong move . . .' Kabir warned him.

Ali had trouble dialling the number, with his teary eyes and trembling hands. Finally, he managed to get through. Kabir instructed him to activate the speakerphone.

'*S-salaam aleikum*,' he said, trying to sound normal. 'Janaab, I won't be able to make it today.'

He choked as he said the words. The headmaster began yelling on the other end of the phone.

'Janaab, please understand. My wife is really unwell. But don't worry, I am sending a cousin of mine. His name is Yusuf. He is very reliable.'

There was a brief silence. And then, after what seemed like an eternity, came the reply.

'How soon can he get here?'

16

12 September 2014
Quetta, Balochistan

'Please leave your bag here,' the guard at the gate of the Fayyaz-ul-Uloom madrasa told Kabir. The last of the students had left the premises. He threw another glance at Kabir and said, 'You're not the usual guy.'

'I apologize, janaab. Usually it's my cousin, Wahab Ali, who comes here. Today, he couldn't make it.'

The grouchy guard inspected Kabir and then tugged the bag with the electrical equipment away from him. Kabir, dressed in a tattered, checked shirt and a pair of loose trousers, a pen perched over his ear, looked every bit the electrician he was supposed to. But now his bag of tools had been confiscated.

He had expected them to search his bag thoroughly, and had that happened, they would've certainly not found anything suspicious. He had dismantled his gun thoroughly, so that even the most obvious parts would've passed off as an electrician's tools and other paraphernalia. But now he would have to think on his feet.

'How do you expect me to work without m
janaab?'

'There's a bag with all the equipment you i
for you inside.'

Kabir nodded, turned away from the guard and began walking towards the madrasa. He wrapped a scarf around his face, as the wind blew hard, sending dust flying into his hair and eyes. As he crossed a fairly large playground, he felt a sense of familiarity. The last time he was at a madrasa, things hadn't gone down too well. *You can't think about that now . . . Concentrate!* But despite cautioning himself, scenes from his past flashed in his mind. The domed structure, the playground, the door to the entrance, they were all too familiar. He looked to the side and saw two identical Toyota SUVs. *So Omar is here.*

'Yusuf?' the headmaster of the madrasa confirmed as Kabir approached. He held a medium-sized, worn-out leather bag.

'Yes, janaab,' Kabir replied. 'Wahabbhai sent me.'

The headmaster handed Kabir the bag with the equipment. He motioned to Kabir to follow him. Kabir walked behind the stout figure into a classroom on the right. There were no desks, just large carpets that had been rolled up and stacked upon each other in the corner of the room.

'Wait here,' the headmaster said as he walked out of the classroom, closing the door behind him. Kabir wondered what was happening. He took the pen tucked above his ear, pressed a button and muttered into it.

'I'm in.'

Suddenly, the door opened. Kabir slid the pen into his pocket quickly. Three large guards followed the headmaster into the room. They looked Pashtun to him. *Omar's guards.*

'Search him,' the headmaster said, fanning himself with a rolled-up newspaper. 'Make it quick, it's getting really hot in here.'

Kabir immediately feigned a worried look. The kind that shows you have nothing to hide, but that you're scared of the three huge guys who are more brawn than brain. The guards formed a triangle around Kabir, examining him. The headmaster walked out, leaving the door ajar. Kabir saw him going down the stairs, through the reflection off the glass panes on the door. *Omar must be in the basement.*

Kabir felt three pairs of hands searching different parts of his body simultaneously. They checked his shoes, his scarf, his shirt and then finally his trousers. One of the guards ran his hands over Kabir's buttocks, taking longer than he needed too. He then did the same thing with Kabir's crotch. He looked up at his friends and cracked a joke in Pashto. Kabir did his best to keep calm and not send his heel into the man's teeth. Kabir noticed that each of them carried a revolver, probably a .38 Webley by the look of things, tucked into the side of their pyjamas. Now that Kabir's firearm had been confiscated at the gate itself, he needed to get his hands on one of these.

'He's clear,' the guard said. He then walked to the door and stuck his head out.

'The Amir is coming up now,' he continued in Pashto, 'after which we'll take the electrician to the power source.'

Kabir looked on confusedly, as if he didn't understand Pashto. He finally saw a tall figure coming up the stairs, in the reflection on the glass. He didn't need to see more to know who it was. Behind the tall figure, Kabir noticed, was another man taking equally confident strides. *Baradar . . .*

'Come on,' the guard said to Kabir. 'Let's go.'

Kabir picked up the bag of tools and walked behind the guard. The other two walked beside him. Kabir felt his temples throb as he followed the guard into the chamber below. A strong stench welcomed him, only growing stronger as he walked into a corridor.

'The circuit control room is at the end of the corridor,' the guard pointed out. Kabir noticed four rooms in the basement. It didn't look like a place that was regularly lit up anyway, with electricity or otherwise. As Kabir walked on, he noticed an empty room, with a lit cigar lying in an ashtray. Kabir deduced that it was the room Omar and Baradar were in. The guard shoved him, urging him to walk faster.

Kabir passed another door. It was locked. *Could the prisoners be in there?* Kabir continued walking and, as he approached the third door on his right, he realized that the source of the smell originated from there. He walked up to it swiftly and, on seeing what was inside, froze momentarily. Four bodies, chained to a wall, drenched in blood, urine and sweat. He couldn't tell if they were alive or dead. *The prisoners. The Indians.*

The guard closed the door quickly on seeing Kabir's reaction.

'They are kafirs,' he growled to Kabir. 'You don't need to look so sympathetic. Do your job and get out.'

Kabir nodded obediently as the guard opened the room for him. Kabir looked at the large board, with switches and wires all in a tangled mess. Kabir walked into the room, and the three guards followed suit.

'It's stuffy in here,' Kabir said. 'I would appreciate it if you could wait outside.'

The guards shot each other a look, shrugged and stepped out. Kabir rested on his haunches, zipped open

the bag and pulled out a torch. He clicked it on and looked
at the equipment inside. A screwdriver, scissors, pliers, a
battery-operated soldering iron with some soldering wire
wrapped around it, and three rolls of duct tape. *Good
enough.*

Kabir stood up, and looked at the circuit thoughtfully.
He scratched his chin and then looked at the guards.

'Bloody Balochis,' he sighed at one of them. 'I will have
to repair the generator, because there's nothing that can be
done here. They've cut off the cables on the pylons from the
main power-grid.'

'Do whatever you have to, man,' the guard said rudely.

'I will,' Kabir said. He bent down and switched it on
and allowed it to heat up. *Don't you worry, I will.*

The guards turned around and began speaking to each
other in Pashto. Kabir looked at his watch. *Ten minutes and
the Balochis will be here.* He looked down at the soldering
iron, picked a bit of wire and touched it to the tip. The metal
glimmered and melted. *Perfect.*

Kabir then lifted the screwdriver with his other hand and
held it behind his back. The guards saw him stand up and
walk towards them. The three of them towered over him, as
he stood about a metre away. It was dark, save for the little
light the torch gave out. Kabir smiled to himself.

'What's the matter now?' the guard asked. The two next
to him glowered.

'The four kafirs in that room are my countrymen,' Kabir
said. 'And I'm here to get them.'

The guards stood bewildered for a split second—more
than enough time for Kabir to act. With one swift motion,
he used the soldering iron in his right hand to stab one man
in the eye, and with the screwdriver in the other hand, he
slashed the man on his left, across the cheek. Both of them

yelped in pain. The third man reached for his gun, and Kabir rammed his boot into the man's crotch.

'That should teach you not to touch other people's balls again,' Kabir said as he kicked the man in the groin repeatedly.

Kabir bent down and picked up the gun. He saw that the guard with the soldering iron in his eye was convulsing in pain, his mouth struggling to scream. The other guard, however, had recovered from the shock and was pointing his gun at Kabir, about to pull the trigger. Kabir somersaulted and speared him into the circuit wall. Kabir didn't want to risk being heard by firing the gun, so he elbowed the man in his face, caught a handful of his beard and twisted his head until his neck cracked. The man slumped to the ground. Within a minute, Kabir had made a heap of the three tough guards.

Kabir picked up the other Webley revolvers as well, and emptied the rounds with the help of some light from the torch. He slipped some spare cartridges into his pocket. He examined the firearm he chose to keep, for good measure. He noticed it was a fake. It looked surprisingly authentic, but the tiny imprint that read 'Made in USA, Birmingham', gave it away. The original firearm was made only in the UK. Gathering himself, Kabir walked slowly towards the prisoners. He pulled out the pen with the audio transmitter and spoke into it.

'I'm with the prisoners,' he said as he entered the room.

'Should we move in?' Isha asked.

'Hold on,' Kabir said as he held his breath. 'Let me unchain them. Move when you get my signal.'

'Roger that,' Isha's voice crackled through the pen.

Kabir slipped the pen back into his pocket and looked at the prisoners, recalling images of them as he had seen them last, as opposed to how they looked now. One of them showed signs of moving. He walked over and bent down on his haunches near him.

'It's all right,' Kabir said as the man flinched. 'You're going to be okay.'

'W-who are you?'

'Major Kabir Anand. I'm here to rescue you.'

The man's thin lips formed a weak smile. He moved with great effort, against the resistance of the chain. He had a broken leg. Kabir felt the blood rush to his head.

'They'll pay for it,' Kabir said through gritted teeth. 'I promise you that.'

Kabir stood up, enraged. He saw a metal chair in the corner of the room. He strode over and broke away a piece. He picked up the iron leg and smashed it repeatedly against the prisoner's chains until they gave away. The other three men stirred slightly before waking up, completely disoriented. They did not realize Kabir was here to save them.

Kabir lifted the pen and spoke into it.

'I've got them. It's time to make your move.'

Kabir waited for a reply, but the pen just crackled noisily.

'Do you copy? Isha? Nihar?'

And then, suddenly, Kabir heard a noise grow louder. It was coming from outside the building.

'KABIR!' Nihar's voice shrieked through the pen. 'THEY KNOW YOU'RE THERE!'

Kabir had just about figured what Nihar said, when the noise grew louder. And then Kabir placed the source of the noise. *A helicopter.*

Nihar's voice screeched through the pen again. Kabir held it to his ear.

'GET OUT OF THERE! THEY ARE COMING FOR YOU!'

'TELL THE BALOCHIS TO ADVANCE!' Kabir bellowed back as he readied his weapon. He knew they were coming to get him. But he had planned it out well enough. It was always going to be hard.

Suddenly, he heard Isha's voice through the transmitter.

'A HELICOPTER IS LANDING OUTSIDE! OMAR IS ESCAPING!'

17

12 September 2014
Quetta, Balochistan

Kabir looked at the prisoners. They were in no shape to move, much less escape. He closed the door and waited behind it. He switched off the torch, deciding to work in complete darkness. The element of surprise was all he had. Within a few moments, the basement would be full of militants and Kabir would have to fight his way to the top alone. He closed his eyes and reconstructed the route from the stairs up to the electrical control room. *Four rooms. One of them is locked.*

He heard some hurried footsteps coming towards the chamber. *Four guards, maybe five.* He picked up the revolver and decided to wait it out. The first move would have to be his. Kabir crouched silently behind the door, waiting for the men to approach. *They'll probably want to kill the prisoners first . . . I'd do that if I were in their place . . .*

The militants reached downstairs. He heard a man speak in Pashto, ordering the men to separate and search the rooms. *That evens the odds.* He heard the footsteps getting louder as he saw little beams of light floating around. He clutched his Webley revolver closer. *It's show time . . .*

As soon as the guard opened the door, Kabir shot him. The bullet tore into the man's skull with ferocity, and blood sprayed all over Kabir's face. He pulled the man towards himself before he fell, intending to use him as a human shield. The guard was rather heavy, and Kabir tried hard to balance himself. There were bursts of fire aimed in his direction as the other men closed in. Kabir staggered out, with the dead man's body shielding him. With one swift motion, he held the gun beside the guard's torso and fired blindly. Bullets flew from both sides and Kabir managed to kill another guard. *Two down . . .* His body-shield had saved him from quite a number of bullets. Kabir was out of ammo and he needed to reload. He grabbed the dead man's gun as well and went back into the room for cover. A few metres away, the two guards who were in Mullah Omar's chamber did the same.

Kabir switched the torch on and looked at the gun he had borrowed. It was an Afghani *jezail.* Kabir looked at it incredulously. It was a long-barrelled handmade gun, not too accurate, and extremely slow. He pulled out the spare bullets he had pocketed for the Webley and realized that they weren't enough. He decided to make do with the jezail. *Just my luck!*

Kabir took a deep breath and decided that attacking would be his best defence. He decided to go for the jugular. He crept up with the gun pointing ahead, towards Omar's room. He knew the two guards would be waiting on either side of the door, planning their move. He had to be swift.

He kicked open the door and pulled the trigger, killing the guard on the right. The gun recoiled jerkily, and Kabir just about managed to keep his grip on it. The man on his left raised his gun and was about to pull the trigger when Kabir slammed the butt of his jezail into his eye, and then, with a hard swerve, bashed it against his temple. The man collapsed instantly. Kabir shot him for good measure. *There will be Afghani reinforcements coming soon.* He had an idea. *Maybe I can shift the prisoners to the other room.*

He shot open the lock on the closed door and held up his torch. There were large duffel bags and huge wooden crates on the floor. On top of the crates he found some jerrycans, each with perhaps 5 litres of water or so. He raised the torch to the label and read, 'Aab-e-Zamzam—Holy Water from Mecca'. Kabir, on seeing this, felt the need to quench his thirst. He opened a bottle, gulped down some water quickly and then poured some over his head. He bent down and unzipped the duffel bags, only to find rocket launchers, rifles and a few loose grenades. He scoffed at the hypocrisy of it all: water from a holy well and weapons of serious destruction, lying next to each other. He bent down to pick up a couple of grenades, put them into a smaller bag around his shoulder, and then loaded the Carbine rifle.

Kabir quickly walked into the opposite room and handed a revolver to the one prisoner who had managed to come to. He decided against dragging the prisoners into the other room.

'Here. In case you need it,' Kabir said. 'I'm sending my colleagues down to get you.'

'Please come back soon,' the man said faintly. Kabir nodded tersely and slammed the door shut.

He went out, stepping on dead bodies as he ran up the stairs. His finger was firmly placed on the trigger of the rifle, ready to fire in an instant. As he reached the top, he looked out of the window at the playground.

The helicopter was all set to take off. One Land Cruiser had broken through the wall and had driven off recklessly. Veer was running to get into the other one. On the ground, around sixty Balochis had swarmed in and had begun fighting Omar's guards. It was a scene from a medieval skirmish, complete with guns, swords and impaled bodies. Everything was going according to Kabir's plan. Except the fact that there was a huge helicopter that was trying to whisk Mullah Omar away.

Kabir ran outside and saw Nihar and Isha take cover behind their car, firing at Omar's men. The total strength of Omar's fighters at that moment, both Pakistani and Afghani, was around forty. He had certainly been caught unawares.

Kabir coughed as he ran outside the madrasa and pointed out to Isha and Nihar. 'THE PRISONERS ARE IN THE BASEMENT,' Kabir yelled, taking in lungfuls of the dusty air. 'GIVE ME THE CAR!'

Nihar and Isha nodded and ran into the madrasa. Kabir tossed the duffel bag with the grenades and rifle to Isha, as he himself got into the driver's seat. He revved up the engine and cast a sideways glance at Veer, who had driven out of the hole in the wall in pursuit of the other car. *What the fuck is Veer up to?*

The chopper's wings began to rotate rhythmically and the helicopter lifted itself off the ground. The Balochis opened fire at it. Kabir revved the engine of his car. He had an idea. *It could get you killed, Kabir. But if Omar and Shehzad are in that chopper, it had to be done.*

'CEASEFIRE!' Kabir yelled at the Balochis through the window. 'Don't shoot the chopper!'

They didn't seem to obey at first. Kabir could see the chopper gain height, bullets ricocheting off it as it did. It was almost six or seven feet off the ground, when Kabir slid open the sunroof of his vehicle, shifted gears quickly and rammed his foot on the accelerator to gain speed as fast as possible. He looked up at the helicopter as he closed in. *It's all about the timing . . .*

His vehicle was thankfully quick to respond, and he saw the helicopter turn midway in the air. Kabir swerved the car, and jumped up on the seat, swiftly climbing out through the sunroof. The whirlwind of dust that the chopper kicked up began to get into his eyes. Kabir closed them involuntarily as he tried to maintain his balance on the roof of his car. He looked up and mentally reckoned the distance between him and the landing-skids of the chopper.

The chopper was almost eleven feet high now. Kabir kept his eyes on the chopper's skids, his heart thumping against his chest. His vehicle was beginning to slow down now and was about to ram into a wall. He would miss his chance if that happened. *It's now or never . . .*

Kabir leapt upwards with his arms outstretched.

18

12 September 2014
Quetta, Balochistan

Isha stepped in, rifle in position. Nihar followed her, holding a pistol up, ready to fire any moment. *Fire blindly when facing hostiles. It's not ideal advice, but there may not be enough time to aim when push comes to shove,* Kabir had told him. As they moved further into the madrasa, the metallic smell of blood welcomed them. They knew Kabir had done a good job of mopping up the madrasa, before he had asked them to help get the prisoners out. But one could never be too sure. *Never know when some gun-toting maulana would step out of the shadows.*

'Cover me,' Isha said as her walk became more brisk. They passed by locked classrooms on their way to the chamber below.

Nihar's face contorted involuntarily at the sight and smell of the pools of blood splattered across the floor and the walls, like macabre Rorschach-test inkblots.

'Isha, why do you think Kabir got into the car?' Nihar whispered as they tiptoed gingerly over a heap of dead bodies.

'I'm sure he has his reasons,' Isha replied, switching a torch on and passing it to Nihar. 'He certainly hasn't taken it for a joyride.'

'But, then, we need a vehicle to get the prisoners into!'

Isha stopped and nodded thoughtfully. They were at the base of the staircase, looking at the hell Kabir had single-handedly raised. As she took some sure-footed strides, she could feel the stickiness of the blood on the floor through her boots.

'Make a call to the Balochis,' she said finally, her voice nasal. She was trying to avoid inhaling the stench that enveloped the entire basement. She pulled out her satphone from the inside of her jacket. Nihar wedged the torch between his teeth as he took it from her.

He looked at the screen as he punched in Nabil Bugti's number. Isha moved ahead, scanning each room as she passed by. She saw the large duffel bags and the jerrycans of water. She turned to the room opposite and, peeping through the door, she saw the Indian prisoners. They looked as dead as the bodies they had just walked over. She took a step inside and saw one of them meekly raise a rifle. His attempt to move was so slow, she could've shot him thrice.

'It's okay,' she said. 'We're here to get you out! Just a few more minutes . . .'

Nihar had crossed over to the room with the water, picked up a jerrycan and was drinking from it even as he spoke to Nabil Bugti.

'Order your men to get us a car, a big one, outside the madrasa. We're with the prisoners, and we're about to move them out . . . Do it ASAP!'

Bugti shouted back something to the effect of asking them to buy as much time as they could, and then disconnected. Nihar lifted two cans of water and walked to the room across. He walked quickly to the unconscious prisoners and splashed some water on their faces. They had to revive the four prisoners, who were in a sorry state. There was no time for sentiment.

After giving them enough water to drink, Isha and Nihar looked at each other and nodded. They helped each prisoner up, one at a time. They struggled and stumbled, manoeuvring to place the prisoners' arms over their shoulders. Nihar helped two soldiers up, simultaneously.

'Be strong, brother. Just a few more minutes to freedom,' Nihar repeated over and over, as he got them to move, finally. Their frail bodies dragged their feet as they slowly made their way out, with a lot of help from Nihar and Isha.

'Thank you,' one of them said wanly. The others repeated after him.

'Not yet,' Isha said.

'We are glad you guys came for us,' another murmured.

'*Jai Hind!*' another said weakly.

And, finally, the four of them were rescued from the prison they had been confined to for what seemed like an eternity, with their faith in their country reinstated.

'We move them to a classroom till the vehicle arrives,' Nihar instructed Isha. The prisoners looked at the dead bodies along the way, twitching involuntarily. One of the two that Isha was supporting threw up, staining her jacket.

'S-sorry.' His lips quivered.

'It's all right,' Isha replied. 'You owe me a new one once we get back home.'

Nihar had reached the top of the stairs, helping his prisoners along towards the first open door they saw. Isha dragged the third man in as well.

'I'll go check if the car has arrived,' she said. 'You keep an eye on them.'

Nihar helped them rest their backs against the wall. He held his pistol loosely as he walked back towards the door to keep a lookout on the corridor. He looked across at the classroom opposite and spotted a packet of cigarettes lying on the mat. *What the hell, I've never needed one more.* He stepped out and strode into the room. His eyes fell on something else.

There was a broken laptop, three bullet holes smashing its screen. Nihar instinctively bent down and picked it up. The screen fell apart, cracking as it hit the ground. Nihar was left standing with the bottom half of the device in his hands. *Someone had shot at it before leaving the room—probably Omar or one of his cronies, upon realizing they had to hurry out of the madrasa. This might just be useful . . .*

'I asked you to stay with the prisoners!' Isha snapped sternly. Nihar turned around and shrugged, holding up the part of the laptop still left in his hands. Isha shot a glance at it and didn't look too amused. 'Help me get them to the car! We have to get the hell out before the Pakistani reinforcements get here!'

She turned and stormed into the other room. She had got another Balochi to help the prisoners to the car. Nihar looked at his latest find thoughtfully. He cradled it between his rib and the inside of his arm. He had almost walked out of the room before he remembered the forgotten pack of cigarettes on the floor.

~

'Shoot at the bastard!' Omar bellowed as he sat low in his seat. 'And drive faster! Let's get to the camp, he won't stand a chance there!'

The Pakistani driver, who was already clocking 145 kilometres on a main road, jammed the accelerator pedal down harder and took a slight turn and went off-road. Besides Omar, there were three others in the car, including the driver. Shehzad had ordered them to get to the madrasa and stand guard around Omar.

'We need reinforcements,' one of them said into his phone. 'There's a turbaned guy behind us. He's got the Amir's other Toyota.'

They turned and looked at the car gaining speed.

'We'll do our best to hold him off,' the man continued. 'But better intercept him halfway. We're driving up to the Amir's camp!'

The man disconnected his phone, lifted his rifle and nodded at the other man beside him. They rolled down their windows. 'Aim for the car, preferably the tyres. I'll try and get the guy.'

Veer had taken the turn as he continued to gain speed. He saw Omar's car going towards a hill a short distance away, kicking up clouds of dust in its wake. It was a good 300 metres away from him and he needed to catch up and knock the car over. *I can't let Omar get away.*

There were large boulders in his way, and Veer had to steer his way around them if he were to get anywhere close to Omar's car. He eased the gearstick into sixth gear and began to close in on his target. He noticed two men from either side of the car stick their heads out and take aim. A flurry of bullets followed. Veer's reflexes led him to duck. Four bullets hit the windscreen. Veer lifted his rifle from the seat next to him and shot at the windscreen himself and then with the butt of the rifle shattered it open. *I've made it easier for you to shoot me. Go for it, motherfuckers.*

The Pakistanis expected Veer to slow down, but he didn't. Veer continued at the same pace, poking his rifle out through the gaping hole in the windscreen and firing at the car with one hand. All his bullets were off-target, but he hadn't expected himself to hit the car anyway. It was just to keep the soldiers from shooting at him for a few seconds. *Sometimes that's all you need.*

Omar's SUV had reached the foot of the hill and was beginning to make its climb. Veer brushed his wild hair aside and looked over at the top of the hill. It wasn't too high, and he saw a group of caves. There was a flat patch of land ahead with barbed wire strung over low walls. A paved entrance led to a large gate. It was a Taliban stronghold. *I have to stop the car from going in, it's not too far away.*

Veer pressed the accelerator as hard as he could and the car's engine roared dutifully. Veer's temples pulsed, drops of sweat fell over his brow. His teeth gnashed and his veins throbbed as he reached closer to the car. He lifted his rifle as he saw the two men appear through the window again. He lifted his hands off the steering momentarily and shot at the car. This time, he managed to hit the glass. The men drew themselves in again, afraid of getting shot. Their car was ascending the hill. *Almost there . . .*

Veer drifted slightly to the car's right, calculating a good angle to make an impact. *If I swerve left and hit it now, the car will probably overturn and fall into the bushes on the side of the hill.* He was about to execute his plan and make the turn, when he heard the distinct sound of a bullet, and lost control over his vehicle. The bullet had hit his tyre, and at the speed at which he was driving, he had to muscle with the steering wheel to stop it from overturning. He did his best and the car lifted off the ground momentarily, before coming to a halt. Another burst of bullets flew at him and he crouched down and looked to his right. Omar's car was way up the hill. Someone else was shooting at him. He lifted his rifle and jumped to the back seat, trying to buy himself some time before making his next move. He looked and saw two black vehicles right opposite him. At least five men stood in a line and fired at him, taking slow steps towards his car. He was outnumbered. His car had started smelling of gas and there was a angry curl of smoke emerging from the bonnet. He looked at his rifle and saw he didn't have enough to fight his way out of this. Even if he did, the Taliban reinforcements were bound to come and get him as soon as Omar made his way through that gate. *This is it, I guess . . . But let's not go down without a fight.*

Veer breathed in heavily and held up his rifle. He exposed himself briefly and fired at the men who were now approaching their prey. He shot six times, and one bullet managed to find its target square in the chest. The man fell, but then rolled over to the side and stood back up with some effort. His bulletproof vest had saved him. Veer was out of ammo. He searched his pockets and found a matchbox.

He lit a matchstick and decided to drop it into the petrol tank of the car, once the attackers were closer. He was going to blow up the car. *If I die, so do they.*

The men walked closer, firing away at the car. Veer lay prone on the ground, waiting for the right moment. And then, suddenly, he heard another spate of gunshots coming from another direction. A small explosion followed. It was the kind of sound a grenade made. Veer was confused. He looked over and saw his five attackers on the ground, parts of their bodies blown up, lying in different places. He looked quickly to his right and saw a familiar figure. Irfan

Baloch Khan was getting out of a jeep along with two other men. He ran right up to Veer and pulled him out of the car.

'Are you okay?' asked Khan.

Veer could not believe his luck. He panted heavily. He turned and looked up at the Taliban stronghold. Omar's car was already inside, safe and sound. 'Give me your weapons,' he said hurriedly. 'Your guns and grenades.'

'Why?'

'I'm going after Omar.'

Khan looked at him incredulously. 'No, you're certainly not. Get in the jeep and let's get the hell out of here.'

'You don't understand!' Veer held Khan by the collar. 'I can't let Omar get away after getting this close to him!'

Khan pushed him away roughly and raised his voice. 'I have not put my ass on the line and saved you here, just so you can walk into the lion's den! What do you think, huh? You'll walk into that place and find Omar waiting for you at the entrance?'

'Let me worry about that!'

'No, fuck you! Get into the jeep!'

Veer punched Khan and quickly grabbed a grenade from his vest. Khan's Balochi friends raised their guns at him. Khan motioned to them to lower their weapons.

'You need to think this through, Veer. They're probably already on their way down to get you.'

'I have one grenade,' Veer said firmly. 'And I will make it count.' He turned around and began to walk up the hill.

'If you take another step, I will shoot you myself.'

Veer ignored him and continued walking. Khan shot at Veer's feet, missing deliberately.

'Going up there is a crazy idea, Veer! You want death? I'll give it to you myself. But I'm not letting you die at their hands!'

Veer continued walking. Khan shot at his feet again. Veer didn't seem perturbed.

'You think you're doing your country any good, Veer? Your country needs you now more than ever. And it needs you alive.'

Veer stopped midway, looking at the gate of the Taliban stronghold. He saw some militants coming out of it.

One of Khan's Balochi members spoke: 'You need to be rational about this. There's no way you're getting through to Omar. They'll destroy you before you reach halfway.'

Veer's body was shaking with anger. He couldn't believe he had let Mullah Omar get away.

'Get into the fucking jeep right now,' Khan ordered. 'Or I will shoot you square in the head myself.'

'I'm doing what is right for my country,' Veer scoffed and turned around, continuing to walk.

'You have been warned,' Khan said. He aimed at Veer's right calf and pulled the trigger.

19

12 September 2014
Quetta, Balochistan

The ascent of the Alouette III chopper was surprisingly swift, once it had generated sufficient downwash. It had risen to a good thirty feet off the ground within seconds of Kabir having made the jump to grasp the landing-skid. The skin on his hands seemed to be tearing away, and his muscles shook violently as he tried to keep himself from falling. But that's not all he had to do. He had to muster up enough strength to pull himself up and into the chopper. Luckily, in their scramble, Baradar and Shehzad hadn't sealed the doors of the helicopter shut yet. But they had noticed him jump up towards the chopper.

Kabir's body trembled violently as he pulled himself up by a fraction and rested his left arm over the landing-skid. He was still an arm's length away from the lower edge of the door. Through his wildly flying hair, he saw an Afghani militant lean out and point a pistol at him. Kabir, who was in the process of lifting his leg on to the landing-skid, saw this and froze instantly. The man had a clean shot, point-blank. In that split second, Kabir ran through all the possibilities in his head, death topping the list. He realized he couldn't jump for obvious reasons. And if he stayed there, the man would shoot him ten times out of ten. These were situations formal training did not prepare you for. Kabir did the only thing that he knew how to do best. *Attack.*

Kabir felt a muscle in his lower back and right shoulder slowly tear as he forced himself up to reach out and grab the man by the arm. He pulled the trigger, but Kabir's tug directed the shot away to his right. And then, using the man's arm as support, Kabir pulled himself up just enough to dig his fingers into a groove on the metal flooring of the chopper. The man began to kick at him frantically. Kabir, mustering up all his brute strength, yanked at the hem of the Afghan's pyjama with his other hand. The man fell forward, yelling and tugging at Kabir's hair in a bid to maintain his balance. Kabir elbowed him sharply in the face, and the man let go and fell out of the chopper, some fifty feet to the ground.

Kabir climbed up inside quickly and rolled over—to see something he least expected. The reaction from the two others in the chopper was the same. There was a stunned moment of silence. The roar of the chopper's engine, coupled with the sound of sliced wind, was completely zeroed out of Kabir's head. Then it all made sense . . . *This isn't Omar . . . It's Baradar . . . Fuck, we got played. Veer must've seen Omar in the car, and that's why he got into the other one to chase him . . .* Kabir looked to his right to see Shehzad in the cockpit, staring back at him incredulously.

'KILL HIM!' Shehzad yelled suddenly to Baradar, pushing some buttons. Baradar searched frantically for a gun, but found none. He picked up his machete, raised it and brought it down swiftly. Kabir rolled over instinctively and missed the blow by a whisker. He then retracted his legs and got himself up. His legs felt heavy, his shoulder unresponsive, his back numb.

Baradar lifted the machete again. There was a 2-metre gap between Kabir and him now. The chopper was a seven-seater, but it was still cramped for space behind the front row. Baradar began to stride towards him, ready to swing the machete across Kabir's neck. Kabir had his back to the glass windshield on the side of the chopper. Baradar swiped and missed again, but managed to chop a lock of hair off the side of Kabir's head instead, as he ducked. Kabir, who was in a low crouch, decided to use his position to his advantage. He speared Baradar on to the seat with all the strength he could gather from his right shoulder-blade. Both men grunted loudly as they threw blind punches at each other. Meanwhile, Shehzad was unstrapping his seat belt, having finally gained enough altitude to activate autopilot. He realized his firearm was in the inner pocket of his jacket, which now lay on the floor. *Not enough time for that . . .*

Kabir bashed his forehead against the ridge of Baradar's large Afghani nose, cracking it instantly. He then kneed Baradar in the pit of the stomach, sending him wheezing and gasping for breath. Kabir turned to see Shehzad surprisingly close to him, in the process of picking up Baradar's machete. The chopper rocked slightly in the air as it moved ahead slowly on its own. Kabir steadied himself and swivelled around, sending his heel into Shehzad's temple. Shehzad fell down, releasing the machete almost as soon as he had held it. Kabir turned his attention back to Mullah Baradar. With gritted teeth, Kabir stepped towards him and tugged at his turban.

'You think you have saved Omar again,' he growled. 'And you might have. But this time, you aren't getting away yourself.'

'I will die for Allah and I will die for my brother, Amir Mohammed Omar.'

'Unfortunately, Allah doesn't quite care about you, if He sent me to hunt you down. Let's hope, for your sake, your brother does . . . if he survives.'

'You can say what you want.' Baradar's lips curled into a bloody smile. 'You're about to lose a whole lot of brothers yourself.'

Kabir's eyes bulged angrily. His clenched fists crashed into Baradar's crooked teeth. Kabir was about to launch another punch, when a sudden shock flowed through his body. Shehzad had lifted the machete and slashed at him from behind, cutting him deeply across his back. Kabir felt his shirt stick to him with the sudden gush of warm blood. His entire body began to feel numb as he dropped to one knee. Shehzad staggered behind him and got ready to launch his machete again. As he raised it and began to bring it down, Kabir pulled Baradar ahead by the nape of his neck in the way of the machete.

There was a lot of blood. The machete went deep inside Baradar's right flank. Shehzad's expression was one of pure horror. He was still gripping the machete as Baradar's body went limp. Kabir was still holding Baradar's nape, supporting himself on his knee. A surge of wind blew in from the open door. Kabir's and Shehzad's eyes met again. Their fierce intensity meant only one thing—one of them was going to die.

With renewed energy, Shehzad wrested the machete out of Baradar's body. Kabir jumped back to his feet and turned around to grab something to fight with. He saw a small fire-extinguisher and kicked it loose. He lifted it as Shehzad began to wildly hack the air with the machete, sending droplets of Baradar's blood flying through the air. Kabir moved around swiftly and swung the metal extinguisher towards Shehzad, who backed up a few steps and swiped the machete towards Kabir again. Kabir shoved the extinguisher in the way, causing a slash in the can. There was a forceful spray of white propellant that Kabir directed on to Shehzad's face. Shehzad dropped the machete to guard his eyes. Kabir slammed the can into the side of his head, causing him to trip over Baradar's body. Kabir flung the can aside and launched a flurry of hard kicks into Shehzad's sides and his face. Once he overcame his feral madness, he bent over him, panting for breath.

'Who killed Sadiq Sheikh?' he rasped.

Shehzad looked at Kabir's sweaty, bloody face. He began to laugh. Kabir punched him.

'Who sold my country out?'

Shehzad's laugh grew louder and more maniacal. Kabir smashed his head against the floor.

'What did Baradar mean when he said that?'

Shehzad continued grinning lamely. Kabir was convulsing with anger. He shot a glance towards the door and dragged Shehzad to the edge. They looked at the distant ground below. Hillocks with weathered rocks scattered all around, dirt tracks, some run-down buildings . . . *Houses of terror.*

'I am going to ask you this one last time,' Kabir growled. 'Who sold us out? Who killed Sadiq Sheikh?'

Shehzad looked around, his eyes bloodshot. His lips trembling but still smiling.

'My dead body has a better chance of telling you.'

'So be it.'

Shehzad closed his eyes, ready to be kicked out of the chopper. But it didn't happen. Instead, he felt his wrists being tied together. Kabir had ripped out the seat belt and was using it as handcuffs.

'W-what are you doing?'

Kabir pulled Shehzad back inside and closed the door.

'Keeping a promise.'

He pushed him on to another seat and used its seat belt to tie him in place. He raised the bloody machete and slashed at the ligament below his kneecap. Shehzad yelped in pain.

'Not like you can run away from a flying copter.' Kabir shrugged. 'But I'm a sadist just like you. In our profession, we learn to be one.'

He turned around and walked to the cockpit and found a cellphone. He picked it up and walked back towards Shehzad. He squinted at it and dialled a number. Shehzad looked on, shivering with pain, wondering if his body would go into shock because of the loss of blood. Kabir, however, who was bleeding profusely from the back himself, seemed composed since he was now in control.

'Salaam, Bugti Sahab,' Kabir said. 'Have I told you the tale of *Macbeth*? In a nutshell, he was this guy who killed his king and a lot of other guys, just to be in power. But it didn't quite go according to plan. His head ended up on a platter. Well, I happen to have someone else whose quest for power went awfully wrong. In fact, he's going to be at your place, all trussed up. You can decide how you want to deal with him yourself.'

Kabir smiled and winked at Shehzad. Shehzad's mouth was agape, lines of bloodied saliva were trickling down.

'I think a six-foot metal casket should be just fine. What? No? It's just five-foot long? It's okay, I don't think he'll mind.'

The bewilderment overshadowed Shehzad's pain. He writhed in agony, strapped to his seat.

'Oh, one more thing. I'll be landing soon in a helicopter. *Khuda hafiz*.'

20

12 September 2014
Mastung, Balochistan

Around a hundred Balochi militants had moved away to the periphery of the training ground as they saw the chopper approach. Along with them stood Isha and Nihar. Veer was with the Indian prisoners at Nabil Bugti's residence, a short distance away. The prisoners were having their wounds treated by the Balochi women on Bugti's instructions. Veer was having his leg patched up by Irfan Baloch Khan, who had calculatedly taken the shot to prevent him from walking into the Taliban stronghold. The bullet had grazed Veer's calf muscle, after which he had been overpowered and dragged back to safety. He scowled at the smiling Baloch Khan.

The helicopter landed roughly, bouncing a couple of times before coming to a halt. Kabir unlatched the door and staggered out. There was a moment of silence as the militants looked at his bloodied state. Nabil Bugti jogged up to support him as he led him to Isha and Nihar. Kabir's shirt was tattered and crimson. Nabil looked at his men, smiled and raised his hand as a signal. His men on the mountain responded by firing their RPGs into the air to welcome Kabir back.

'How many men did you lose?' Kabir asked Bugti softly, struggling to speak.

'Ten at the most,' Bugti replied, directing them to the car. 'But you need not worry about them. They're warriors who were trained to die. Your friends and you should go back to my place and get patched up quickly. After that, you can come back here.'

'Baradar's dead,' Kabir told Bugti. 'Shehzad is in the chopper.'

Bugti's nose flared. His pink face grew red with fury at the mention of Shehzad. He helped Kabir into the car and then turned and walked away. Nihar took the wheel, and Isha sat beside Kabir, helping him lie down, resting his head in her lap.

'You're losing a lot of blood,' she said.

'No shit,' Kabir murmured.

'I noticed you got a new haircut.' She smiled as Nihar pulled out of the premises.

'Yeah,' Kabir replied meekly. 'Now I've got a crazy hairdo like the kids at my college. Maybe it'll help me fit in. It's funny, though. I've got a slash across my back, a few cuts on my cheek, and you still notice that clump of chopped hair?'

Nihar shared in their laughter as he guided the car down the hill.

Nihar asked, 'How do we get out of here?'

'The way we came in,' Kabir said. 'Ask Joshi to organize a flight for us at Chabahar, Iran.'

'It'll be a task to drive back into Iran.'

'Who's gonna drive back into Iran? That's what we've got the chopper for,' Kabir said.

Within the next ten minutes, they were at Bugti's residence. Kabir's back didn't allow him to stand any more. His shoulders were throbbing with the strain they had been put through—hanging off the side of the helicopter. He crumbled to the ground. Isha and Nihar supported him back to his feet as they led him into Bugti's house. Irfan Baloch Khan rushed to help him. They took him to the room where the rescued prisoners and Veer lay. The prisoners were asleep. Veer was sitting on the mattress, frowning and with his arms crossed.

'Omar got away,' was the first thing he told Kabir. He didn't acknowledge Kabir's state or ask him how he was.

'I'm sure you tried your best,' Kabir said as Khan ripped open his shirt. Isha brought disinfectant and cotton out of her toolkit, and poured it over his wound. Kabir writhed in pain as he felt the liquid burn his broken skin.

Veer went on to narrate what had happened. Kabir, though still in pain, turned to Baloch Khan and said, 'Thank you, you did the right thing.'

Khan nodded and went out to bring Kabir a fresh change of clothes. Isha ran some water over Kabir's grimy face, getting all the dried blood out of his hair. Kabir was breathing heavily. The cut was burning and his muscles were sore. He was having great difficulty moving his right arm in particular. Nihar sat down beside him.

'I got my hands on a bullet-riddled laptop,' Nihar said. 'It might be a long shot, but maybe I could recover something useful from it.'

'Check my pockets,' Kabir said. 'I have Shehzad's phone in there. That may be useful as well.'

Kabir held off telling them one thing, though. The thing that irked him the most. *Baradar's last words . . . it may as well be of no importance . . .*

Irfan Baloch Khan tossed a fresh set of clothes to Kabir. Isha and Nihar stood up. Veer stood up swiftly as well. If there was pain in his calf, he didn't show it.

'Now let's get ready to leave. We cannot afford to miss the show.'

~

The local Balochis had gathered around silently. The militants had brought along their families to witness what was about to happen. It was their moment of sweet redemption. For years, the Balochis had been the oppressed ones. Today, however, they might just be one up. It was understood that this wasn't going to change anything for them drastically. But they knew that there was nothing much that they could have done other than staging their little uprisings from time to time, which would only be subsequently crushed mercilessly. Today, they were going to make a statement in a way they had not been able to do before. Today, the BLA was going to hit the ISI and the Pakistani government where it hurt.

Two men dragged a tied-up body along the rocky ground. The face was covered with a jute bag, but they knew who it was. Some knew more than the others, but they knew enough to be vindictive enough to witness what they were about to. Nabil Bugti stepped out of a car, with four others behind him. Not everyone realized who the four were, but again, they knew enough to make them feel thankful. Bugti's nephew came running up and embraced him. Bugti rested his hand on his nephew's shoulder and then cleared his throat to help him speak loudly to his people.

'Salaam aleikum, my brothers and sisters,' Bugti began. There was a tinge of excitement in his voice and his eyes gleamed. 'Today we mark an important day in Balochi history.'

The crowd looked at Bugti, then at the man who lay at his feet, and then at Bugti again.

'For years, we have been the oppressed. And the Pakistanis have been solely responsible for this. Our lands have been stolen, our minerals and resources have been snatched away, our men have been killed, our women molested and our children's lives snuffed out. And this has gone on for years and, unfortunately, will carry on happening, as sad as that truth may be. But we have stayed silent too long. My brave father, Akbar Bugti, was killed treacherously by the same men who tried to buy his trust. Warriors of the Marri tribe and the Bugti tribe have been ruthlessly torn to shreds by the ISI and the Pakistani Army.'

Bugti stepped closer to Shehzad.

'And the man who played a huge role in doing all this in the recent past . . . lies here at my feet. He has been responsible for the death of my father, my brother and many of my men—each and every one of whom was a true Balochi, with nothing but love for his motherland. My father, as you all know, was assassinated in the mountains, and what remained of his body was locked up in a metal crate and sent back to us, so that we could not even honour him with a dignified burial. But look at this sweet turn of events. Today, that murderer's fate lies in my hands.'

Bugti held a key in his raised hand. He beckoned to one of his men. The man dragged a medium-sized metal crate along the ground. Bugti leaned over and whispered something in his nephew's ear. The boy nodded promptly and took a few wary steps towards the tied-up man. He bent over and pulled the jute bag off Shehzad's face.

Shehzad's eyes were half open. His mouth was caked with dried blood. He looked confusedly at the young boy as if it were all a dream. He squeezed his eyes shut . . . The silence around him was unearthly. He couldn't figure out if he was in a quiet place, or if it was all happening in his head. He opened his eyes again, slowly, and blinked them back shut. He saw the distant orange sunset . . . A whole lot of people . . . mountains . . . and a man pulling a metal crate towards him . . . A *metal* crate . . .

'Do you think we should have another crack at him? Maybe we can get something about Sadiq's killer?' Nihar whispered to Kabir.

'He'd talk if he knew there was a chance out of this. And even then, it would all be a lie. That's what I would've done if I were in his place.'

Veer rested against the car, smoking and looking at the scene with a hint of interest.

'Thanks to these men,' Bugti said, pointing towards Kabir and his team, 'I can finally quench my thirst for revenge. And because of them, I will do to Tanveer Shehzad what he did to my father.'

Bugti walked over the crate and opened it. It made a creaking sound.

'But there is a small change,' Bugti said, pinching two fingers together on his raised hand. 'My nephew, Azaan, will elaborate.'

'Chachu is going to lock this man alive in the crate. And then I will go with him to the top of that mountain and throw away the key.'

Shehzad shook violently. Fear was beginning to get to him. He didn't mind death at all. But he had always pictured himself dying a quick one. A bullet to the head, perhaps. But this was going to be quite the opposite. He mustered up enough strength to turn and face Nabil's bloodshot eyes.

'Kill me now, Bugti.'

Bugti's ferocious, unforgiving eyes showed that he could've ripped Shehzad's heart out of his ribcage with his bare hands. But he remained silent and swallowed his anger. He caught a handful of Shehzad's hair and lifted him up. He clenched his large, clammy hand into a fist and punched Shehzad in the face. He lifted him off his feet and thrust him into the crate. Shehzad's entire body didn't fit, so Bugti forcefully turned and twisted Shehzad's legs until he was all boxed in. Shehzad rattled against the walls of the crate as Bugti slammed it shut. He took the key and locked the violently shaking box. Bugti himself was trembling with an uncontrollable rage. He held the key up to show his men, who were still uncharacteristically silent, and then dropped it into his nephew's hand. The boy held it indecisively for a few seconds, looked at the box and then turned and began to run towards the hill.

That evening, the Director-General of the ISI, Azhar-ul-Islam Tayyab, had been busy attending several phone calls at the same time, trying to figure out what had happened in Balochistan. Omar was safe, luckily. But he hadn't yet received a proper debrief from his main man on the spot, Tanveer Shehzad. He was about to light a cigarette as he swivelled around in his chair impatiently, staring at the portrait of Mohammad Ali Jinnah on his office wall. There was an urgent knock at the door. The man from his front desk stormed in and placed a crumpled envelope on his desk. Tayyab opened it quickly and pulled out a folded note.

Tanveer Shehzad's body lies in this coffin. Inshallah, his soul will find its way to the pits of hell.

Tayyab dropped the letter and pulled out a fresh, glossy photograph from the envelope. He let it drop to the floor as he rubbed the bridge of his nose. He looked at the picture of the lifeless metal crate again.

~

12 September 2014
Indira Gandhi International Airport, New Delhi

They should be here any moment now. By the look of things, the operation went all right. The news describes it as a little skirmish between the Pakistanis and the Balochis. There will be a lot of questions thrown at me very soon. They'll ask me about our involvement, and I'll have just one thing to say. If I say anything at all, it'll be about 'non-state actors'. Isn't that what they had said after 26/11? He wished he could claim credit for this act of daredevilry on his team's part, but as is the norm with all covert operations, victories are celebrated silently.

Arun Joshi had his arms crossed as he glanced at the clock. It was close to midnight. He was waiting for Kabir and his team to get back. The last he had spoken with them, they had been boarding the flight back from Chabahar.

They should be here any minute . . . Should I tell Kabir? Or has he figured out enough himself? I could have captured that snake that moment and grilled him thoroughly . . . But that would've definitely rubbed Kabir the wrong way. I may not know Shakespeare that well, but who's not a fan of poetic justice? Kabir will kill him on his own. Let the son of a bitch die.

There was a quick rattle at the door. A guard stuck his head in.

'Sir, they are about to land.'

Joshi got up gracefully and put on his coat. He walked out of the door and towards the runway. Through the glass wall he saw the plane landing smoothly. He walked outside into the chilly night, watching the door of the plane open. Isha was the first to step out, followed by Nihar. They walked down the short metal staircase and turned around to wait for Veer and Kabir. Veer, who was limping a little himself, helped Kabir out of the aircraft by letting him rest his arm on his shoulder.

Joshi looked at all of them, allowing himself a small smile. *It's just been a few days, but they look much older than their usual selves. He looked at Veer in particular. The man had become a shadow of himself—if one looks at the file pictures we have of him on record.*

Veer looked back at Joshi and nodded. He breathed in deeply and looked up at the sky. *Looks just the same as it did there. Then why does everything feel so . . . different?* He shut his eyes. *Let it sink in . . . You're back where you belong.* He opened his eyes and they fell on the Indian tricolour fluttering wildly from the side of a parapet.

Joshi strode up to them and shook hands with Isha and Nihar. His gaze moved on to Veer and Kabir. He noticed that Veer's homecoming had moistened the corners of his eyes.

'It's good to have you back, Veer.'

'Thank you, sir.'

Joshi looked at Kabir's gaunt face.

'Before we exchange pleasantries,' Kabir said, 'the prisoners are still in the plane, too drained to move. Send in the medics to get them out.'

'Good job, Kabir.'

Kabir glanced sideways at his team.

'It would've been impossible without them.'

Joshi patted Kabir on the back. 'I have something important to discuss. We will have a debriefing session soon.'

Kabir groaned.

'Trust me, it cannot wait.'

'We can do it next week.' Kabir sighed. 'I need some rest. I'm an old man now.'

'The day after tomorrow, then,' Joshi said with finality. 'I have a lot on my plate. There is unrest in Ladakh. Chinese troops have breached the Line of Actual Control. There is a major face-off between us and them in Chumar. The Chinese President is coming down to Ahmedabad soon to meet our prime minister and sort out certain issues.'

'If you insist,' Kabir said resignedly.

'Sir,' Nihar said, 'we have managed to lay our hands on something extremely useful. Kabir got hold of Shehzad's phone, and I managed to get—what I think may be—Omar's laptop. It's damaged, but I may be able to recover some data.'

'That's great. Get on it ASAP.'

'I'm going back to my wife and son, sir. First things first. If I stay away any longer, she'll be a threat to national security.'

Everyone laughed as they entered the air-conditioned airport building. Isha turned to Kabir. He looked back at her, his gaze softening.

'I wonder if you saw the obvious reference to Shakespeare today?'

'No.' Kabir shrugged.

'It took us twelve days in Balochistan. And we're back home on the twelfth night. *The twelfth night*, get it?' she said playfully.

Kabir smiled, letting the lame joke pass.

In peace there's nothing so becomes a man
As modest stillness and humility
But when the blast of war blows in our ears
Then imitate the action of the tiger . . .

PART III

The Crack of Doom

21

14 September 2014
RAW HQ, New Delhi

'Bro, there's a lady outside waiting to talk to you.'

Ivan had broken Nihar's concentration. It was eight in the evening. Nihar had been fixed to his chair in the dim control-room since the past few hours. He had made many attempts to recover every bit of data he could from the damaged laptop. He had failed initially, but had managed to find a way through by extracting solely the hard disk, opening it up and examining it further. He decided not to do it in a hurry, lest he lose something vital. He had utilized all the software at his disposal, but the procedure was painstakingly long. He had searched thoroughly for any viruses, just to be doubly sure. Once he realized that he hadn't found any threatening malware, he decided to initiate the recovery program. The process had taken up a chunk of his time and wasn't even halfway towards completion.

'Lady?' he asked, sounding disoriented.

'Her name's Isha. She's quite . . .'

'Pretty? I know,' said Nihar, completing Ivan's sentence. 'Call her in.'

'I was going to say "impatient", but you decided to fill in the blank. Good to know, I wonder what your wife will think though!' Ivan sniggered.

'Send her in and get back to cracking the phone I gave you,' Nihar said with an embarrassed smile.

Ivan laughed and called Isha in. She was elegantly dressed in a black shirt and black trousers. She pulled up a chair and sat down beside Nihar. Ivan tried hard to catch Nihar's attention, to pull a face or make an inappropriate gesture. Nihar saw this from the corner of his eye and ignored him. *Gosh, how I've missed my little control room and its little eccentricities.*

'Any progress?'

'Just a few documents here and there,' Nihar said. 'I'm afraid of opening them now, in case it interferes with the backup.'

'How long will that take?'

'I've been at it since morning,' Nihar said. 'Might take a couple of hours. Maybe more.'

'What about Shehzad's phone?'

'It's password-protected. Plus it has additional software which the ISI seems to have installed on the Android device, which could wipe out the data on the phone if you get the password wrong more than five times. Ivan's working on it. There's a special software to jailbreak such phones.'

Ivan swivelled around in his chair and held the phone up. It was attached to a cable that led to a device, which in turn was connected to a laptop.

'So far, I've managed to back up a little bit of the data from the phone,' Ivan said. He clicked on a document that had links to four websites. 'Looks like your spymaster

Shehzad was fond of Bollywood films. His browsing history shows that he was looking for illegal torrent links.'

'He had these on the phone?'

'Yeah,' Ivan said, clicking away on his computer. 'Let's open them up with the browser.'

There were five links in all, and all of them opened on separate pages.

'Ha! So he wants to watch *Life in a Metro*,' Ivan said, looking at the poster of the film. He clicked on another link. This time the poster of the film *Murder* popped up, and with it was a huge sequence of numbers in a document. Once he clicked on the document, under a random sequence of numbers, there was another link to download a document.

'That looks like another file,' Isha said, rolling her chair towards the computer. 'Click on it.'

'It could be a virus,' Ivan warned her. 'But what the hell . . . I have a backup of the data.'

The file downloaded. Another random sequence of numbers opened up. Nihar squinted at the screen. *ND28617720.*

'Open the other links,' Nihar said. 'We're on to something. This is a smart way to share information. Since most people around the world are busy downloading movies or music from torrent sites, you can slip in a document totally unnoticed along with a film.'

Another link opened up. It had an image from the Michael Jackson album *Bad*, released back in 1989.

'Well, I'd never imagine a Paki spy moonwalking,' Isha said. 'Scroll down . . .'

Ivan downloaded the file. Within minutes, the entire music album was on the computer. He skimmed through each song to see if it was another audio file disguised as music. It wasn't.

'Well, at least he had good taste in music. There's another image here, probably of the cover of the album.'

He clicked on it and up cropped an image of a line going straight and taking a right. There was a red dot on the line before it turned to the right. They looked at each other and shrugged.

'That has to be something,' Nihar said. 'Download all the films. Maybe there's some encoded data on the video. Maybe those numbers above are the durations at which the message will be revealed. Or maybe there's something that tells us what this line is.'

'Well, maybe this is just Shehzad's torrent wish-list. We are barking up the wrong tree.'

'Do as I say, Ivan. Enough of your fucking around.'

Isha raised an eyebrow at Nihar. Ivan didn't seem too perturbed.

'Well, it'll take ten–fifteen minutes to download the films,' he said, lighting up a cigarette.

Nihar walked back and slid into his chair. Isha followed suit. 'You done with your debriefing?'

'I was the first to go,' Nihar replied. 'What about you?'

'Joshi's busy right now,' Isha said.

'Oh yeah,' Nihar said. 'He's expecting Kabir here. They'll be discussing something really important, apparently. Maybe it's something on Sadiq's killer.'

Isha nodded thoughtfully. Nihar asked her if she'd like some coffee. She said she would, and they walked down to the end of the corridor and got themselves a cup each. Nihar got one for Ivan as well. They walked back into the control room and Nihar placed Ivan's cup in front of him.

'Thanks, man.' Ivan smiled. 'The movies have downloaded. There are five in all. And each one of them has an attachment with a random line.'

He opened the photos and scratched his shaven pate. Isha leaned forward and looked at them. Then he dragged the cursor to the video itself and clicked.

'Play them,' Isha said. 'Note down any text you see that has been added externally.'

The cult film *Enter the Dragon* began to play. The first thing to pop up in the movie, right under the credits, was this sentence:

Torrent uploaded and seeded by AngeliqueX123

'That's French for "Angelica",' Ivan said quickly. He added, 'Let me check the other video.'

The Hindi movie *Murder* played, and in very tiny font they noted the words on the top-right corner of the screen:

hooray

'That term is synonymous with "yahoo",' said Ivan instantly. 'They're probably using a Yahoo email address! AngeliqueX123 must be their username! We need the password!'

Nihar and Isha frowned at each other. Ivan held his breath as he opened all the images they had obtained. They were beginning to enjoy the puzzle, but feared, slightly, what they'd end up finding. Ivan jumped up hurriedly and pulled out three loose A4 sheets from his printer. He kept one for himself and handed one each to Nihar and Isha. He printed the random lines and separated them out.

'Write down all the words we just saw,' he said. 'And everything they could possibly mean. Clearly, there's some code. And these lines definitely have something to do with it.'

'Maybe we'll get a better idea if there's a connection between the data from the laptop and this,' Nihar said. 'Let's just wait it out.'

Ivan ignored him and started scribbling things on his sheet of paper. Isha chewed the end of her pen thoughtfully. Nihar sipped his coffee, trying to join the dots in his head.

~

One hour later

The atmosphere in Arun Joshi's cabin was tense. Joshi examined Kabir. The last time they had met in his office, before Kabir embarked on the mission, he had looked rather different. But today, even though he was less scruffy, Kabir looked exhausted. He had shaved off his beard to expose his pale sunken cheeks, and had chopped off his hair to match the side that Baradar's machete had clipped off. He smelled heavily of muscle-relaxing balm. He had suffered a muscle tear in his lower back, a severe sprain in his right shoulder, and inflammation in his right elbow and biceps, which had forced him to put his arm in a sling. There were several bandages covering the cuts. With his free hand he lifted his cup of black coffee and sipped it, thoughtfully chewing on what Arun Joshi had just told him.

'So where is he now?'

Joshi told him.

'How did he get there?'

'We know for a fact that the ISI has played a role in getting him out of the country.'

'Ridiculous!' spat Kabir. 'You guys didn't do anything about it?'

Joshi smiled. He clasped his hands together, leaned forward and spoke. 'I let him go, Kabir. He has always been under constant surveillance. I could've picked him up any time I wanted.'

'So you let him live . . . for me?' Kabir raised his arched eyebrows.

Joshi shrugged and nodded. 'I'd like to think you've earned it.'

'Thank you. I'm sure you may have had the urge to pick him up and adhere to the law, which would've taken an eternity to take its course.'

'Can't say it didn't cross my mind,' Joshi said. 'So will you go?'

'It has to be done,' Kabir said firmly. 'And I have to do it. For Sadiq. And for myself.'

He remembered his favourite line from *Hamlet*. *Revenge should have no bounds.*

'Good,' Joshi said with an air of finality. 'I'll have it fixed, then.'

Kabir shifted in his chair uneasily and stood up slowly. Joshi could tell he was having some trouble moving.

'You want to wait before I organize your trip?'

'No,' Kabir replied. 'I don't want that bastard to live any longer, now that it's under my control.'

He walked sluggishly towards the toilet next to Joshi's cabin. He went inside and closed the door behind him. *Nobody would've dared to enter that loo without asking me first.*

Kabir locked the door and switched on the light. He looked at his haggard reflection in the mirror. His eyes were bloodshot, and open only because of the caffeine. He looked at his hairline and noticed it was greyer than when he had left for Balochistan. His jaw was locked in a cruel grimace, and his lips were thin and cold. He shut his eyes and tried to remember what he had looked like twenty years ago. His hand slipped into his pocket. He pulled out a container with three vials and some cotton. From the other pocket, he pulled out an injection. *Another dose won't hurt. You need it more than anyone else in the world.*

He quickly rubbed some solution over the veins near his elbow. He pulled the liquid out of the vial and into the syringe. He pushed the liquid into his bloodstream through the needle. He closed his eyes, leaned against the wall and breathed in deeply. His mind blanked out momentarily. Then he heard a knock outside. He realized it wasn't coming from the bathroom door. *Someone had come to see Joshi . . .*

He opened his eyes swiftly, leaned into the washbasin and splashed water wildly on to his face. He ran a hand through his scruffy hair and shot one final look at himself. He pulled the flush on the commode, so that Joshi would think he had used it. And then he stepped out.

It was Isha and Nihar. Both looked at him as if they didn't know him. It took them a while to place him. Without the long hair and the beard, Kabir was unrecognizable. On seeing them a genuine smile appeared on his face. They smiled back. He looked at Isha.

'How are you?'

'Not too bad,' she said, noticing him. 'Better than you anyway.'

Kabir smiled, shook hands with Nihar and took his seat. Joshi was looking at Nihar's iPad thoughtfully. Isha examined Kabir's soulless eyes above his well-defined cheekbones, trying to replace the image she had of him in her mind. *There's something dangerously alluring about him. He looks like a man who needs company. But then again, he is a man who is better off alone. Nothing gets in his way. And he wants nothing to get in his way.*

'This is serious.'

Joshi slid the iPad towards Kabir. Kabir looked at the various words. Nihar went on to explain how Isha, Ivan and him had managed to procure the data that had led to this deduction.

'We found various coloured lines from the different links,' Nihar explained. 'There were five in all. We superimposed them all, and this is what we got. It's a map!'

Nihar continued, 'The coordinates in New Delhi make the password for the email address AngeliqueX123@yahoo. com. This is the single email address used by the mujahideen to communicate amongst themselves. So what they do is they set up one ID and share the password. And then they save a message as a "draft". After everyone has read it and replied to it in the "draft" itself, the message is deleted. This is an easy way to avoid detection. One of the mails we found, and it was saved earlier today, had just one word: "Tomorrow".'

Kabir swallowed, his Adam's apple bobbing up and down. He shot quick glances at Isha, Nihar and Joshi. He was beginning to go numb. *Is it the injection or is it the apprehension?*

'Go on,' he said in a gruff voice, swiping at the iPad.

'It's a fairly simple message,' Nihar continued. 'One of the movies we downloaded is called *Murder*. The other is *Life in a Metro*. Say them together.'

'Murder life in a metro,' Isha said softly. 'Tomorrow!'

They knew instantly what this could mean. And their first reaction was one of denial. *Another 26/11!* There was a pregnant pause. Kabir lifted the iPad again and glanced at it. It confirmed his fears. The red dot on the bottom-right line was where the attack was scheduled to happen.

Joshi broke the silence. 'According to Nihar, all we have for now is this. Once he recovers the data from Omar's laptop, we might just find out more.'

Isha's eyes were on Kabir, as if he was the one with a solution.

'I'll take charge of the security around the metro with the red dot. It's the Nehru Place Metro Station, if I'm not mistaken. One of the most crowded stations,' Kabir said thoughtfully. 'Security in and around every other station must be beefed up, too.'

'Thanks, Kabir, but we'll take it from here. You don't need to be a part of this. You've done enough already,' Joshi said dismissively as he got up from his chair.

'Did I hear you correctly, Mr Joshi?'

'Yes, Kabir.'

Kabir's eyes narrowed, his face grew red. He stood up and blocked Joshi's way.

'Look at yourself,' Joshi said. 'You're not even in a state to stand.'

'I was in no state to go to Balochistan either. There wasn't an iota of concern about my welfare then. And I believe my team and I have done an exceptional job of pulling off a mission as tough as that.'

'Yes,' Joshi replied. 'And I applaud you and your team for that, Kabir. I do. This is something I can get my other agents to handle. And, frankly, a man with his hand in a sling, a rebellious attitude and a penchant for recklessness cannot be appointed for a job as crucial as this. The reason you were sent to Balochistan is the same reason you cannot be sent to the metro station: you flirt with danger!'

Kabir took a step closer to Joshi.

'I have never been reckless unless the situation demanded it,' he said, tightening his jaw. 'And I'm afraid the situation is beginning to demand it.'

'Is that a threat, Mr Anand?'

'It's a polite request. You've made me a part of this, and I will see it through.'

Isha and Nihar threw each other nervous sidelong glances. Isha realized she needed to stop this from getting out of hand.

'Sir, can Kabir be a part of the team? Don't isolate him at this crucial stage!'

Joshi took a deep breath and huffed. He held Kabir's gaze and then nodded.

'You will be with Nihar in the control room throughout,' he said, and walked away to alert the other agencies about the threat. Kabir's temples throbbed with the sheer thought of the imminent emergency as he saw the map of the Nehru Place Metro Station again. *There was very little time left.*

22

15 September 2014
Nehru Place Metro Station, New Delhi

Nehru Place is a large business and commercial centre situated in South Delhi. It was but natural that the Nehru Place Metro Station, one of the most sophisticated in Delhi, was going to be crowded with commuters at eight in the evening. The younger lot, who had managed to make their way into multinational companies, but weren't in positions high enough to be chauffeured around in their own sedans, looked grimly similar, ticking mechanically to their clocks. Their ties were loosened, their first two buttons undone and their laptop cases hung limply by their sides, as they entered the metro that was praised for being as regular as its international counterparts. They greeted each other politely and discussed their work superficially, trying to make themselves sound important, all the while looking at the indicator for the next train's arrival.

'There are a lot more cops around here than usual,' one such youth muttered to another. Another young man nodded in agreement, sipping at a pricey cappuccino from the Starbucks nearby.

'Wonder what that is all about,' he said, slurping his coffee, a tinge of genuine concern in his voice. 'Hope everything's okay.'

Everything, as it turned out, was not okay. Kabir and Nihar had spent the entire day in the control room. Nihar chatted with the technicians who controlled the automatic trains. He did a great job of playing mediator between the various security agencies they employed. Kabir kept to himself, keeping an eye on the proceedings from a chair in the corner of the room. He was at his introspective best. He thought about everything that had happened in the recent past. It passed by in a blur. He had risked his life on more occasions than one in a span of twelve days. But the way things were moving, it looked like he would have to wait a while before he got back to his college with his copy of *Macbeth*. He had taken another dose from the vial. It definitely helped calm him down.

Veer and Isha were on the ground, alert as ever, dressed in their regular clothes. The cops had been told that they would be supervising matters as well, and their needs were to be catered to. Even though all the stations were being guarded and watched vigilantly, the focus was on the Nehru Place station. The red dot on the part of the line on the map that Ivan had found corresponded almost exactly to Nehru Place, and probably meant that it was the target. It was a large station, and Isha and Veer had split up to even things out. They were connected through discreet transmitter–receiver devices, routed via Nihar's laptop.

'Anything?' Isha asked.

'No,' Veer replied bluntly.

Isha didn't reply and continued to pace away. She began to get tired of the nothingness. She watched a group of five khaki-clad cops walking in through the entrance, chatting away. She was glad the security had been doubled. *The terrorists were probably spooked away*. She turned her back to the cops and began to walk towards a snack bar to get herself something to munch on, when she heard that dreaded, unmistakable sound. *A gunshot.*

Her hand involuntarily went to her hip, pushed behind her jacket and drew out her pistol. She turned to look and saw one of the policemen standing with a rifle over a dead man's body. The four cops behind him had split into two groups, cocked their guns and had begun to walk briskly. At first, she thought the cop had spotted a terrorist and done the job. But when the other policemen opened fire indiscriminately, the real horror of what was actually happening dawned on her. Bodies began to drop to the ground immediately. She rushed for cover. There was chaos. The terrorized commuters began to rush out towards the exit, screaming in panic. There was a near-stampede. The metro security rushed to the spot and helped the bewildered crowd out of the station with great difficulty.

'Veer, they are here, dressed in police uniforms!'

Kabir and Nihar stood up and listened to her voice.

'Lock the station down. Set up a perimeter outside,' Kabir instructed. 'Any trains that are coming in now need to be stopped. We can't let more people arrive on the scene!'

A technician replied, 'It's too late. One is just about to reach!'

'Then keep the doors locked,' Kabir said. 'Isha, get to cover. We are watching the CCTV footage. I'll direct you around. Veer, you stay put. One of them is coming towards you.'

Both nodded. Isha hid behind a wall, took aim and fired at the hostile cop. She missed. The cop turned, raised his rifle and shot at her. The bullets embedded themselves in the wall. The cop drew closer. Isha stuck her hand out and fired blindly.

'Don't fucking do that!' Kabir snarled in her earpiece. 'You might hit a civilian. Take the shot when I tell you to. He's ten steps away. On my count . . . Three . . . Two . . . One!'

Isha bent down and rolled over to her left. She took a clean shot, hitting the cop in the stomach. She fired again. The cop dropped down to the ground. She saw Veer at the opposite end, running swiftly to switch cover, firing at a couple of cops who had their eyes on him.

'Kabir, please do something about the real policemen. We are getting confused.'

Kabir looked at Nihar. He was breathing rapidly.

'Make an announcement! Call them up! No more cops should come in wearing their uniforms. Seal the perimeter. Alert all the stations now. Freeze every metro.'

'There is one train leaving Nehru Place right now,' Nihar pointed out, as the doors of the metro opened and the passengers rushed inside for cover.

'Let them all go inside,' Kabir said. 'Then send it to the next station. It's the safest bet. The civilians inside will survive.'

Veer still had his back against a narrow pillar. Two of the 'cops' split up and were coming towards him from both sides. If he killed one, the other was going to kill him. He decided to take the chance and go for the one on the left. *He's walking faster than the other. If I get him, I might still have time to kill the other one.* A furious spurt of gunshots followed. Veer heard two bodies drop to the ground. The real policemen had shot them dead. They had their uniform on inside out, and it was also unbuttoned to reveal a bulletproof vest. Veer came out of cover. They still had their guns pointed at him. They recognized him and lowered the gun. He gestured to them to walk away and evacuate anyone they could. He saw National Security Guard commandos rush in from the opposite side.

He held the transmitter up to his mouth and said, 'Kabir, how many more do you think there are in here?'

Kabir watched the CCTV footage from the control room. He noticed the policemen with the unbuttoned shirts from the grainy footage, his eyes cancelled out the few strewn dead bodies and, suddenly, in the sweep of his gaze he saw the cop who was channelling everyone into the metro. *He's wearing a buttoned shirt.*

'Veer! Isha!' Kabir shouted. 'The cop who is sending everyone into the train isn't a real one! Get to him now! I'm closing the doors! Don't let him get in!'

Veer and Isha looked at each other from the two ends of the station. He motioned her to stop and began to run towards the end where the cop was sending the last of the civilians inside. A few still jostled to get in. The cop pushed them aside and went in as soon as he saw the doors were about to close. Veer galloped furiously, yelling. He held up his pistol and fired at the glass windows of the train. It was beginning to gain speed. Veer managed to get a grip through the broken window and jumped up and inside the train. He fell to the floor with considerable force, but quickly and nimbly brought himself back to his feet. The wind swept inside as the train left the station. It soon started ascending slightly on to an elevated track. There were around twenty civilians in the train, Veer estimated from a cursory glance.

The gunman looked at him, momentarily taken aback, and then realized the only possible solution was to shoot the intruder to his little party. He cocked his AK-47 and aimed it at Veer, who was about a metre away from him. Between them was a puny man who was sweating profusely, too petrified to move an inch. Veer realized he was too far to attack the gunman. He acted on impulse and sent his boot into the back of the little man between them, who in turn stumbled ahead and sprawled over the gunman, throwing him off balance. The little man had completely lost his bearings and rolled on the floor. Veer saw his chance and ran head-on, ramming the gunman into a metal pole. The man pulled the trigger defensively and fired at the lights. A brief shower of sparks flew to the ground, causing the lights inside to fluctuate. Veer sent his knuckles crashing into the gunman's nose. He was about to deliver a fatal blow when he felt a blunt thud on his head.

Veer lost his vision momentarily and began to feel dizzy. There was another attacker in the train as well. The second man held the butt of the gun and slammed it against Veer's face again. Veer felt a tooth loosen. A gush of blood rushed out. The man was about to deliver a third blow, when Veer retaliated by kicking him on his knee. The man reeled backward a couple of times, against the inertia of the train. Veer rolled aside and pushed himself up. His vision was hazy. He heard the passengers yelling and pleading for mercy. He vaguely noticed the gunman pick up his weapon and get ready to fire. Veer charged at him, head-on, like an enraged bull. He shoved the man into the wall, pinned him against it and pummelled him in a fit of blind, brutal rage. The man fought back, but was no match for Veer's ferocity. Veer wrapped his right arm around the man's neck and crushed his windpipe, rendering him lifeless in an instant. Veer shot a final glance at him and saw an amulet hanging around his neck. He was about to rip it out, when he heard the shrill scream of a woman. He turned around to see that the other gunman had stood back up. Blood dripped from his disfigured nose and stained his khaki uniform. But then Veer saw something he didn't like. The man didn't have a gun on him. He had something much worse. He held a small switch. *A detonator.* Veer's gaze followed the wire connected to the switch. It went through the gap between two buttons. *A suicide vest.*

Veer's fierce eyes met the man's steady, glassy gaze. The wheels in his mind whirred, processing information and performing calculations. The man had just said his prayers. His thumb was about to come down and push the button. *A single click, and at least twenty people would die.* The train was speeding over a busy road. If there was a blast, a few compartments of the train could easily topple over the bridge on to the cars below. And there would be an explosion soon after. *The body count would rise. There is no alternative. I have to do it.*

As the man's fist tightened around the detonator, Veer ran towards him and speared him upwards, off his feet and through the gap in the window from which he had earlier muscled his way in. It wasn't a neat sight. The wind blew in through the broken glass. The direction the train was taking didn't help either. But straining every sinew in his body, Veer managed to grab the man and jump out. The bomb went off. There was an explosion in mid-air. To the onlookers and commuters on the street below, it would've looked like an extremely loud and flashy firework, a bit too close for comfort. People gathered to look as the train sped across. None of them, at first glance, would've been able to guess what it really was.

A flash of light. A deafening sound. A huge sacrifice.

23

17 September 2014
Islamabad, Pakistan

'Is there anything else that I should know of?' Rameez Nawaz, the incumbent Prime Minister of Pakistan, asked tersely. His steely gaze was met with an equally steady one from the Director General of the ISI, Azhar-ul-Islam Tayyab.

The atmosphere in Nawaz's cabin was tense. Both men were seated. The air conditioning was doing its job well enough, but there was a stifling silence for a few moments.

'I know nothing, Wazir-e-Azam,' Tayyab replied, his liver-spotted hands resting on the table.

He did a good job of remaining unfazed. He headed a highly efficient organization, which had the reputation of being one of the deadliest in the world. He had been instrumental in building the ISI to what he proudly thought of as a 'state within a state'. This wasn't the first time a prime minister had sat opposite him, questioning him about some of his lesser-known activities.

'Tayyab,' the prime minister growled as he wiped away beads of sweat from his thinning, henna-dyed-orange hairline. 'There are better ways to tackle a problem than play dumb.'

Tayyab simply shrugged.

'Wazir-e-Azam,' he said, leaning in, his voice intense, 'whatever it is you suspect me of you know very well you would've done the same.'

'No,' Nawaz replied. 'You have been reckless throughout your career.'

'I'm loyal to my country, Wazir-e-Azam. I do what I do for Pakistan alone.'

'This was our time to lie low, Tayyab. We fucking hid Osama. We are actively involved with al-Qaeda. You are covertly hiding Mullah Omar. That skirmish that broke out in Quetta could've brought hell down upon us, had Omar not escaped. I know you couldn't resist the urge to exact revenge for what they did in Balochistan. But this soon? I'm amazed at your capabilities, and disgusted at your insolence.'

It never was meant to be revenge for Balochistan. The plan was always in place, still is . . . Tayyab looked back at Nawaz, who had got off his chair and was pacing around the room.

'I still don't understand this conversation, Wazir-e-Azam.'

'Take a fucking hike!' The PM kicked his chair. 'The train that blew up? The gunmen in Delhi?'

Tayyab maintained a stony silence.

'If I had informed you about what was going to happen, would you have approved of it?'

'I wouldn't have let you do it right away,' Nawaz said. 'There is no love lost between us and India. But there's a way things are done.'

'If there's anyone who knows how things are done, Wazir-e-Azam, it's me.'

'Imagine, Tayyab, had one of them been caught, it would've been a Kasab-like situation all over again. He would surely have spilled the beans sooner or later. And this time, we would've been in deeper shit. India and America would've joined forces to wipe us off the map! Is that what you want for Pakistan, you son of a bitch?'

Tayyab remained quiet and looked down at his feet, trying to feign shame. The prime minister stood still, glaring at Tayyab. His clenched fists and knees shook violently.

'I could have you arrested for treason,' he said through gritted teeth. 'I could serve your head on a platter to the rest of the world!'

'That wouldn't be a good move,' Tayyab replied sardonically.

The prime minister fumed away. Tayyab got up and walked towards him.

'You could do that if you think I'm guilty of treason. But then, fighting an enemy isn't treason,' he continued. 'If the world fears Pakistan today, it is because of the ISI.'

'We could well be on the brink of war because of your short-sightedness,' Nawaz replied.

'And it's my job to ensure that it remains at just that.' Tayyab's voice dropped as he scratched his silver stubble. 'There are days I fear myself, Wazir-e-Azam. I make cruel decisions that are more often right than wrong. Since you brought Balochistan up, don't you think my operations there are justified? We are only taking our land back from some ill-mannered villagers . . .'

'I'm not talking about that. Balochistan is justified. What about India? I agree that there's no love lost between us. But these are fragile times and I would like to be kept in the loop before you take such a drastic step.'

Tayyab shrugged.

'It was a train blast. That's it. You have plausible deniability.'

The prime minister scoffed. *Plausible deniability.*

'I want you to tell me everything,' the prime minister said as he sat down. He gestured for Tayyab to begin.

'There is nothing to tell, sir.'

'We've been going around in circles for far too long,' said Nawaz, banging his fists on the table. 'You may enjoy taking innocent lives. But I don't. Especially if I'm going to lose my countrymen to some sort of retaliation!'

'You won't. I assure you.'

Tayyab's defiance was getting to Nawaz. He poured himself a glass of water, spilling some on his table, and chugged it down. He began to understand why Tayyab was always in people's bad books, from ex-PMs to various political executives. But at the same time all of them respected and admired Tayyab for the job he was doing. He got his hands dirty. And he enjoyed doing it.

'Tell me one thing, Tayyab.'

Rameez Nawaz's voice was artificially calm. Tayyab nodded fervently.

'Is there anything else I should know?'

'I don't get what you mean.'

'Anything else up your sleeve! Any future attacks you have masterminded along with the brainwashed militants you have trained!' snapped the prime minister.

'That sentence is heavily peppered with conjecture, Wazir-e-Azam.'

'You're pushing me to the limit, Tayyab.'

'Well,' Tayyab said stoically, 'there is nothing up my sleeve. And there are no future attacks that I have masterminded with my brainwashed militants.'

With that, he swivelled around and closed the door shut behind him. The prime minister breathed in deeply and buried his head in his hands. *Tayyab has lied through his teeth. Again.*

~

17 September 2014
RAW HQ, New Delhi

'I still can't believe he's gone,' Isha said solemnly.

'He had told me in confidence about his plans once he returned to India,' Nihar said in a low voice. 'Unfortunately, they weren't meant to be.'

'What do you mean?' Isha asked.

'He had plans to marry a girl before his stay in Afghanistan got extended. After Balochistan, he was going to go back to Mohali and meet her. If she wasn't married, he said he would walk up to her and coax her to take him back. If she was, he said he would never cross her path again. He wanted a shot at a normal life.'

The sides of Nihar's eyes were moist. Isha wore a grim expression. Just like the grieving families of the dead, they only mourned the person they had lost. That was the harsh reality. No matter how much one sympathizes for the others, one always tends to mourn what one has lost more. Veer Singh was one of the eighteen dead. He was reduced to a mere number for those who didn't know him. But for those in the train, he was a hero. He had jumped out, unflinchingly, in an attempt to save their lives, even if it had meant sacrificing his. And he had succeeded.

Kabir had his back to them as he looked out of the window on to the desolate streets. He did his best to never wear his emotions on his sleeve. He had never cried even when he had witnessed gruesome deaths of people he knew before. But they always did take a part of him away with them. *Like Vikramjit . . . Sadiq . . . And now, Veer . . .*

Cry woe, destruction, ruin and decay;
The worst is death, and death will have his day.

'We didn't know him for too long,' Nihar said, a lump forming in his throat. 'But he might've just been the best friend I've ever had. He makes me proud to be an Indian.'

Isha was reduced to tears, which she quickly wiped away with the edge of her shirt. She had been taught never to succumb to emotion when on the job—be it deep sorrow or uncontrollable rage—because it made you weak. It clouded your judgement. Kabir was still frozen in his posture. His free arm rested in his pocket, while the other hung in a sling. He hadn't slept in days.

'We will mourn Veer when circumstances allow us to,' he said finally, his face still turned. 'Just as we will mourn every other innocent life that was lost yesterday and any time before that. But more importantly, we have screwed up. We knew they were coming. And we couldn't stop it.'

He banged his fist on the window in disgust. Nihar nodded as he lifted his iPad and swiped at it. Isha crossed her hands and looked at him. It was well past midnight. The city was hauntingly silent. None of them had had adequate rest since they had got back from Balochistan. If anything, they had rested more there.

'Where's Mr Joshi?'

'He's gone for a meeting with the senior officials of other agencies. NSA, IB, DIA, you name it . . .' Nihar said. 'They're deciding their next move. Besides, the PM doesn't want the attack to get in the way of the meeting in Ahmedabad.'

'Do you think Mr Joshi will tell them about my involvement?' Kabir asked.

'No,' Nihar replied. 'Not unless he has reason to. In fact, he's keeping his cards close to his chest.'

'And no terrorist group has taken responsibility yet, either,' Isha said.

Kabir walked back, pulled up a chair and sat beside them. He shot a quick glance at the newspaper that was lying on the coffee table. Entire pages were filled with reports about the incident. He diverted his gaze to the computers running a program in the background.

'Have you found anything else?'

Kabir had a nagging feeling that it wasn't over yet. Even though he desperately wished it was, he knew the ISI always had tricks up its sleeve. Nihar nodded as he passed his iPad to Kabir. A few images appeared. They were hand-drawn maps.

'Here's something else we found in their email drafts. Omar's laptop has crashed, but from what we could recover, we found similar images.'

'These are floor plans of some kind.' Kabir frowned. 'Did you figure out more?'

'Ivan managed to get these out a few hours ago,' Nihar said. 'He is at the Defence Intelligence Agency office right now, trying to pull out a match and revive the disk to get more data. They have advanced technical equipment there.'

Kabir scratched his chin. He felt his hands tremble, and clenched his fists to stop anyone else from noticing. He could feel the vial in his pocket beg to be injected into his bloodstream. He needed his fix again. *I need to stop before I go out of control . . . A few last hits . . .*

'Kabir, are you all right?' Isha asked.

'Of course,' he replied.

'You're sweating.'

'It's nothing,' Kabir said, getting up. He walked into the toilet, the door slamming behind him. Isha and Nihar shot each other confused looks.

'He's been through a lot.' Nihar shrugged. 'Just when he thought he had gotten out of it for good, circumstances thrust him back into the game. That must be affecting him.'

Isha nodded and was about to speak, when Nihar's phone rang. He picked it up quickly. It was Ivan. Isha looked at the washroom door. Kabir had left it ajar. *He's forgotten to lock it.*

She got up and walked slowly towards it. Meanwhile, Nihar had rushed to the computer and begun typing furiously. Ivan was explaining something to him on the other end of the phone. Isha peeked through the gap in the door. Kabir was leaning over the washbasin. The tap was running and he was splashing water on his face wildly, wetting his T-shirt in the bargain. Isha pushed the door open and looked at him. Kabir looked up, his eyes bloodshot. He was trembling violently.

'Get out, Isha!'

'You have to tell me what's wrong, Kabir!'

Kabir was silent. On his drenched face he wore a guilty look. Isha shut the door behind her.

'Tell me, Kabir. I won't tell a soul. What's the matter?'

'I don't know, Isha . . .' His voice was far away. 'It's this entire thing. And I have to stay strong and see it through to the end. I know how these people are. It's not over. It's never over.'

Isha took a step closer to him. Her eyes met his. She looked at them. *Fierce, cold, lonely and, for the first time . . . vulnerable.* And then her eyes slipped lower and she saw something on the ground. *An empty vial.*

'What is that?'

Kabir kicked the vial away. Isha turned and was about to pick it up, when Kabir grabbed her by the arm and drew her close. She looked at him unfazed.

Her voice was stern. 'What was that, Kabir?'

'Painkillers,' Kabir said. 'For my arm and back.'

'Why are you hiding them, then?'

Kabir was silent. He was still holding Isha tightly. She looked down at his arm and noticed the reddened skin around the tiny needle-punctures.

'I've been using them more than I have been instructed to,' Kabir said finally. Isha glared at him. 'Don't worry. I'll get done with them soon,' he said.

'Kabir, I am taking you to a doctor right away. This can prove to be fatal!'

She turned around and tried to free her arm. Kabir held it tight and pulled her back. She was inches away from his face.

'Isha, I can do it myself. I don't need a doctor.'

'That's not for you to decide.' Her voice softened. She could feel his breath against her face. Kabir's eyes were intense.

'I'll quit,' he whispered. 'I promise.'

She closed her eyes and tilted her head. Kabir drew her closer. She could feel his beard touch her face. His free arm held her by her waist. She could feel his breath against her forehead. Her pheromones soothed him. He ran his nose down the side of her neck. She closed her eyes as their lips met. They didn't know how long it lasted, but they drew apart because of a knock at the door. Kabir bent down and picked up the vial. Isha opened the door hastily. Nihar shot

them a questioning look. He wore a harassed expression.
Isha opened her mouth to explain.

'It's okay, I don't want to know.'

He lifted his iPad and pointed at the screen. It just had
the 'play' button.

'A downloadable link just dropped into the mailbox.
I traced it back to a source in Ahmedabad,' Nihar said
quickly. 'I clicked the link and it led me to this video. They
have come to know that we've found an entry into their
email account.'

'What's the video about?' Kabir asked, towelling his
face dry.

'It's a message,' Nihar said solemnly. 'From the al-
Qaeda leader, Ayman al-Zawahiri.'

24

18 September 2014
RAW HQ, New Delhi

A massacre of Muslims is being carried out these days by you, and most of the Muslim world is totally oblivious to it.

The footage was clear in terms of voice and video quality. The elderly man's droopy eyes looked right into the camera. He wore a skullcap and a clean white kurta. On his forehead was a dark spot, probably gained from the number of times he pressed it to a rock-hard floor during namaz. His neat, steel-rimmed spectacles rested halfway down the bridge of his nose. If he wasn't the man he was, he would probably come across as a harmless old man, popular among the children of his area for his eccentricity and storytelling. But this man was no ordinary storyteller. He was none other than Ayman al-Zawahiri, the chief of al-Qaeda. The man who had once been Osama bin Laden's trusted aide and was now his successor. *One of the most feared men in the world.*

A brown curtain behind him shimmered as he continued.

And on our part, my warriors and I have pledged to make a serious effort to bring an end to this wave of oppression on Muslims in Bangladesh, India, Myanmar and Sri Lanka, with everything in our capacity. As for our brothers and our people in Kashmir, Gujarat and Assam who are living under the dark shadow of Hindu occupation, I would like to say that the crimes that they have witnessed, and that are still taking place before their eyes, expose the extent of deception of the nationalist democratic way, which calls for their participation, side by side with the Hindus, in a system that brings together Hindus and Muslims. If they haven't already noticed, they should realize that this so-called 'democracy' brings Muslims and Hindus together only to present the Muslims as an easy target for the Hindus.

He swallowed and continued with gusto.

My respected Muslim brothers, in the face of adversity, we must firmly hold on to the creed of loyalty to the believers and disassociation from the kafirs! I will make sure that every kafir pays for the injustice that has been meted out to my fellowmen.

He raised his forefinger and steadied it towards the camera as his voice boomed on.

I would like to remind the oppressive and criminal government of India that every crime has a punishment. The new prime minister is our sworn enemy, but he better remember that the one who sows thorns never reaps flowers. My Amir, Mullah Mohammed Omar, my late brother, Osama bin Laden, and myself have always believed that the oppressed will get their rights back, even if does take some time. We have made our sacrifices and, inevitably, we will make some more. But understand one thing, the time has arrived! Prepare to repent. A tempest is about to shake you soon. The little incident in Delhi was just a prelude to the chaos. A mere taste of things to come. Get ready for the beginning of the endgame.

Zawahiri breathed in deeply, his face calculatedly calm. He was about to conclude.

Allah the Glorious has stated the truth, 'Those who do wrong will come to know by what a (great) reverse they will be overturned!' My fighters of al-Qaeda, all of you who have worked tediously for years to set up a base in your wretched country, India, are all set to prove Him right.

~

It was five in the morning. Kabir's face was morose as he sipped another cup of black coffee. He stood upright, behind Joshi, Nihar and Isha. He still smelled strongly of the muscle-relaxant balm. They had seen the entire video five times since it had been downloaded. For Kabir, watching the footage once was more than enough. Zawahiri's words were set in his mind. There was no cryptic element in the message. The man conveyed what he wanted plainly. What angered him more was the fact that al-Zawahiri, just like every other terrorist, had quoted Allah out of context. *No god has ever told his creations to kill one another.*

Isha broke the silence, directing a question to Joshi. 'So is he accepting responsibility for the metro incident?'

'In a roundabout way, yes,' Joshi replied. 'But that doesn't matter any more. What matters is what's about to happen. A threat like this cannot be taken lightly.'

'He's probably being hidden by the ISI in Pakistan itself. This statement has certainly not been issued from Iraq or Syria,' Nihar added. 'I won't be surprised if al-Zawahiri is firmly ensconced in some safe house not far from an army facility in the Gilgit–Baltistan area or some such godforsaken location.'

Kabir walked up slowly and pulled up a chair.

'He's probably enjoying Omar's hospitality in Balochistan, for all we know. The Quetta Shura, Haqqani Network and al-Qaeda are all, at the end of the day, headed by Omar with varying degrees of separation.' Kabir paused and looked at the frozen frame of al-Zawahiri's wrinkled face. 'They may not be directly associated, but they have pledged their allegiance to each other. It's one large mushroom of terror.'

'Pakistan is preparing itself for the withdrawal of US troops from Afghanistan, and part of the preparations are the way and means to ensure that India does not get the upper hand in Afghanistan,' Joshi said, adjusting his spectacles. 'They want the army to remain in control of the situation when it comes to dealing with India and Afghanistan. They will ensure this by keeping the Haqqanis and Quetta Shura untouched. On the Indian front, Lashkar-e-Taiba is no longer potent enough in the present international environment to be seen as encouraging Pakistan-sponsored terrorist organizations in India.'

'And by putting out this video, they have ensured that they have thrown in al-Qaeda for greater effect,' Nihar said. 'They are, after all, an organization feared worldwide.'

Kabir sighed. 'Now that we're done playing analyst, it's time we see the video for what it really is. They are a step ahead of us. They know we have broken into their email account. Zawahiri has personally threatened us. It's not something to be taken lightly.'

Kabir directed his gaze at Joshi. 'Sir, we must not waste a moment now. We don't have much time on our hands.'

Joshi nodded in understanding as he saw his phone buzzing with calls from the heads of various security agencies. He was in the midst of organizing the functions for the next three days. The President of the People's Republic of China was scheduled to fly down to Ahmedabad to meet the Indian prime minister the following afternoon. The agenda was to discuss and peacefully sort out the Sino-Indian border conflict that had broken out in Ladakh. The buzz was that they even planned to sign a few important deals. *As if I didn't have enough on my plate already.*

Kabir stood up. His eyebrows were stitched in a frown. Something had just hit him.

'Nihar, the video was uploaded from Ahmedabad, right?'

'Not uploaded,' Nihar said. 'It was routed through a server in Ahmedabad. They wiped out all traces of the account after the video was put up, so I can't track it back any further. It wouldn't have been easy to get more anyway, considering they merely dropped the link in the drafts.'

'And do you remember all the films that we had found on Shehzad's torrent list?'

'Yes,' Nihar continued. '*Murder, Life in a Metro, Enter the Dragon* . . .'

'Exactly,' Kabir said. 'I know this isn't a strong enough connection. It might be the stupidest of hunches ever. But maybe . . . just maybe, the last film had some cryptic yet simple message to it.'

'*Enter the Dragon?*'

'Yes. Tomorrow our PM is meeting the Chinese President. It could be nothing, but it could be something. Every other movie on that list added up to something. Except this one.'

Kabir turned to look at Joshi. They all wore a similar, grim expression. The same thought shot through their minds.

'Sir, I request you to keep me on this case,' Kabir said plainly. 'I want to be a part of tomorrow's security detailing. It might come to nothing, but the fact that the video links back to Ahmedabad is reason enough to believe something might just happen. And if the shit hits the fan again, we'll have only ourselves to blame.'

There was a brief pause. Joshi rubbed the bridge of his nose and closed his eyes. 'Don't make me regret it. Isha and Nihar will be with you, too.'

'You won't, sir. I promise I will stop this. Even if it's the last thing I ever do.'

~

18 September 2014
Ahmedabad, Gujarat

A tall man sat cross-legged on the reddish stone steps, watching the tranquil Kankaria Lake. He soaked in the calm—even though all he stood for was destruction. *This is it. Today I'm going to wrap up an important chapter in my life.* He had waited for the perfect opportunity for years. He was never afraid of death. He was only afraid that he would die before he had exacted his revenge. Revenge for his father. Revenge for his mother. Revenge for his Muslim brethren. There will be death. There will be a sea of innocent blood as well. But a *qurbaani*, a sacrifice, had to be made for the greater good. He closed his eyes and relived that day again—the day that had transformed him into the merciless man he had now become.

~

He remembered the picturesque landscape of Kashmir, his birthplace. He remembered the humble yet beautiful cottage in Srinagar. His father was a local Kashmiri. His mother was a Hindu lady who had converted to Islam after meeting his father. There had been no compulsion as such from his father himself. But his parents wouldn't accept a Hindu daughter-in-law. In the heart of a conflict-ridden Kashmir, this was a small problem, which was resolved soon enough.

Just like any other day his mother had helped him dress up in a woollen muffler and a monkey-cap. He wanted to go out and play. He liked collecting acorns from the oak trees nearby. Little did he know then that what was about to happen next was going to replace the acorn with a grenade—for the rest of his life.

As he stepped out through the back door, he saw three Indian soldiers hop out of their vehicle. Their cruel faces were still etched in the corridors of his memory. They pulled his father out of the house and threw him on the snow-covered gravel. His face was severely bruised. One of the soldiers dragged him through the snow, leaving behind the torturous trail of a man resisting them as they did so. They took him to the doorstep and knocked at the door. He saw his mother rush to open it. Had he been a little older, he would've probably warned her against it. But then, he was told by his father that the Indians were good men, that the soldiers were men of integrity. His father was one of the few pro-Indian ethnic Kashmiris—and ironically, he was the one who paid for it.

He watched through the window as they butchered his father in front of his eyes. They accused him of despicable things. His father was a simple man. He ran a grocery store. He was certainly not a terrorist. Not a bomb-maker, like they insisted. He was a simple Muslim. And that was his only fault. His mother had cried her lungs out. She was called names for being a Hindu and yet marrying this wretched Kashmiri.

They poured on her the scalding tea that simmered on the stove. They beat her as she bawled in frenzy. Ripped off her clothes. They took their time with her. One by one. Next to her dead husband. She fell unconscious. And then her life slipped out of her. He saw all of this from outside the house, shaking and trembling, but doing his best not to make a sound. And that day, seething with rage, he had made himself a promise. A promise that had led him to this juncture of life where he stood right now. He became everything his parents didn't want him to. But he did it for them. Maybe they would understand, watching him now from the world above.

~

The memories were as vivid as ever. The man looked down at the clear waterbody. A tear rolled down his cheek and fell off his pronounced jaw and on to the red steps below. He had risked his life every single day ever since, waiting for this day to come. He picked up his phone, opened an application that used the Internet instead of cellular networks. He dialled a number and called his mentor, whom he fondly called Chacha.

'Chacha . . . Kankaria Lake in fifteen minutes,' he said and closed the call. He looked at his phone and started to watch the al-Zawahiri video. In the fifteenth minute after the call, he felt a hand rest on his shoulder.

'How are you, Shiv?'

'Did I ever tell you why I picked that name for a cover ID on this mission?' The tall man's concentrated gaze was still directed at the water in the lake.

The mentor was slim, short and in his early sixties. He had a thin, wavy beard, no moustache, and an amiable look. Nobody would suspect him of even swatting a fly.

'No,' Chacha replied.

'He was the man who murdered my father. The man who raped my mother to death. Colonel Shiv Singh and his two cronies.'

'It's strange that you chose his name, then. Why would you do that?'

'It gives me purpose. The hatred gives me strength to do what I am about to.'

'So today's the day we have been working towards,' Chacha said. 'We have immense faith in you, beta.'

The tall man looked down at his shoes. His fingers were intertwined with each other.

'Is everything in place?' Chacha asked.

The tall man pointed to the lake. His mentor's eyes followed his forefinger. He saw a faint white streak coming towards him.

'And what about Tayyab Sahab? Any contact with him?'

'He's given the go-ahead,' Chacha replied. 'No complications there.'

The tall man stood up and walked down to the lake. He pulled his trouser-legs up to above his knees, removed his slippers and took a few steps into the lake. He stood in the same line as the trail of white light. He heard a slight buzz. In a few moments, the trail had completely died away and the buzzing had stopped. The man put his hand underwater and felt a large, smooth, streamlined metal object. He smiled to himself.

'Is it working?' the mentor asked him from behind.

'Like a charm.' The tall man smiled.

25

19 September 2014
Ahmedabad, Gujarat

'President Bocheng has just left the Sardar Vallabhbhai Patel Airport. He should be here within half an hour.'

It was two-thirty in the afternoon. The Chinese President, Zhou Bocheng, had arrived right on schedule. The Indian prime minister, Shailendra Patel, had already checked into the Grand Hyatt Hotel to welcome him. The security detail organized for both the leaders was impenetrable. The meeting was absolutely necessary and had been planned weeks in advance.

The primary agenda was serious. A face-off had ensued between the Chinese and Indian troops in the Chumar sector of Ladakh. More than 200 troops of China's People's Liberation Army had entered the region and begun to build a 2-kilometre road within the Indian territory. India and China have had long-standing differences over the demarcation of the boundaries along the Himalayan region, dating back to the late 1950s. After the initial conflict in

1962, a demarcation then known informally as the Line of Actual Control—the LAC—was chalked out to prevent any confusion. In 1993 its existence was formally accepted in a bilateral agreement. However, the problems never stopped. India accused China of repeated violations of the LAC in certain sections of Ladakh. Chumar itself had witnessed several situations in the last three years. The two leaders had decided to talk it over amicably, before taking any radical step. The enterprising Indian prime minister also decided to talk business and development, amongst many other things.

Kabir, Isha and Nihar waited in an OB van, the size of an ambulance, outside the main entrance. On paying it more thought, they had begun to realize that the ISI certainly did have a trick up its sleeve. The timing of the al-Zawahiri video . . . the movie links . . . the metro station incident . . . Everything was a way of messing with India. And they weren't done yet.

The team had been holed up in the van since eight in the morning, poring over every minute detail. Nothing seemed out of place. Nihar kept a strict watch on the email ID. It had been inactive since the al-Zawahiri video. The timing of the video, the content, all pointed at a possible attack on the PM. The metro attack had already shaken them up, and they knew they couldn't afford to have another such incident on their hands—let alone one involving two of the most powerful men in the world. And God forbid, if something happened to the Chinese President on Indian soil—the aftermath would be calamitous. *The dragon would crush them.*

'It's a funny thing,' Isha said. 'You spend a few days away from this country and you miss a lot.'

Kabir shrugged. He tightened the knot of his tie and put on his blazer. His hair was smoothed down to the left. He was categorically told by Joshi not to turn up in a pair of 'trashy' jeans and an 'apology for a T-shirt' like a 'vagabond'. He looked at his watch.

'Well, that's the reason we love our country, don't we?'

Isha smiled. 'Looking smart. You should wear such clothes more often.'

'Get a room, the two of you,' Nihar scoffed, as he watched the CCTV footage. 'Wait . . . What the hell?'

Kabir stood up and looked at the screen.

'Why is the PM coming out of the conference room? Isn't he supposed to wait there until Bocheng arrives?'

Kabir eased on his earpiece and pressed a button. He asked his point of contact the same question, and sighed and disconnected the call.

'He wants to greet Bocheng at the entrance.'

'It's things like this that make it dangerous,' Isha spat. 'Why does he have to do such stuff?'

Kabir tucked his gun under his belt and buttoned up his blazer to hide it.

'This is politics, my friend,' Nihar said. 'Every minute move has a detailed agenda.'

'Personally, I prefer a PM who is less of a showman and more someone who puts his money where his mouth is. But, well, clearly the others don't.'

'We haven't given the man enough time to show what he's capable of, though,' Nihar argued.

Kabir got ready to leave the van as he saw Bocheng's convoy of identical Mercedes limousines enter the gate. Simultaneously, he saw that the doors of the main entrance to the hotel open and watched the PM stride out confidently. He turned around at Isha and Nihar and raised an eyebrow.

'We live in a country where politicians divide us and terrorists unite us,' he said, slamming the door of the van behind him.

Zhou Bocheng, turned out in a sharp suit, stepped out of his Mercedes with his rather glamorous wife, who was known to be on *Vanity Fair*'s best-dressed list. Prime Minister Patel, who wore his trademark *bandhgala* suit, stretched out his right hand, which Bocheng grasped firmly. It was as perfect as any political reception could be. Both men smiled at each other. The photographers clicked away, capturing this picture-perfect moment. Kabir's eyes shifted from one photographer to another. *The same guys.* Just as a precaution, he had earlier checked each camera and tripod personally. He knew of instances where a disassembled gun had been stored in the hollow legs of a tripod and the remaining bits had been strategically placed within the camera itself. But he was glad that he had found nothing. After exactly a minute the Chinese power couple was led into the Hyatt hallway by the gracious prime minister. Bocheng's wife was led into an extremely lavish suite, while the PM took him into the conference room for a session of diplomatic discussion.

It was going to take a while. Kabir summoned Isha and Nihar to the lobby, from where they went into a conference room adjacent to the one where the PM and the Chinese President were. If they had to wait, it was better they waited in the comfortable confines of a five-star hotel. Kabir had a look at the official itinerary again. A photo-op session had been scheduled after the meeting, followed by a banquet spread at the Sabarmati Riverfront. After this, the two leaders would fly back to Delhi. Kabir was to accompany them, staying close to the PM throughout. But the fact that the terror video was traced back to Ahmedabad still worried him. He wasn't going to relax until the PM was back in Delhi.

So far, so good. Everything was going according to plan. But he had to wait and see for how long things would stay that way. *That's the worst part of being a man in the intelligence game. The wait. Minutes turn into hours, which turn into days, which turn into months and, sometimes, even years. But then, all of it boils down to those few seconds. The seconds that justify the wait. The seconds that make or break. The seconds that determine life and death.*

~

At exactly ten minutes to five, Kabir got a text message that told him the meeting was over. The prime minister stepped out of the conference room first, leading Bocheng on his way out. They continued to smile as they made some small talk. The PM told Bocheng of his plans to treat him to a lavish dinner by the picturesque Sabarmati Riverfront Park. Bocheng nodded and thanked him appropriately. His bodyguard, who was probably a Chinese intelligence agent of the Ministry of State Security, or MSS, whispered something in his ear. Bocheng frowned and nodded.

'Is everything all right?' the PM addressed a slightly perturbed Bocheng.

'Yes,' Bocheng replied. 'I'm afraid I will be slightly delayed for dinner. I shall see you at the venue. You please carry on. Sorry for the inconvenience.'

The PM nodded and said that it shouldn't matter. He walked away to the lobby. He looked at Kabir's stern face and acknowledged it with a nod and a polite smile.

'Good evening, sir. Please come this way.'

Kabir led the PM to his armoured navy-blue BMW. He let the PM's security open the door and let him in. He turned around and informed Nihar and Isha about Bocheng and his slight delay. They decided to move to the venue and scan it for any discrepancies one more time. He informed the representatives of the local police, the Intelligence Bureau and state intelligence before leaving the hotel for the waterfront. On the way to the venue they learnt about the three memoranda of understanding that had been signed. Bocheng and the PM had struck deals that envisaged promoting bilateral trade, setting up of industrial parks and developing cultural ties. They had also nominated Guangzhou and Ahmedabad as 'sister cities'. Another detail, which hadn't quite made it out into the open yet, was a probable nuclear deal. They decided to discuss it in more detail once they were in New Delhi, before announcing it formally.

'What about the problem in Ladakh?' Isha asked as Kabir drove the van to the venue.

'Oh, they spoke about that right up front. Bocheng has agreed to pull back all his troops.'

'And just the day before yesterday he asked the People's Liberation Army not to back down in their fight! Well, our PM is certainly a charming man.'

Kabir looked at her and smiled.

'Not as charming as you, of course, Kabir,' Nihar chimed in from behind. Isha threw him a questioning look. 'What? I'm just telling Kabir what you might've told him anyway,' quipped Nihar.

They took a smooth turn and passed through a few barricades, Kabir flashing his credentials. They were allowed to park in the designated area, being an official security vehicle. Kabir parked and got off. The prime minister's BMW was parked neatly in place, with many policemen surrounding it. An empty space was reserved for Bocheng's Mercedes. A nice breeze blew across the space. Kabir took a step and leaned over a ledge, looking down at the calm Sabarmati river. He wished he had the time to admire the beautiful sunset.

'Mr Anand, the prime minister is in the tent already. Let us know when to activate the signal jammers,' a senior official of state intelligence whispered to Kabir. 'The Chinese are breathing down my neck, too.'

'Has Mr Bocheng left the hotel?'

'Yes. He just got into his vehicle.'

'Good. As soon as he's here, activate the jammers. Run me through all the security arrangements again.'

Kabir turned away from the river and began to walk alongside the official, who recounted all the arrangements that had been implemented. Kabir looked around to see if he could spot their two snipers holding position. He couldn't. *Perfect.* The official then directed him to a spot at the opposite end of the park that lay ahead. He asked him to set up his equipment there, because that would be just beyond the jammers' range. Kabir thanked him and walked back to Nihar and Isha.

'Take your equipment to that platform there,' Kabir said, pointing to an amphitheatre in the park. 'We have to stay right behind the jammers. Bocheng will be here any moment and we might not have any network.'

Nihar picked up his laptop and locked the van. Kabir called Joshi and updated him about the proceedings. They passed by a dance troupe which was rehearsing a traditional Gujarati folk dance to entertain Bocheng and his wife. An array of Gujarati dishes, prepared by the best chefs in the state and the prime minister's personal cooks, were being trolleyed into the luxurious tent where the dinner banquet was being hosted.

'Bocheng is about to get here,' Kabir told Nihar. 'Security is tight. Difficult to reach the PM. Just keep an eye out for anything untoward.'

'Isn't that what we have been doing all day?' Isha replied tiredly.

Kabir pulled a chair and sat down. He tugged at his tie and loosened his collar. *Fuck this. I'm not here for a magazine shoot.* He thought about his classroom back in Mumbai. He couldn't wait to get back.

~

Zhou Bocheng's convoy was fifteen minutes away. Kabir got the jammers activated. Nihar had his laptop right inside the jammers' radius. The sole purpose of the jammer was not to stop phone calls, but to stop something far more serious, like a remote-controlled detonation. The Chinese security personnel were busy on their phones, communicating with the personnel that accompanied Bocheng and his wife. The others were busy supervising the meals that had been laid out. The dinner, right from its preparation stage, had been under immense scrutiny, lest someone attempt to poison the fare. Nothing of that sort had happened so far. The cooks were even made to taste each dish in advance, to be doubly sure.

Kabir began to walk back towards the designated parking area, where Bocheng's car was about to arrive. He reached the river and leaned against the railing. Nihar and Isha stayed by the amphitheatre. Isha was speaking to Joshi, keeping him in the loop. Nihar typed away at his computer. He clicked open the signal radar, just to see if the jammers were doing their job properly. Bocheng was going to be there in ten minutes, and they could not afford any slip-up. *That's good. All the signals are being emitted and received outside the radius. Most of them are security guys making calls.* He minimized the program window.

A few Special Protection Group commandos swept the grounds with Deep Search Metal Detectors, DSMDs, highly powerful metal detectors that were located at the end of a long rod. The main stage was clear. One of the commandos walked towards the parking lot, with the DSMD, to tell Kabir all was clear. As he walked by the railing, the DSMD beeped faintly. The commando frowned to himself. He walked by the same spot again and there was nothing. But Kabir noticed the commando retrace his steps.

'Is something wrong?'

'The metal detector beeped as I passed that spot,' the commando said, pointing at a bare, concrete platform. The platform was not too far away from a large swing-seat that was caparisoned with flowers and awaited the Chinese President, so he could sit there and watch the picturesque river in the company of the Indian PM, while savouring the local fare. Kabir took the DSMD from the commando and walked towards the spot again. There was no beep, no detection of any metal. Kabir looked up and shrugged. From the corner of his eye, he saw three Chinese men, part of Bocheng's security, who he deduced were MSS men, walking urgently towards him. Behind them Nihar scurried towards him as well. Before the Chinese could speak to Kabir, Nihar pulled him aside and spoke in Hindi instead.

'I was looking at the radar for any phoney signals or waves, when I found one coming into the jammer radius,' he said, shocked.

Isha was having a quick word with the MSS, after getting a brief from the commando with the DSMD.

'So you mean to say some unidentified object is closing in on us?'

'Yes,' Nihar murmured.

Kabir closed his eyes. And then the image of a faint, white streak in the river popped into his head—something he had earlier dismissed as some form of aquatic life swimming through the river water.

26

19 September 2014
Ahmedabad, Gujarat

'What if it's a bomb?' Isha said in a low whisper, sounding worried. Behind them, there was a sudden frenzy as Bocheng's car turned into the street leading up to the Sabarmati Riverfront.

'A submersible carrying explosives!?' Isha continued with bated breath.

The three Chinese men were speaking animatedly to Nihar. 'We detected some unusual activity on the radar,' one of them said. They had identical frowns.

'Nothing to be worried about,' Kabir replied. 'But I'm going to check on it anyway.'

'I think we should stall the President until you do that.'

'You don't have to,' Kabir replied. 'Unless it's something serious—which I doubt it will be.'

The three men had a brief discussion in Mandarin and walked away with purposeful strides.

'They're probably going to hold Bocheng back,' Isha said.

The Chinese President's convoy had arrived and was about to drive through and park. Kabir turned and looked back at the river. And then he shrugged off his jacket and unbuttoned his shirt. He knew Isha could be right about a submersible explosive. *Plus the DSMD had beeped. That doesn't happen too often. What if it is some metal object under the mortar?* He had never encountered such a thing in the past, but he knew of its existence.

'Kabir? What are you doing?'

'There's only one way to find out,' he said plainly. He threw his clean shirt on the ground and stood only in his vest and trousers. The veins bulged in his lean and muscular frame. The adrenalin was pumping through him.

'We can't risk it. Alert Mr Joshi. Don't let the Chinese guys know about it. This will cause unwarranted panic if it's not what we think it is.'

'And if it is what we think it is?'

'All the more reason not to tell them. See what they're up to and let them resolve it amongst themselves. Nihar, try to convince them it's nothing. Cook some story up if you have to.'

The President's car entered through the gate. Kabir hoisted himself over the railing, turned to see if anyone else was looking and then dived into the river. He was a fairly good swimmer, though he had never liked swimming, especially when on a mission. But he had learnt to do it. *Besides, it doesn't look like I have a say in making my own decisions any more . . . The circumstances are doing it for me.*

He moved comfortably with a fluid breaststroke once he was under water. The undercurrent of the river was helping him speed up in the direction he wanted to go.

Nihar watched him, leaning over the railing. He turned around to go speak to the Chinese men. Isha had walked back to the part of the promenade from where she could get cellular coverage. She updated Joshi about what had transpired. He gave her a set of instructions. She got down to executing them immediately, gathering a few senior members of security. Bocheng's car was now through the gate. The prime minister was still in the tent, waiting for Bocheng to be escorted in.

Kabir heard a buzz through the whoosh of the flowing river. He began to descend further underwater. It was coming from behind him. He realized he was swimming in the wrong direction. His sore back and injured shoulder began to ache. He realized he needed a shot of his painkiller immediately. *Just hold on for a while.* He took a deep breath and went below. He moved lower, and squinted to look through the water. He saw a streamlined object, vaguely like a mini-submarine. It had slowed down as it approached the concrete wall of the waterfront. He went back to the surface and gasped for air. It had been a while since he had done this. He shook his head violently, cleansing his irritated eyes, and took another deep breath, and dived back underwater to get closer to the object.

He realized he needed to swim very low. Moreover, the wall of the promenade caved inwards, being almost concave in profile. He held his breath and pushed himself lower. He had to turn and swim against the undercurrent that offered a fairly strong resistance. The object was parking itself against the wall, almost attaching itself to the upper end. Kabir could feel the pressure building. His ears felt the piercing force of the water, his heart was pounding against his ribcage. His brain was beginning to feel the oxygen deprivation. His eyes burned as he opened them ever so slightly. Against every bodily impulse, he pushed himself further to get within reach of the object. He deduced that he couldn't resist the pressure any further. He decided to take a wild swipe and grab the object. At least get a hand to it.

He turned his body downwards and made the attempt. He managed to grasp it for a fleeting moment, but it escaped. He saw the rotor spinning furiously. He turned around to make it back to the surface to get some air. But as he turned he decided to make another attempt. This time, as he moved up, he used his legs like pincers and wrapped them around the object. With great effort, he managed to change its course. He pulled it to a higher level, before it slipped out again. *Another second, and a nerve would burst.* He went back up to the surface, gasping for breath. He spat out some water and began to feel a little dizzy with the sudden exertion. He felt blinded, felt his vision turn achromatic. He waited for a moment and took another deep lungful of air. *This time I'm going to get that contraption back up with me.*

He pushed himself below. The object was lowering itself back to its initial level to park itself against the wall of the waterfront promenade again. Kabir lunged at it and grabbed it with both his hands. It hadn't gone back to its original position yet, and so was higher than it was before, and a tad easier to get to. He wrestled with it as the rotor began to slash away at his skin. He saw the blood mingle with the water. He opened his mouth slightly, to bubble some breath out, and with all the strength that he could muster he overturned the object, the blunt, smooth end facing him, and pulled it up to the surface. He held the object tightly as his feet paddled recklessly to stay afloat.

'Kabir, hold on!'

He didn't hear Isha calling out. His senses had pretty much given up on him. But he clutched the vibrating object close to him to prevent it from letting it loose. The rotor chopped at the river wildly, sending short spurts of water into the air. The object was beginning to break loose. It was too heavy to grab on to. Kabir's teeth gnashed, his face reddened. And then he felt it being tugged away from him. He looked up clearly to see Isha pulling it out of his hand with the help of two other men on a fisherman's boat. They scooped it up and then pulled Kabir up as well. He coughed wildly, thumping his chest and spitting out the river water he had ingested. His body shook violently as he lay in a heap in the boat, drenched to the bone. The blood from the gashes began to drip on to the wood. Isha and the other men were busy tending to the object. They had switched the motor off.

'What is it?' Kabir spluttered.

'A submersible vehicle laden with explosives,' the man replied. *Isha was right.* The object, around five feet in length and about a foot in diameter, now lay in the boat.

'It was geo-tagged towards the promenade. So it doesn't need a signal or remote control to direct it. It has enough liquid explosive in it to blow that entire section up!'

Kabir looked in the direction in which the man pointed. President Zhou Bocheng had just got out of his car a few minutes earlier. Had Kabir not brought it out of the water, the bomb would've continued on its destructive, watery course and torn apart that part of the promenade, taking with it the Chinese President and his wife. *And very soon, the country itself.*

The boat was directed to the opposite shore by the men. They got off and pulled up at the deserted promenade. The area had been kept out of bounds for the general public today. Surprisingly, only the regular guards were on duty. Kabir found it difficult to move, and had to be helped off the boat and on to his feet. They dragged the object to an enclosure, so that nobody could see what was happening. Nihar was calling Isha, but she didn't answer. She was bent down over the object and was tinkering with it for a good two minutes, while the other two officers continued staring at it, clueless. She pointed to a steel case attached to the streamlined object. Her eyes were full of fear.

'What's the matter, Isha?'

'Nothing,' she replied unconvincingly. 'You're bleeding! Guys, please fix him up.'

'Tell me what you found, damn it!'

'The liquid explosive is encased in this thick steel case, so that the water doesn't seep through. It was poured into it in its liquid state, so that there's no scope for oxidation to deteriorate the compound.'

Kabir read her worried expression. *There's something she isn't telling me.*

'All three of you look concerned,' he growled. 'Tell me what it is!'

'There's a timer attached to it,' Isha said tersely. 'I tried disabling it, but there is a tricky tamper-proof anti-handling device around it. As it stood, the bomb was meant to assassinate President Bocheng! Since it was geo-tagged, a timer was meant to go off as soon as it reached the location. And unfortunately, it did reach its final docking location.'

'Which means the timer must have been set off,' Kabir said solemnly.

Kabir's thoughts were in a whirl. *The First World War that started in June 1914 was triggered by the political assassination of Archduke Franz Ferdinand of Austria, the heir to the Austro-Hungarian throne, in Sarajevo, by a Yugoslav nationalist. Within weeks the world had been plunged into turmoil as the conflict spread. Had the bomb*

set off now, the Third World War would've effectively begun.
China would've vowed to vanquish this country. Pakistan
would've joined them—after having secretly ignited the fire.
The Chinese wouldn't care to find out who was responsible.
The fact that Bocheng was killed on Indian soil would have
been enough to set us on a collision course. But there's a more
immediate problem at hand . . . The bomb . . . It is war's prize
to take all vantage.

'The anti-handling device, which is attached to a bomb
to prevent it from being tampered with or disarmed, is in
place. It's very tricky to bypass this magnetic fuse, because if
we move it out of place to disarm it, which we have to, it will
definitely detonate,' another agent next to Isha said. 'And we
have less than thirty minutes before it goes off! There's no
way to work around this. A trained bomb squad may have a
10 per cent chance, but we might run out of time!'

Kabir got back to his feet with renewed energy. He
asked Isha for a phone, so that he could tell Joshi about the
situation. She handed it to him reluctantly. He stepped out
of the enclosure and made the call. He noticed a van pull
up at the entrance. He took a step back and cut the call. A
man came running out, looking through binoculars at the
opposite area, where the function had begun.

~

'What do you mean?' the voice at the other end of the line
cried. 'Why have the celebrations not begun?'

'They got to it. The bomb will probably go off anyway,
but the target will remain unharmed!'

The tall man put down his binoculars. He was
completely bewildered himself. He had bided his time with
the members of the press in a tent reserved for journalists

and reporters, waiting to witness the assassination of Zhou Bocheng in person. He hadn't managed to get a good view of the river, but he trusted his plan completely. He seldom made mistakes. He had orchestrated the entire thing perfectly—building the device, testing it, planting it. It was a foolproof plan. He had set the wheels in motion for the world's biggest war yet. And now someone had thrown a spanner in the works. *It's still not too late, though. The bomb is going to go off anyway. My sniper-rifle is still in the car. I need a good vantage point, that's it.*

'Chacha, I have no idea. Things should've gone smoothly.'

'Is there a Plan B?'

'It's like an alarm. In half an hour it will wake you up.'

'No,' the man replied exasperatedly. 'That's not good enough. Do the honours yourself. I don't care about the risk involved.'

The tall man disconnected the phone. He saw a police combat vehicle approach, accompanied by three policemen on their bikes. He hurried back into his van to avoid arousing any suspicion. His rifle lay in a duffel bag in the trunk. He needed to assemble it quickly. He needed to take the shot himself. Pull the trigger on Bocheng. And if possible, on his wife as well.

Should I take the shot from somewhere nearby itself? No! Can't risk being spotted. A security sniper will take me out in no time.

He had left the engine of the van running, in order to make a quick getaway. He pushed the pedal to the metal and set off. Little did he know that the main reason why he had to improvise had already spotted him.

~

Kabir came rushing out of the enclosure. Isha and the two men were still with the bomb. The armoured combat vehicle screeched to a halt and two officers jumped out, followed by a bomb squad. They saw Kabir's lithe figure rushing towards them. He was still in his vest, which was completely drenched and had several stains of blood on it.

'Give me the keys to your bike,' he gasped. 'Quick! My colleague Isha is in that enclosure. She'll explain everything to you.' The man handed him the keys. 'And the gun,' he asked as he hopped on to the bike. The man handed him his pistol. Kabir revved the bike and sped off. His eyes followed the van all along. Now he had to catch up. In his head he made a mental calculation of the time left for the bomb to set off. *Twenty-five minutes . . . A man to catch . . . A political assassination of insanely epic proportions to be averted . . . A bomb to be deactivated . . . A war to be prevented . . . And all I have is twenty-five minutes . . . A man I am cross'd with adversity.*

27

The van wove through the traffic effortlessly. The assassin had reached the junction where he needed to take a U-turn and cross over to the other side of the river. He made a quick turn and got on to the bridge. He picked up speed and cast a quick glance at his wristwatch. He needed to scout for a good vantage point and then assemble his sniper-rifle. There was a lot of work to do. He had a good twenty minutes in hand. After that the bomb would go off. And then they would whisk away the PM and President immediately, before cordoning off the area. *This has to be quick and precise.* He looked at his rear-view mirror out of sheer habit, to see if anyone was following. Nobody was.

As he crossed the bridge, he cast a glance at the riverfront promenade. He had half a mind of stopping the van there, assembling his rifle and taking the shot. But he needed to be quick about it. And stopping his vehicle midway was bound to arouse suspicion. The good part was, if he did manage to make the shot, it would've been a clean getaway. *No security on the bridge. No CCTV. The cartridge of the bullet would fall in the vehicle itself. No trace left behind.* He had slowed down as he continued to mull over his options. He decided against it. He put his foot back on the pedal and zoomed ahead. *All I need is a high building.*

He had crossed the bridge and was on the main road. He kept a mental track of his position vis-à-vis the position of the podium on which the PM and President were to stand for their photo-op. According to the itinerary, the folk dances would probably be on right now, followed by a quick photo session and, ultimately, the grand dinner. He scoffed to himself. A frivolous thought crossed his mind. *They're going to feed the poor Chinese President vegetarian dishes. If I don't get a good shot, I'll probably have to wait for him to choke over the dinner he's served.*

He moved ahead and saw that the signal at the next crossing was about to turn red. He accelerated, manoeuvred the van skilfully and took a sharp left. He passed a few local stores and a few high-rises. They looked too busy to walk into. Even if he did successfully make his way into such a building, it wouldn't be long before some resident alerted the guards. He needed something quieter. Stealth was a priority. At least until he got his bullet into Bocheng's gullet. After that he had no issues creating a ruckus, even if it resulted in his own death. He was prepared to die, as long as he had done what he had lived for in the first place.

He cruised along until he found the perfect building, so to speak. A construction site. *It's evening, and the workers look like they're on a break. The guard is still at the gate. Need to find a way around.* He parked the van and stepped out. He lifted his duffel bag with the rifle over his shoulder and walked along the dusty pavement. Luckily, not too many people were around. He turned again to check if he was being followed. Since he couldn't enter through the main entrance without drawing attention, he decided to climb over the aluminium sheets and get inside the compound. He took the support of the rusty metal frame that held the corrugated sheets together and pulled himself up. He threw his bag down and jumped over to the other side.

A solitary worker with his protective headgear and jacket was walking by with a shovel. He looked at the assassin confusedly. The assassin, however, had made his decision. He punched the bewildered worker, breaking his nose. And then he choked him to death. He dragged the body into a corner and pushed it into a pit. He pulled out the worker's jacket, strapped it on and put on his helmet. He picked up his bag and resumed his path. He walked, concealing his face from the few workers that were sitting in a group as they sipped from small glasses of tea between the shifts. He saw just what he wanted. *Two elevators made especially for the workers.* They weren't the normal kind. They were merely a metal frame with a steel mesh all around, but extremely sturdy, so that heavy loads could be carried up easily.

It was a high building, twenty floors, probably. The framework had been laid out. The tall man activated the lift and it sped up quickly to the top. Within thirty seconds he was on the top floor. After climbing a short flight of stairs, he pushed open a flimsy door and walked out on to the terrace. He stepped on to the mortar and cement, leaving behind a trail of footprints. He hurried to a spot and pulled out his scope. There were small mounds of debris all around him, little tin and plastic containers, cylinders of steel and other construction material. He found a short wall of bricks, which hadn't been set with cement yet. It was the perfect support for his rifle. He unzipped his duffel bag.

The McMillan Tac-50 Caliber Sniper Rifle. Fifteen parts when broken down. A minute and a half to assemble. The same rifle with which the world record for the longest successful tactical combat shot was fired by a Canadian soldier, who was more than 2 kilometres away. I'm definitely within one and a half. He gets to keep his record.

The man quickly looked through his scope. He could see the riverfront. It was going to be a difficult shot. But he backed himself up to make it. He needed to take the shot when Bocheng was on the stage. That would give him a good time-frame and a wider target. He had almost assembled the rifle. Just a few screws left to tighten. A bullet to be loaded. He had one shot, and he had to make it count. He looked at his watch. *Seventeen minutes before the bomb goes off.* He mounted the gun on the brick wall and clasped his hands. They were clammy with perspiration. He breathed in deeply. And then he heard a faint metal clank. His lift had made the same noise when it had reached the floor before the terrace. *Someone's here.*

~

Kabir had tailed the assassin successfully. He rode his bike into the compound and asked every worker to get out immediately. They looked confused and scoffed at the shabby man in a vest, mistaking him for a drunkard. And then he showed them his gun and led them out quietly, lest the assassin get alerted. Isha had followed Kabir in a police car. She had been on a call with Joshi throughout. She relayed his instructions to Kabir. She wanted to join him.

'No way,' Kabir rasped. 'Where's the bomb?'

'Where we left it. A bomb squad is dealing with it.'

'Do as I say. Listen to me very carefully.'

He instructed her briefly and walked away. He used the other construction elevator and sped up to the top floor. Every muscle in his body ached. But that could be repaired. An international disaster of this scale couldn't.

Kabir stepped out of the elevator, his gun in position. He noticed that a flimsy door to the terrace was ajar. *The assassin is here.* He climbed two steps at a time, stealthily. It was beginning to get dark outside. A faint light-bulb, hanging from a couple of wires, flickered. He decided to walk through the door. It was eerily silent on the terrace. He could see the Sabarmati from where he stood. He took another step ahead. And then another.

And then he fell to the ground with a dull thud. His brain shook within his skull. He could taste the mortar. He felt the warmth and wetness of blood oozing out and soaking his hair. The assassin stood behind him with a metal spade. *Maybe this was it . . . This was where I fail . . .*

The assassin lifted the spade again and was about to bring it down, when Kabir rolled over. The assassin missed. Kabir's vision was blurred. Kabir launched a kick into his shin that made the assassin stumble forward. He kicked him again, dropping him to the floor, right next to him.

The mauve sky offered just enough light for him to see the assassin's face. His body went numb as their eyes met. Both of them froze with disbelief, simultaneously. Their bodies lay on the wet cement, refusing to budge. Kabir's bloodshot eyes widened as his vision began to come back to normal. He couldn't quite process what he just saw. Or whom he just saw.

Vikramjit Singh.

28

19 September 2014
Ahmedabad, Gujarat

There were a few more seconds of stunned silence. Vikramjit was the first to recover. He rammed his fist into Kabir's face. Kabir felt a sharp pain in his cheekbone. Vikramjit slid away and got back on to his feet. Kabir rolled over sluggishly, trying to get up. His body refused to comply. Vikramjit launched another kick into Kabir's ribs. Kabir dropped back on to the ground. Vikramjit grabbed a handful of Kabir's hair and dragged him up. He took Kabir's pistol, dropped the magazine out and threw it aside. Kabir's eyes burned with hatred.

'Well, it's been a while . . . Adonis . . .'

Vikramjit smiled and kneed Kabir brutally in his solar plexus. Kabir clutched his stomach and stumbled backwards. He spat blood out as his back hit the wall.

He let out a single blood-mingled word: 'Why?'

Vikramjit looked at his watch. He looked down from the terrace. There were a good ten minutes. *And he's not brought backup. Some things never change.*

'No backup? Your arrogance has proved to be your undoing. Same old overconfident Kabir,' Vikramjit said with a wry smile. 'Always wanting to be the hero.'

'*Why?*' Kabir shivered with rage. A stream of blood flowed through his left nostril. 'Why did you do this to your country?'

'This is not my country. I am an orphan thanks to this country.' Vikramjit's words spewed bitter venom. 'My father was an honest Kashmiri Muslim. In fact he was one of the few Kashmiri Muslims who supported the Indians. And my mother was a Hindu who converted to Islam. It was all going well, until you people came into the picture.'

He paused. His eyes glimmered with rage as he told his tale.

'One fine day, three of your soldiers stormed in and accused my father of being a terrorist, because of his religion. They killed him and raped my mother to death. They planted evidence to suggest he was indeed what they claimed he was. I was young. I watched all of this from outside the house. Had I been in our cottage, they would've killed me too. Unflinchingly.'

His eyes were blood-red. His strong jaw set firmly. He swallowed to clear the lump in his throat.

'But I lived. I lived to exact a cruel revenge—vendetta. Ever since that day I was bound by the darkness of revenge. And God knows I had to wait a long time for the day to come. But today I will get the revenge I have been seeking when I put a bullet through Bocheng's skull. China will annihilate your country, and there will not be a thing you can do about it.'

'Those three soldiers don't stand for the rest of us,' Kabir said, crawling in an attempt to push himself back on his feet. 'There are people like that on every side. Evil isn't bound by a country or a religion. You don't have to do that, Vikramjit.'

'That is not my fucking name. You never knew me, Kabir. It was all an act. I was well trained in Kashmir, in the harshest of conditions, to deal with the most unthinkable of pain. To work my way out of the trickiest of situations. I'm bound by Allah's course. The course of jihad. And He will guide me through this.'

Vikramjit lifted his rifle and adjusted the muzzle. He walked ahead and jammed the muzzle into Kabir's neck. Kabir coughed uncontrollably.

'Allah doesn't teach his children to kill innocent people. No religion, no God has ever taught anyone to kill innocents. We use this as an excuse to quench our thirst for blood,' Kabir growled through gritted teeth, his voice trailing away. 'The difference is that some of us accept the reality, the destructive power of human beings, the others pin it on God. A god whose words they twist to suit their fucked-up mentalities!'

Vikramjit took the butt of the rifle and rammed it on Kabir's forehead. His head hit the cement with a dull thud.

'Exactly, Kabir. I'm not killing anybody innocent here. None of you are innocent,' Vikramjit roared back. 'I have lived to avenge my innocent parents and every innocent life that has been taken by your country! Where was your quest for righteousness then, you bastard? I have been burning with a desire to see your country up in flames! And today is that day! I will kill Bocheng and then I will kill you. Spare you the pain of seeing your country torn to shreds in war!'

Vikramjit tightened the scope and kept the gun leaning against the brick wall. He walked towards Kabir. Kabir realized he had to stall him. Muster up enough strength to go and attack him. Vikramjit threw a punch at Kabir, which he evaded. Kabir, in turn, jammed his fist into Vikramjit's ribs. And then dug his nails into the hollow between the breastbone and the Adam's apple. This unsettled him a bit, as he gasped for air. Kabir threw another quick set of punches. Vikramjit blocked them and moved away, as Kabir staggered ahead. Kabir swung his arm, but Vikramjit was quicker. He stepped aside, bent down and pulled Kabir's leg towards him with his right hand and pushed his chest away with his left, in a clinical takedown. Kabir rolled on the ground. Vikramjit launched his heel into Kabir's weak lower back, sending him flying into the flimsy terrace door. The door broke and some plaster dropped on to Kabir. *I can't give up. I have to stop him. And then, if the beating of my heart stops, so be it.* He pushed himself up with the support of the loose door-frame.

Kabir sprang up, clutching a rusty metal rod. He charged towards Vikramjit and clubbed it against his knee. Vikramjit fell to the ground. Kabir lifted the rod above his head and brought it down on his skull. Vikramjit groaned. Kabir lifted it again, to go for the jugular. Vikramjit got hold of a rock and flung it at Kabir's chest. It bought him enough time to move aside and tug Kabir by the shin and drop him down.

'Kabir, you're not going to make it out alive this time,' Vikramjit said. 'This is God's script. And this is how it ends.'

He picked up a spade and swung it at Kabir. Kabir ducked, missing it by a whisker. He picked up a handful of cement and flung it at Vikramjit's face. It went into his eyes and mouth, and he moved away reflexively. Kabir realized it was his chance to get rid of the rifle. Probably throw it over the wall and off the terrace. He ran to grab it, when Vikramjit tripped him. He fell forward, face down. Kabir managed to get a hold of the rifle and pulled it towards him. He hit it hard against the ground. Two loose pieces separated, because they weren't tightened well enough.

Vikramjit was quick to grapple with him and push the rifle away. Kabir slithered out and got hold of a loose brick. He hit it against Vikramjit's head. A stream of blood followed a dull noise. He caught him in a chokehold.

'How did you do it?' Kabir growled.

'You think I'm the only one?' Vikramjit's smile was bloody. 'Years of training. I was planted into India. I was an orphan with no traceable background. A new name, a new identity. No records. I studied and worked to get into the Indian forces. I did the unthinkable by getting into your system. I sacrificed one of my own operatives, Haneef Sayyed, to climb up the ladder and win your trust. It was all like a one-sided game of chess, but nobody ever looked at it that way. After I had proved my mettle, I got the posting of my choice: Balochistan.'

Vikramjit broke into a wild laugh, as Kabir tried to choke him harder. His shoulder, however, had given up on him. It couldn't produce the strength he needed. Vikramjit realized this and bashed the back of his head into Kabir's face. Kabir coughed blood. Vikramjit turned around, picked up the spade again and slammed it into Kabir's dead shoulder. Kabir yelled in pain. His body was momentarily paralysed. He could barely move a finger. Vikramjit lifted the spade and brought it down on Kabir's right knee. Kabir grimaced.

'Balochistan!' Vikramjit laughed. 'I was doing a fine job in Balochistan. A double agent in the midst of one of the most conflicted regions! I withheld information from India. I leaked every bit of intel that came my way to the ISI and every jihadist outfit. I pledged allegiance to the Amir himself. I was deemed one of the most skilled operatives. I was held back to destroy your country when the opportunity was right. And I could do it from the inside, without even raising a few eyebrows! In fact, I was quite at ease with myself when I taught at the madrasa. Until you came along. Sadiq Sheikh's blue-eyed boy. The flamboyant Kabir Anand!'

Vikramjit's face was inches away from Kabir's. Kabir could feel the tang of the sardonic words on Vikramjit's breath, as he writhed in pain. His mouth fell open, blood-tainted saliva dripped out.

'That old bastard sent you and then it all went awry. You got in the way of my work. I had to rework my strategies. Be careful about things. I couldn't leak intel as easily any more. And if you remember, I had even tried to discourage you from going into that madrasa on that day.'

The pieces of the puzzle all fell into place. Kabir remembered Vikramjit's contribution to that fateful mission. He had portrayed himself as someone who was afraid of killing, when he was the one who had orchestrated it all along. Or maybe he was afraid, because Kabir had killed more than he expected. Kabir remembered every move Vikramjit made, every word he spoke when he was in Quetta. Right from the Arabic nuances to the way he placed the Holy Quran on the table.

'So it was you who sold us out?' Kabir's voice was hoarse. He was in agony. The blood rushed through his veins. He wished it was all a bad dream. *I need to buy time.*

'Ladies and gentlemen, we have a winner here.' Vikramjit grinned maniacally at an immobile Kabir. 'We had to do something, so that you never got your hands on all the intelligence stored in those computers. That Claymore bomb behind the door was planted. As soon as you left, one of my men behind the door deactivated it. We had cleared the computers by then and fled the scene, setting the madrasa ablaze. We never expected you to get past the front door. But you were good. You killed so many of ours and managed to escape. But I realized that the best way to punish you was to implicate you. Make you look like the man who sold us out. As far as it went, I was dead. And then, of course, the Afghani defector was killed too. It all worked so perfectly against you, Kabir, that I realized you didn't have to die at all!'

Kabir closed his eyes. The one missing link in the answer to the diabolical riddle that was unfolding, something that had needled him throughout his life, was someone he had considered a brother in Balochistan! The reason he had to step down and cut his career short. The reason he had to hang his head in shame. It all boiled down to a betrayal by someone he had thought of as a brother. Vikramjit looked at his watch. *Bocheng should be on stage now.* He picked up the rifle, looked through the scope and zoomed in. He saw the Indian prime minister go up to the podium with a great degree of pomp.

'You got Sadiq killed, you son of a bitch! You were the mole,' Kabir groaned. 'You were always the mole.'

'You think there aren't more like me, Kabir?' Vikramjit said, getting Bocheng in his cross hairs. He looked up and placed the bullet. He placed it and loaded the rifle. *Perfect.* He turned to face Kabir, one last time. 'As far as Sadiq goes, unfortunately, a close associate of mine did the job. But you killed someone whom I held in high regard as well. The old principal at the madrasa. You didn't think about that twice, either.'

Kabir's jaw trembled. His body was convulsing. His heart was beating rapidly, aching as it thudded against his chest. His body was losing blood at a rapid rate. The bomb was about to set off in another two minutes.

'One last thing,' Kabir said meekly, closing his eyes. 'What's your real name?'

It was a feeble attempt from him to buy time. *But then, I never expected this.*

Vikramjit snorted.

'I guess you'll never know,' he said contemptuously, screwing back the pieces that Kabir had managed to break off the rifle. 'It was good knowing you, Kabir Anand. You tried your best. Now, watch as I fire a bullet and seal your country's fate. After this, a bomb will go off. The one by the waterfront. There is no way you can disarm it. And then I will put a bullet in your head. I must say it was a pleasant surprise catching up after all these years. *Jai Hind!*'

Vikramjit placed his finger on the trigger. He aimed, making a mental calculation of the trajectory of the bullet. *The wind, the velocity, the curve the bullet is likely to make.* He watched Bocheng stand next to the prime minister as the shutterbugs clicked away. His shot was clear. *One . . . Two . . . Three . . .*

Kabir's eyes closed as he heard *the* gunshot.

29

The sound of the gunshot still resonated in Kabir's ears. His eyes were closed. His bloody face twitched and then curled into a smile. *Yes. It's the right sound.* He tilted his head, opened his eyes, and saw what he wanted to see. *The right kind of gun makes the right kind of sound. Isha has made it in time.*

Vikramjit had fallen to the ground. His left hand clutched his right one as he shrieked in anguish. Tears of pain rolled down. His hand was nearly blown off. It hung loosely, his cracked bone held together by a few thick strands of sinew. His body convulsed violently in a spreading pool of blood. Kabir looked to his right, at the area where the flimsy door had once stood. Isha still held her pistol in position, about to fire one final shot.

'NO!' Kabir bellowed. 'Don't shoot!'

She looked at Kabir and lowered her gun. She ran to him hurriedly and helped him up. Kabir was on his feet, shaking uncontrollably.

'Were you able to bring the bomb here?'

She looked at her watch and nodded affirmatively.

'We have exactly a minute and twelve seconds, Kabir. Let's get the hell out of here!'

He yelled at her. 'You weren't supposed to come up!'

'Come on, quick! We can make it out in time!'

Vikramjit's painful roar brought a wide grin to Kabir's crimson face. He staggered towards him and bent down on his haunches. He took the rifle that had fallen to the ground and placed it in Vikramjit's lap. He looked at Vikramjit's pale face, laced with blood that trickled down from his head.

'Kabir, hurry!'

Kabir's eyes bore into Vikramjit's. Vikramjit's mouth was agape and stayed frozen there.

'There are fifty-five seconds to the bomb,' Kabir whispered. 'Unless you can take the shot with your toes, I would advice you to say your last prayers. Here, let me help you.'

He pulled Vikramjit's right hand and took his left and joined them by their sides. Vikramjit's painful bellow was music to his ears. Kabir's grin grew wider.

'There you go. I've made your job easier! Fold your hands, say your prayers to a God who's about to send you to Hell. The bomb is on the floor right under this one. This time, though, you won't be able to trick me and run away. You like outwitting people, don't you? Let's see you weasel your way out of this one, you bastard.'

Vikramjit's eyes widened as his body began to shake violently. He began to foam at the mouth.

'Like you said a few minutes ago. This is God's script. And, *I am the hero*!'

Isha pulled Kabir away by his blood-soaked vest. She put his arm around her shoulder and helped him move quickly. 'We have forty seconds left! We have to hurry!'

They scampered over the debris and broken stone. Isha transferred some of Kabir's body weight on to her as they climbed down the stairs. She dragged him to the lift and pushed him in. She pressed the large red button to take them down. Kabir lay on the floor, smiling at her. Her face was worried as the lift began to move sluggishly at first and then gained speed.

'Why are you smiling?' she asked worriedly, looking at her watch.

'You look prettier when you're hassled,' he replied.

'We have ten seconds before the bomb goes off, Kabir!' she said. 'We might not make it down in time! Hold on to the side of the grilles!'

She realized Kabir was in a critical condition and needed immediate medical help. A hundred thoughts flashed through her mind as she weighed all the possibilities. Kabir, on the other hand, was blank. The lift had just crossed the fifth floor. The bomb went off.

They heard a loud thud, a sound very similar to the one made by a thundercloud. The deafening explosion was a high-intensity one. They felt the lift oscillate violently. And then the cord snapped, sending them plummeting to the ground. They felt the reverberations. They were about to hit the ground in a millisecond. But they gripped the side of the lifts. And then suddenly, their bodies bounced off the ground and hit the ceiling of the lift.

Nihar saw the lift hit the ground. He saw Kabir and Isha get thrown about like toy figurines. In his mind he hoped for the best. He prayed they'd survive. He rushed to see that Kabir lay on the metal floor, stirring slightly. His eyes were closed, his mouth open. Isha stirred slightly as Nihar summoned a medic team. They lifted Kabir quickly and hurried away with him on a stretcher. Nihar and another policeman lifted them up and began to run outside the compound. A load of debris came falling down. Behind them, the other lift came rocketing down, too. There was a cloud of dust and a shower of glass and stones as the building began to finally give up.

'Quick! The building will collapse completely any moment!'

As they moved away, they saw six floors on top of the incomplete building crumble down like a sandcastle into nothing but a heap of construction material.

Nihar got into his car and called Joshi immediately. 'Yes, sir. Kabir and Isha are being rushed to the hospital. It was Kabir's plan, sir. He asked us to transfer the bomb to this construction site and put it in the building as soon as we could and then evacuate the area. He had planned to stall the assassin for long enough until it went off. Isha went up and brought him down in the nick of time. Yes, very good, sir. He's in extremely poor condition. Will he survive? I hope for the best.'

Kabir was in an ambulance that was being driven to a nearby hospital. Isha lay beside him. She realized she may have fractured a few bones. She had great difficulty moving. She turned to look at Kabir, whose face remained impassive. His body smelled of stale blood. The medics checked him for a pulse. It was faint. His heart rate was below normal on the electrocardiogram. Tears rolled down Isha's cheek. He opened his eyes, turned to look at her and smiled.

'Your life is nothing short of a Shakespearean drama, Kabir Anand,' said Isha, her voice husky with emotion. 'Revenge, betrayal, dignity, indignity . . . You've seen it all.'

'Come here.' Kabir choked and then burst into a bout of violent coughing. He gestured Isha to bring her head closer.

He held the back of her head gently and pressed his lips on her forehead. She smelled the coppery blood, and smiled back.

The medics held him still and injected him with a serum. They wiped the blood and tied his open wounds up with tourniquets. He opened his mouth to speak again and then realized he was too weak to utter a word. He gasped for air. He closed his eyes as he felt a darkness overpower him . . .

All the world's a stage, and all the men and women merely players: they have their exits and their entrances; and one man in his time plays many parts . . .

30

1 October 2014
RAW HQ, New Delhi

Isha and Nihar were in Arun Joshi's cabin. He had briefed them about what was about to happen. About who had killed Sadiq Sheikh and how it all added up, once the missing link—Vikramjit Singh—was discovered. *Vikramjit didn't work alone. All these years that bastard mole was right under our noses and we never knew it. And now he has defected. He's living a happy life. But not for long . . .*

Isha looked at her watch. 'Do you think he'll come?'

'It's been over an hour since we've been here,' Nihar said, tapping his feet impatiently.

Joshi, however, was in a genial mood. 'Don't worry.' He smiled. 'He will come. He'd be foolish not to. It's the reason he signed up for this in the first place.'

Joshi's phone rang. It was his secretary. He looked at the phone and shrugged. He pressed a button and without waiting for the secretary to say anything, said: 'Send him in.'

A few seconds later the door opened. The man in front of them stood a little under six feet. He wore a white shirt and grey trousers. His beard was neat, and his ashen hair was tied up in a short ponytail. The eyes beneath his arched eyebrows were cold. His face was impassive. He limped in with the help of a crutch. He reeked of musk, in an attempt to overpower the smell of the balms and medicine he had to apply on his injuries. He acknowledged Isha and Nihar with a nod. It had been fifteen days since he had seen them last.

'Named your kid, yet?' he addressed Nihar with a smile.

'Yes.' Nihar smiled. 'I named him Veer. I hope he is as brave as the real one.'

There was a minute of solemn silence. Joshi adjusted his spectacles.

'It's good to have you back, Kabir.'

'It's good to be back, sir.'

Joshi looked at Kabir, motioning to the empty chair. A lot had happened since his face-off with Vikramjit Singh on top of that building.

'I have a proposition for you, Kabir. *We* have a proposition for you.'

Kabir let out a deep breath. 'Sir, if you wouldn't mind, I need a cup of black coffee.'

'That can wait,' Joshi said flatly. 'So, Abdullah Abdullah and Ashraf Ghani have signed a power-sharing agreement, with the latter being named President, and Abdullah taking on an important position in the government. This could either be good or bad for the dynamics of world politics. Only time will tell us about how the Taliban continue and what America's next move is.'

Kabir nodded tersely, wanting to tell Joshi he knew, but not meaning to be rude.

'Do you know about the Islamic State of Iraq and the Levant, Kabir?'

'I happen to read the newspapers, sir. But I'm afraid I haven't bothered to catch up much since we got back from Balochistan.'

'So then you all know that the self-proclaimed caliph, Abu Bakr al-Baghdadi, is trying to bring all the Muslim-inhabited regions under ISIS's political control. And, well, he is the new self-proclaimed Amir al-Mu'minin.'

'Well, even I'm contemplating calling myself that now.'

'In fact, ISIS is a direct threat to India. Those few Indian boys who left to join will soon multiply into many more. We may just be on the edge of falling into a deadly abyss.'

'Haven't we been there before, sir?'

'I'll cut to the chase, Kabir. I would like to thank you, Isha, Nihar and Veer for the exceptional job that you all have done. For the bravery that you all have shown. For the selflessness that you all have displayed. For the sacrifices that you all, especially Veer, have made. Right from Balochistan to the attempt on President Bocheng. I have already discussed my plan with Isha and Nihar.'

Kabir looked sideways at Isha and Nihar. They avoided looking back at him.

'Investigations have suggested that this entire plan was orchestrated by the ISI well in advance. They had planned an explosion at a mall in Pune, as Isha knows. Followed by the incident at the metro station. And then they got wind of the high-level meeting between President Bocheng and the PM, thanks to the insider. We are a country with dangerous enemies, Kabir. Enemies who will stop at nothing to see us go up in flames.'

Kabir retained a sphinx-like expression. Joshi's eyes were expressive.

'I want you to be in charge of a small covert team that is completely off the books. You will have all support from the government. Your team will consist of highly trained military commandos and will have direct access to RAW.'

Joshi let the words linger in the air as he gazed at Kabir. Kabir matched his gaze with an equally piercing stare.

'My children are waiting to be taught Shakespeare, sir.'

Joshi smiled and leaned back in his chair.

'Let me know if you change your mind, Kabir. The country is at great risk with the various elements of terror raising their ugly heads.'

Kabir remained quiet. Nihar and Isha looked straight at Joshi.

'Anyway,' Joshi broke the silence, as he stood up, 'it was great working with you, Kabir Anand.'

Kabir stood up and extended his hand, which Joshi shook firmly.

'Likewise, sir.'

Isha and Nihar stood up, ready to leave the cabin. Joshi nodded to them briefly, indicating that he wanted to speak to Kabir in private. They thanked him and walked out. Joshi pulled out a brown folder from his drawer.

'You have a loose end to tie up,' Joshi said. 'And don't worry, you'll get your fix of black coffee outside.'

Kabir swallowed lightly as he balanced himself on his crutch. Joshi held the brown envelope firmly, keeping it close to him.

'I hope you're off the painkillers, Kabir.'

Kabir looked a little surprised.

'Isha told me,' Joshi said, addressing his furrowed brow. 'She's concerned about you. And it would be a pity if you died of an overdose of painkillers after defying death at every step that you took in the past few days.'

'I will stop, sir.'

Joshi's lips curled into a half-smile as he held the brown folder forward.

'Your passport, cover IDs and two tickets for an all-expenses-paid trip to Dubai.'

'Two tickets?'

'Coincidentally, Isha is also in the mood for a holiday,' said Joshi, smiling knowingly.

Kabir smiled back. And then Joshi's smile vanished.

'Make sure he gets the death he deserves.'

'You can count on that.'

Kabir turned and began to walk away.

'I wish you the best, Kabir Anand. And think about my offer.'

'Yes, sir.'

Kabir shut the door firmly behind him. He had no intentions of going in ever again or thinking about any offer.

~

Kabir got out of the sedan and nodded at the driver. He rested on his crutch as he frowned to himself. He looked at the rusty gate, slightly ajar. He leaned ahead and pushed himself forward. The door creaked as he pushed it and limped in. The leaves rustled under his feet as he looked down at the brown mounds strewn with rose petals. Kabir put his hand in his trouser pocket and pulled out a little plastic bag. He stepped gingerly past a fresh mound of soil and stopped in front of a spot that was relatively flat. The chirping of sparrows punctuated the silent evening.

'*Salaam aleikum*, Sadiq Sahab.' A lump formed in his throat as he dropped his crutch and sat down beside the mound. He looked at it for a few more seconds.

Nothing can we call our own but death

And that small model of the barren earth
Which serves as paste and cover to our bones.

'You were a brave man, sir. You inspired me. At my best, I couldn't be half as good as you were.'

Kabir picked up a yellow leaf and looked at it. He closed his eyes as he remembered the first time he had met Sadiq. He was a hard man to impress on the training ground. And while the others were trying to work hard to show Sadiq how good they were, Kabir worked to prove it to himself. Sadiq liked that about him. Kabir found the corners of his eyes moistening.

'I apologize if I ever did something you didn't approve of. You were like a father to me.' His voice trailed away. 'And you still are.'

He sat there for another five minutes, enjoying the calm of the graveyard. He pulled out a handful of rose petals from the plastic bag and dropped them evenly all over the mud under which Sadiq's body decomposed peacefully.

'They were right in front of us, and the two of us couldn't recognize the two of them. They did their jobs well, sir. And Vikramjit is dead now, for real.'

He rubbed the bridge of his nose.

'I promise you one thing. The other bastard won't live for long either. He is going to pay for what he has done, in the worst possible way.'

He clutched a handful of soil and let it slip through his hands, back on to the mound. He pushed himself off the ground and picked up his crutch.

'Until we meet again, sir. *Khuda hafiz.*'

He trudged out with a heavy heart. But he was more determined than ever to kill the bastard who did this. He opened the door of the parked sedan and got in.

~

3 October 2014
Mumbai

Kabir had waited another day at New Delhi before he flew back to Mumbai with Isha. They went straight to his apartment. They had a quick lunch and spent some time together, after which she left for Pune to meet her mother. Kabir, on the other hand, hoped to go back to the college to have a word with the Principal. After that Isha and Kabir planned to meet again in the evening and spend the night until they had to travel.

Kabir went to the college. He was able to walk better than before, but still felt he needed the crutch. The watchman wished him a good afternoon. Kabir acknowledged him with a curt nod. He walked up the dusty wooden staircase and through the stony corridor before stopping outside the Principal's cabin. He knocked sharply. There was no response. A peon passing by informed him that the Principal was on his rounds since the examinations were on, and he was taking a round of the classrooms to check if everything was in order. Kabir thanked him and walked towards the classes. He passed by the examination halls. The students, distracted at the drop of a hat, looked at him and then at each other.

One mumbled to another, 'Ha, one game of football and he's got a crutch.'

Kabir continued walking till he saw the tall Principal in a classroom. The Principal turned around and his eyes widened in surprise. He walked out with his characteristic stoop.

'Hello, sir,' Kabir said. 'It's been a while.'

'Kabir, the way you left baffled all of us! And what has happened to your leg?'

'I wish I could tell you, sir.'

'What was it with the PMO? Why did they call you?'

'I'm not at liberty to say, sir.'

'Why are you here, Kabir?'

Kabir arched his eyebrows.

'I would like to continue teaching the kids, starting next semester.'

The Principal looked thoughtfully at him.

'Will there be any more phone calls?'

'Only if you don't take me back,' Kabir quipped.

'I've got a very good teacher to step in,' the Principal said. He turned around and gestured to a lady dressed in a crisp shirt and long skirt to join them. She walked towards them quickly.

'This is Professor Pallavi Pawar,' said the Principal, introducing them. 'And this is Professor Kabir Anand. He taught the kids literature before you were asked to fill in.'

There was an awkward silence. Professor Pawar broke the silence.

'Does that mean my services aren't needed any more?'

'No.' The Principal smiled. 'Since the both of you are so good at what you do, you get to divide the workload and teach the kids.'

Kabir's face relaxed into a dimpled smile. He didn't want the poor lady to lose her job because of him. But he wasn't feeling generous enough to let her have it at his expense.

'Is that okay, Kabir?'

'As long as I teach Shakespeare, I have no problem.'

The Principal smoothed his wavy grey hair and smiled. He began to walk away to check the other classes.

'See you next semester, then.'

Kabir and Professor Pawar stood looking at each other.

'Well,' Kabir said, smiling, 'you can take over the poetry bit of the subject.'

She shrugged.

'I quite enjoy teaching Shakespeare myself, Professor Anand.'

Kabir smiled at her. She found him quite charming. The ponytail, the black T-shirt. The casual jeans. He looked nothing like a professor.

'Well, you might just have to do that again. If I'm not available. *When* I'm not available.'

'And when would that be?'

'If only I knew.'

Epilogue

One week later
Dubai

Not a day had passed that he hadn't looked over his shoulder. He knew he was relatively safe. The ISI had taken care of that. They had completely wiped him off the map, set him up in a good apartment, the perfect cover. He was given enough capital to start his own restaurant in the area of Al Shindagha, a beautiful neighbourhood in the traditional centre in the city. His restaurant was doing extremely well. He offered authentic South Indian fare in the middle of a marketplace not too far away from the Gold Souk. People poured into the little stylized restaurant to eat some vegetarian food on a banana leaf, in a city known for its meat preparations. Ashwin Narayan was not just a defector, or a traitor, as his country saw it, but a successful restaurateur as well.

It was midnight. Ashwin was cleaning up after the last customer had left. He looked at the time on his Rolex and decided it was time to go back home. He lived in a posh apartment in the Al Karama area, that he had bought with the money he had made selling secrets over the years. He pulled the shutters down, stepped into his Chevrolet sedan and turned on the ignition. He put on the radio to listen to the latest Bollywood tracks. He dialled a number on his phone and smiled to himself.

'Can you come over within the hour? I'm in the mood for a little fun.'

'Sure, darling.'

Money. Women. A great house. Ashwin had it all. He parked the car and went into the low-rise building. It wasn't too flashy from the outside. It was just the way he liked it. The ISI had put some thought into it before transferring him there. He had been of great help over the years. He unlocked the door and stepped in. He began humming to himself as he switched on the dim light near the shoe rack. He took off his shirt hurriedly and decided to have a shower, before the call girl came knocking at his door. He began to sing a love song loudly as he undressed. He felt a coin drop out of his pocket and switched the light on to pick it up. His eyes fell on a ponytailed man with a beard, sitting comfortably on the couch with his arms crossed. Ashwin's bare legs began to shiver.

'Good thing you've got your undies on,' Kabir said. 'I wasn't quite prepared to see you soil your carpet.'

'W-who are you?'

'Kabir Anand. Does the name ring a bell?'

Ashwin's eyeballs bulged out of their sockets.

'Of course it does, doesn't it? You were the man Sadiq trusted that day in the control room when he spoke to the Americans, when I was in Quetta with Vikramjit Singh. And by the way, this time he's dead for real.'

Kabir stood up. Ashwin noticed he was wearing surgical gloves.

'You were the man who killed Sadiq in cold blood after luring him into a trap.'

Ashwin trembled as Kabir walked up to him. He stumbled backwards and then rushed to a drawer nearby, searching frantically for his gun. Kabir stood with his hands in his pockets. He shrugged. The drawer was empty.

'Just stop,' Kabir said. 'There's no way you're getting out of this alive.'

Narayan looked at Kabir and opened his mouth to say something. Words failed him.

'No point begging for your life either.' Kabir took a step closer. Ashwin looked at Kabir's unforgiving eyes under his perfectly arched eyebrows.

'You've sold your country out,' Kabir continued. 'You've killed a man like Sadiq Sheikh, who made the mistake of trusting you. And why did you do all this? For the money?'

Ashwin nodded feebly.

'Good you accepted that,' Kabir said. 'I'm really sick of dealing with terrorists motivated by their religious ideals. Nice little apartment you've got here. Al Karama. Here's an interesting fact. *Al Karama* literally means *dignity*. Want to know another interesting fact? Your death will be nothing close to dignified.'

Ashwin hung his head, feigning shame. He sneaked a quick look at his watch. *Maybe if that girl gets here in time, there might be a way out.*

'Oh, I'm sure the delightful lady who is supposed to come tonight won't quite make it upstairs. Thing is, I've asked a lady friend of mine to send her away.'

'You'll never get away with this, Anand!' Ashwin spluttered uncontrollably.

'That's for me to worry about,' Kabir said nonchalantly. 'Within a few hours your bloated dead body will be floating in the waters of the Persian Gulf, never to be found again. If at all your carcass is found, it would be classified as a case of suicide. Which isn't too far from the truth. The moment you killed Sadiq, you were a dead man yourself.'

'You're making a terrible mistake! They'll hunt you down and tear you apart, piece by piece!'

'Well, I wish them nothing but the best in their endeavours.'

Kabir took another step and leaned towards Ashwin. His voice lowered to a chilling whisper.

'Do you remember Sadiq's last words before you pulled the trigger?'

Ashwin's jaw trembled. Kabir grasped his neck.

'No? Well, I'm here to repeat them. I'm here to complete the lines he had left unfinished.'

'Please,' Ashwin gasped, 'I have secrets! I can tell you things about Pakistan that you'd never know otherwise! About China as well!'

Kabir clucked his tongue.

'Unfortunately, such negotiations can't bail you out. Especially if you're hoping for help from me. You've made a grave mistake. Luckily, you won't live long enough to regret it. So now I'm going to ask you one final question. *Any famous last words?*'

Ashwin tried to wriggle himself free. He tried to scratch at Kabir and loosen his grip. Kabir clenched his fist and rammed it into Ashwin's temple with one solid blow. Ashwin dropped to the ground. He began to lose consciousness. Kabir bent down over him and, like a lullaby, softly recited.

Cowards die many times before their deaths;
The valiant never taste of death but once.

Of all the wonders that I yet have heard,
It seems to me most strange that men should fear;
Seeing that death, a necessary end,
Will come when it will come.